To Lena,

Wake Up, Brandy.
it's time to
fight!

Royalty
Crew

A Royalty Crew Novel

SAVAGE
QUEEN

To Lena,

Wake up Beauty,
its time to
feast!

SAVAGE QUEEN

A Royalty Crew Duet

_____

ALLEY CIZ

HOUSE OF CRAZY
PUBLISHING

Also by Alley Ciz

The Royalty Crew (A #UofJ Spin-Off)

Savage Queen

Ruthless Noble- Preorder, Releasing June 2021

#UofJ Series

Cut Above The Rest (Prequel) Freebie

Looking To Score

Game Changer

Playing For Keeps

Off The Bench- #UofJ4 Preorder, Releasing December 2021

BTU Alumni Series

Power Play (Jake and Jordan)

Musical Mayhem (Sammy and Jamie) BTU Novella

Tap Out (Gage and Rocky)

Sweet Victory (Vince and Holly)

Puck Performance (Jase and Melody)

Writing Dirty (Maddey and Dex)

Scoring Beauty- BTU6 Preorder, Releasing September 2021

I grew up a queen among men.

Proud.
Strong.
Royalty.

I'll do *anything* for the ones I love, even if it means allowing myself to be forced from my kingdom.

I may be stuck having to play Samantha St. James inside the gilded halls of my new school, but I'll always be **Savvy King** at my *core.*

Now Jasper Noble and his merry band of douchebags expect me to yield.

That's funny.

They think they're tough.
Gods among men.
I know they're *nothing* but ordinary bullies.

With threats coming from all sides, my adversaries will come to learn—**I *don't* bend the knee for false kings.**

SAVAGE QUEEN is book 1 in the Royalty Crew Duet. It is a #UofJ Spin-off and is a non-dark high school bully/enemies-to-lovers romance filled with hella sexual tension, an alpha-hole hero, and a Boss B heroine. Book 2 is releasing June 2021.

Savage Queen (A Royalty Crew Duet)

Alley Ciz

Copyright © 2021 by House of Crazy Publishing, LLC

Copyright © 2021 by House of Crazy Publishing, LLC

Paperback ISBN: 978-1-950884-20-9

Ebook ISBN: 978-1-950884-19-3

Cover Designer: Julia Cabrera at Jersey Girl Designs

Cover Photographer: Wander Book Club Photography

Cover Models: Joey Lagrua and Kennedy Moran

Editing: Jessica Snyder Edits, C. Marie

Proofreading: Gem's Precise Proofreads; Dawn Black; My Brother's Editor

❀ Created with Vellum

This one is for the ladies! Never be afraid to let your inner boss bitch shine!
#GirlPower
(yes I totally said that like a Spice Girl I don't care if that shows my age lol)

Author Note

Dear Reader,

SAVAGE QUEEN is book 1 in the Royalty Crew Duet. It is a #UofJ Series Spin-off. You do not need to read them to understand the story, you just get to know them a bit more. All are available in Kindle Unlimited.

The Royalty Crew

1. Savage Queen
2. Ruthless Noble- Preorder June 2021

#UofJ Series

1. Cut Above The Rest (Prequel) Freebie
2. Looking To Score
3. Game Changer
4. Playing For Keeps
5. *Off The Bench*- #UofJ4 Preorder, Releasing December 2021

If I'm new to you and you haven't read my #UofJ books
you're fine.
If you have met this crazy cast, this book takes place the
school year after PLAYING FOR KEEPS.
XOXO
Alley

Playlist

- "Women Like Me"- Little Mis
- "Not Your Barbie Girl"- Ava Max
- "Queen"- Loren Gray
- "Games"- Demi Lovato
- "Castle"- Halsey
- "You Should See Me In A Crown"- Billie Eilish
- "Crown"- Camila Cabello

FIND THE FULL PLAYLIST on Spotify.

CHAPTER 1

SENIOR YEAR.

It's supposed to be epic. Filled with parties, prom, and all sorts of debauchery.

God! I was *so* looking forward to living out my teenage drama dreams.

Yeah…

Now though…

Not so much.

All thoughts of what I envisioned my first day of senior year would be like dissolve as our driver pulls through the wrought iron gates of Blackwell Academy and the butterflies in my belly turn into fire-breathing dragons. I shouldn't be here. This isn't me.

The luxury vehicle, the uniform, the most expensive private school on the east coast—*all* of it, wrong.

This isn't my school. No, mine is on the other side of town. Why the hell do I have to spend my last year of high school at this uptight prep school instead of Blackwell Public? Just thinking about it has the potential to make me rage like the Hulk.

I have friends at BP.

A crew.

A legacy.

I was Savvy-fucking-King.

Here? I have nothing, am nothing.

Actually…if I'm being honest, it might even be a little bit dangerous for me to be here, though I expect that thought is more my brother's paranoia rubbing off on me than actual reality.

I get it. At BP, my name alone demands respect, not to mention there's a system in place to help remind those who need it that being an asshole for assholerly's sake is an automatic way to get yourself canceled.

Here at BA? Who the hell knows. For all I know, I could be walking into a *Lord of the Flies*-type situation. Fun times.

"Miss?" The voice of Daniel, my stepfather's driver, startles me. Looks like I was lost in my thoughts and didn't hear him open my door.

It's going to be a *long* day; I can already feel it.

"Ready, Samantha?" asks Mitchell St. James, my new stepdad.

I grit my teeth. Why *she* insists on people calling me by my legal name is *beyond* me.

"Yes. Coming." I loop the strap of the black Nappa leather messenger bag—another insistence from *her*—over my shoulder and slide out, using my hand to smooth my pleated schoolgirl-style skirt that hits me mid-thigh.

Ugh. This damn uniform. Like seriously? What am I, auditioning to be in a Britney Spears music video?

I do have to give credit where it's due. The pretentious people who run this place picked some high-quality materials for us to wear. The white button-up is silk, and my gray blazer is made of the softest cashmere. I was also surprised by the staggering number of possible combinations for a school with a uniform.

I walk around the back of the Bentley, the silver shiny enough I can see my reflection in it, and join the reason for my upheaval.

Okay, I may be acting a tad dramatic from still being salty about this latest development, but who the hell wants to be uprooted from their school *senior* year? *points with both thumbs* Not this girl.

Things would be a lot easier if I hated Mitchell St. James, but alas, I don't. And...

To be fair, *he* isn't the *real* reason for this life change. Nope. That honor falls firmly on *her*—Natalie King. For a woman who didn't give two shits about me for most of my life, this demand—threat—to have me fall in line and live with her straight-up pisses me off.

The thing I haven't figured out yet—and yes, let me tell you, it frustrates the fuck out of me that I haven't—is why the sudden push to act like mom of the year? I honestly have a hard time recalling an instance when I saw her as a parental figure. When he was alive, it was Dad, then the Falco family and my older brother Carter after his death.

It's actually quite fascinating to watch how Natalie transforms into what most people would think is a "normal" human being when Mitchell is around versus the devilish bitch we've always known her as.

Her attempts at rewriting history have also been commendable. Make no mistake, her pretending *she* was the one who made sure I was cared for, ensured I always had my meds, took care of me if I got sick, and taught me how to take care of myself is *precisely* that—pretending. Try as she might, she can't green-screen herself into a role filled by Carter and others.

I'm seventeen years old, a few months shy of being an adult, and capable—at least legally—of making my own decisions. So why? *Why* is it *now* that Natalie King, now St. James, insisted—again, made threats—I fall in line and pretend to be a model daughter? *She's* the real person I'm pissed at. The only good thing that woman has done for me was giving birth to me instead of aborting me.

"This will always *be your home whether you live here or not."* My brother's promise echoes in the back of my mind. It's one I've been playing on repeat since Natalie called us to the house neither one of us has called home to drop her bombs like Blackwell was all of a sudden the Middle East.

"I got married." She wiggles the fingers of her left hand, the giant rock on the fourth one practically blinding us.

To say Carter and I were surprised would be the understatement of the century. Sure we aren't the sit-down-to-dinner-together type of family, at least not with her, but we weren't even aware she was *dating* someone, let alone seriously enough for him to put a ring on it.

"Who did you sucker into marrying you, Natalie?" My lips twitch at the way she bristles at Carter using her first name. I don't blame him; even when I think of her as 'Mom,' the sarcasm is thick.

Marrying into a founding family of Blackwell, Natalie had grown used to a certain level of status. The grass hadn't had a chance to grow over Dad's grave before she started her hunt for husband number two all those years ago.

I dip my chin to study my new stepdad out of the corner of my eye. I gotta hand it to her—it took her *years* to reel in husband number two, but she certainly landed herself a whale in Mitchell St. James. In a custom-tailored suit that must have easily cost five figures, the hotelier radiates luxury and power. *Gossip Girl* is my go-to show to rewatch with my bestie Tessa, and he gives off massive Bart Bass vibes.

"Samantha"—Natalie has always *refused to call me by my Savvy nickname*—*"you will be moving to the St. James with me, and I'll be transferring your enrollment to Blackwell Academy."*

I tried to fight it, but it was no use. Within two weeks, I

was moved out of my brother's place and into the penthouse residence at the St. James and was a registered senior of Mitchell's alma mater.

"Follow me," Mitchell instructs, and again, I do as I'm told.

The BA campus is like something out of a movie. The stone steps at the entrance have to be a hundred feet wide, and the three-story gray stone building beyond them is equally impressive. The doorway I follow Mitchell through is big enough to drive a truck through.

Geez, are we overcompensating for something?

My dark purple Chucks—a nod to my Blackwell Public roots—squeak on the white marble floors, because of course they're marble. Yes, I'm aware I sound like a judgy bitch, but in my defense, *everything* about the place *drips* money. There's no fake lemony scent of floor cleaner here, only a fresh one that manages to make me feel like I'm still outside. Even the hallway's metal lockers look more like high-end appliances than a place for students to store their belongings.

Also…we're late.

Classes started thirty minutes ago, and not one person is in the hall as I follow Mitchell to Headmaster Woodbridge's office. Of *course* they have a headmaster. God forbid they went with a simple principal like BP.

I snort, and out of the corner of my eye, I can see Mitchell's mouth twitch at the sound.

Fuck I'm so bitter about having to be here.

We step inside a room that is—unsurprisingly given everything else so far—beautifully decorated. There are two tufted black leather couches mirroring each other and a large desk set up in front of a wall of windows overlooking the state-of-the-art football stadium and hockey arena. That's what happens when the average person would have to sell their soul to afford the cost of tuition here—though I can't help but smirk thinking of how both places looked the last I saw them. If you ever need to know how much toilet paper is required to TP a football stadium or the best paint to use on ice, I'm your girl.

Actually…

I wonder how the BP start-of-the-school-year prank is going over. I also need to remember to pay extra-close attention to the bathrooms when I need to use one.

"Ah, Mitchell." Headmaster Woodbridge rises, rounding his desk.

"Jonathan."

They shake hands, and by the use of first names, I can only assume the leader of my new school is golfing buddies with my stepfather. *Awesome*—not.

"Samantha." Their attention turns to me. "It's a pleasure to meet you. And let me say, we are honored to have you joining the ranks of our student body."

Honored? Laying it on a little thick, don't you think?

"Umm…thank you?"

"Jonathan." Mitchell speaks to cut the awkwardness. He may be pulling me from everything I've known, but unlike Natalie, he is perceptive enough to read me. "How about we let my daughter"—just daughter; I've noticed he never uses 'step' when he speaks of me—"get settled in before you start any sales pitches."

"You're right, you're right." Headmaster Woodbridge claps him on the back in a good-ol'-boys way. "I've arranged for one of our top students to show you around—teach you the ropes of BA, if you will." He flicks his wrist, checking the gold Rolex on it for the time. "She should be here any minute."

Again I'm hit with a wave of *I shouldn't be here*. I don't want to "learn the ropes." BP is my turf, my kingdom to rule. I want to be sitting in class, passing notes to Tessa. Instead, I'm stuck here in a place where it feels like my Royalty status could bring on a wave of *Off with her head* as opposed to the *Oh shit, Savvy's coming* I'm used to.

For all the stories I've heard about the great pranks of the past, I never fully understood how the *Romeo and Juliet*-esque feud started. I always assumed it was mostly a case of a school that could afford to recruit some of the best athletes from across the country being butthurt because the public school could claim more alumni playing in the NFL.

After I was told I would be transferred to this place that mostly boards—and let's not forget how it boasts about having—some of the brightest and most connected young minds on the east coast, I decided it was time I needed all the facts if I were to come up with a proper plan of attack.

My brother and his friends may have nicknamed me Savage—Savvy for short—for my boss bitch personality, but I know how to turn on the girl-next-door charm when needed. My connections may not come from being a child of the upper one percent like my new school chums, but I *am* a child of a Blackwell founding family, and I exploit the shit out of it.

Not to bore you with too much detail, but here is the gist of Blackwell's history.

The town was founded in 1866 by five families: the Falcos, the Princes, the Castles, the Salvatores, and my family, the Kings. Together they worked toward creating one of the oldest municipalities in the state. Even today, it is a major bedroom suburb of New York City.

Blackwell, at its core, is a town deeply rooted in its citizens. It's why generations later, those founding families are held in such high regard. It also helps that the great-great-grandfathers of the Kings, Princes, and Castles banded together to create Royal Enterprises, a technology and industrial research powerhouse that employs hundreds of locals while giving back to the community.

I also learned from the mayor, my "Uncle Chuck," that most of the town's residents look down on how uninvolved

Blackwell Academy is and how it doesn't give back to the community it resides in. Not one of the limited scholarships the school earmarks for Jersey residents has ever gone to someone from Blackwell.

Knock-knock.

"Ah, there she is now." The headmaster holds an arm out like he's a game show host presenting us with the grand prize. "Samantha St. James, I'd like you to meet Arabella Vanderwaal. Miss Vanderwaal is student body president and the *perfect* person to be your tour guide."

We eye each other warily. She's exactly what I would have expected given my past interactions with the student body of BA—aka Prep School Barbie. She's pretty, gorgeous even, with long chestnut waves that could make a shampoo commercial jealous. She wears the same uniform configuration, but unlike me, her shirt is tucked in where I left mine to drape over my skirt. Her tie is cinched tight at her throat instead of the knot hanging between my breasts. She also has on a killer pair of Mary Jane stilettos—the same ones Natalie tried to get me to change into.

And yes, before you ask, I totally stole my sense of style for the day from my girl Serena van der Woodsen (Blake Lively's character on *Gossip Girl*). What can I say? I'll conform, but only to a point. *Sorry not sorry, Natalie.*

The way Arabella's highly glossed lips twist into a frown, I can tell she too finds my appearance lacking. Too bad, so sad for her—I don't give a fuck.

CHAPTER 2

FOR THE BETTER PART OF three hours, Arabella takes me on what feels more like a world tour than a school tour given the campus's size. *Ho. Lee. Shit.*

BP is one of the nicer public high schools in the state. The deep roots of the town's founding families plus generous endowments from Royal Enterprises have made sure the buildings were updated and added to over the years. Add in both strong football and baseball programs that allow the athletic boosters to bring in money, and the whole school prospers.

But BA? *Dayum.*

How can this possibly be real life?

I may not have attended any of my classes yet, but it's going to take me *days* to remember where they all are despite Arabella pointing each classroom out. There are too many hallways, too many buildings to keep track of.

Headmaster Woodbridge may have chosen Arabella as my tour guide because of her extensive knowledge of the campus, but I have found her more valuable when it comes to all the things you can't find in a textbook.

The bell rings, bringing another period of class to an end —one more I've missed—and Arabella turns on her heel.

"That's the bell for lunch. We get forty minutes. You can leave campus if you want, but anyone who is *anyone* eats in the cafeteria because the school employs Michelin-starred chefs," Arabella explains. "Though you'll have to be careful where you choose to sit. And FYI—"

I don't know what makes me want to roll my eyes more, the statement itself or how she speaks. This chick is a walking, talking cliché of every Queen B in a teen drama. My palm literally itches to smack her as I say, *Stop being so two-dimensional.*

"—most of the hockey and football players are taken, so don't even bother."

I'll give her this—she plays the role to perfection. From the angle of her chin in the air down to the seductive sway of her hips, she has a commanding presence. If she hadn't spent our entire time together making passive-aggressive remarks to make sure I know her place at the top of the BA hierarchy, I might even respect it, but I can't.

Besides, I'm a dragon through and through. I may have to go to school here, but I'll be cheering for BP come game time.

As if on cue, two girls—one blonde, one redhead, both from a bottle—who I can only assume are Arabella's minions if we're sticking with the banality of the morning, strut over and flank her sides.

I finally give in to the urge to roll my eyes when Miss Bottle Blonde shoulder-checks me out of the way. She seems less than impressed as she looks down her nose at me, and her expression only gets worse as I smother a laugh behind a hand and not-so-subtly flip her off by scratching the side of my jaw with my middle finger.

Fuck, I *really* miss Tessa and the Royals.

Bullshit like this would never stand at BP. Hell, I swear one of the main reasons Carter started his crew was to protect the "little guy" from the bullies and mean girls of the world. Between the King name and people loyal to him, my brother has built a system that not only withstood the gap year our five-year age difference caused in a King being a member of the student body at BP, but that still stands to this day.

Now that I'm officially being ignored, I slip my phone from my bag and check the slew of text messages waiting for me. I have a handful from my brother and the other Royals, but the bulk of them come from Tessa. Ignoring the rest, I open up the thread from my best friend.

LITTLE MISS EXTRA: This is crap. *poop emoji* YOU should be sitting here.

LITTLE MISS EXTRA: *picture of an empty school desk*

LITTLE MISS EXTRA: I miss you *sad face emoji*

LITTLE MISS EXTRA: *TikTok video of Tessa lip-syncing to "I'll Be Missing You" by Diddy, Faith Evans, and 112*

LITTLE MISS EXTRA: Do you think I would get in trouble if I took a roll of ARSON INVESTIGATION tape from Pops and used it to block off my new locker neighbor's locker? #AskingFor-AFriend

LITTLE MISS EXTRA: Do they make a patch to help you deal with missing a bestie? You know, like a nicotine patch? Seriously, Bitchy, I'm going through Savvy withdrawals. *GIF of Stewie rocking back and forth in his crib*

I can't help but snort at that one and get another scathing glance from the trio in front of me. *Whatever.* I'm not going to let them judge me for finding amusement in my best friend. Tessa can be so extra at times (hence the text handle), but it's one of the many reasons I love her.

I snap a quick picture of Arabella and her posse's backs and send it to Tessa.

ME: TRUST me, I miss you more. I've spent the morning learning all the ins and outs of this pretentious prep school from Miss Head Bitch herself. And not sure if you knew this, but *whispers* anybody who is ANYBODY stays on campus for lunch *eye roll emoji*

ME: Ohh *stop sign emoji* *no sign emoji* and both the football and hockey team are "off-limits."

LITTLE MISS EXTRA: Yeah, like if you were going to go for a jock, you would go for a subpar football team *eye roll emoji* Please….how about you ask her when was the last time one of their graduates won a Super Bowl? Don't worry…I'll wait.

Only seconds pass before the next message pings through.

LITTLE MISS EXTRA: Oh? Could they not think of one? Didn't think so. But here's ours. *GIF of Eric Dennings doing a touch-down dance*

Of all the BP alums who've gone on to play in the NFL, it comes as no surprise she chose a GIF of Eric. He may not be her blood brother, but he might as well be given the way the Taylor and Dennings families were raised.

After walking for what feels like miles, we finally come to the end of another long hallway at a set of open twenty-foot carved oak doors. I swear everything about this place is steeped in Hollywood theatrics because now I feel like I've stepped onto the movie set at Hogwarts.

I snap another pic, this one with a message that we need to hit up our favorite coffee shop Espresso Patronum as soon as possible. The suggestion is enough to cheer up Tessa if the GIF of a dancing Snape is anything to go by.

Distraction is typically the name of the game with Tess. As the future valedictorian of what would have been *our* graduating class at BP, she sometimes gets so caught up in her head you need to redirect her. With the combined promise of amazing coffee, eclectic and mostly *Harry Potter*-themed decor, and the chance of possibly getting a glimpse of one of her favorite romance authors working, I know I hit the trifecta.

My steps come to a halt as I cross the threshold of the cafeteria.

Holy shit! We're not in Kansas anymore, Toto. I whistle as I take in the vaulted ceilings with their wooden beams and over-the-top crystal chandeliers.

This is *nothing* like any cafeteria I've ever been in. There are no laminate-topped metal folding tables and cheap plastic chairs—nope, only rectangular wooden tables and matching wooden chairs with gray padded seats.

To the left is a wall of glass with doors that open to a stone patio section filled with umbrellaed tables for outdoor eating. I guess going picnic-style on a blanket is too low-class for those who pay over sixty K a year in tuition.

Shit, Savvy. Eat a Snickers or something because even in your head, you sound like a judgy bitch.

Rolling my shoulders back, I do my best to shake off the negativity that's been coating this whole experience. Just because I've been ripped from my old life doesn't mean I lost it. If I ever had any doubts of that, the way my phone is doing its best impression of a vibrator about to bring a woman to orgasm would put them to rest.

Off to my right is the first "close to normal" cafeteria feature with the assembly lines of food selection. I air-quote around the description because instead of smiling lunch ladies in aprons and hairnets, the employees serving the food wear white chef's coats and hats. Everything about BA is pure class.

As my gaze scans over the already half-full tables, I silently curse Tessa and her insistence that we watch *Mean Girls* this past weekend in preparation for me being the new girl because all I'm wishing for right now is a GBF and his artistic partner in crime to draw me a map to where I should sit.

It feels like a hundred pairs of eyes are on me. Who knows? Given that I'm the aforementioned new girl, there might be.

One more pass of the room and my eyes stutter over a light, almost iridescent pair, but I force myself to move on before bringing attention to myself.

"Savs?" a hesitant yet excited voice sounds from my left.

When I look over, the first genuine smile I've had since walking through these hallowed halls spreads across my face. Tinsley Warren, one of Tessa's teammates for the New Jersey All-Stars, more commonly known as NJA, eyes me like she can't believe I'm really standing here.

I completely spaced that she's a student here. Since NJA is a club team, they have athletes from all over. School pride—or in this case, old rivalries—don't come into play when you learn to bleed the blue camouflage of NJA.

Once it dawns on her that I am, in fact, who she thinks I am, Tinsley launches herself at me, her toned arms wrapping around my neck.

"Hey, Tins." I return her hug with slightly less enthusiasm. Having been friends with Tessa most of my life, I've grown used to dealing with more pep in a high ponytail than I'll ever possess in my entire body.

"What the hell are you doing here? BA isn't your kingdom."

I run a hand through my hair, tugging on the strands to keep my amusement in check. I know our last name is King, but did my brother *have* to name his band of merry idiots the Royalty Crew? *You can probably blame your ancestors for that one.* For real, though…the monarchy puns are out of control.

"I know you hate that Natalie and stepdaddy dearest call you Samantha, but maybe it's best you keep the Savage side of your identity a secret at BA," Carter muses, rolling a bottle of beer between his fingers.

"You can't be serious." My jaw practically falls to the floor.

"You'll be less at risk of someone going after you in a power move—"

"Yeah"—Wes snorts—"because that *wouldn't be misguided or anything."*

Carter's lips twitch at the accurate statement from his best friend and number two, but he smothers it quickly and focuses his attention back on me when I ask, "Don't you think they'll recognize me?"

The only thing my questions earned me was one of his *Don't you think I thought about that?* side-eyes. I'm not looking forward to the moment when I have to admit he was right. So far, no one has batted an eye in recognition.

To think, I was all worried he was going to crack a tooth from a clenched jaw when I told him that not only did Mitchell enroll me at BA, Natalie also convinced him it would be best if he did so with St. James as my last name. The only reason *I'm* any sort of calm is that he didn't change my name legally. I still haven't managed to reconcile Carter's sudden maybe-play-along-that-you-aren't-a-King stance on life. Then again, most days, anyone with a Y chromosome doesn't make much sense in general.

"Oh my god"—Tinsley reaches up, flipping the ends of the hair hanging down by my boobs—"when did you dye your hair?" I glance down at my new silver locks. "I can't believe Bette agreed to it."

Bette Dennings, Tessa's pseudo-sister-in-law, is a kick-ass hairstylist. She straight-up refuses to go anywhere near Tessa's strawberry-blonde hair with dye, but I was able to convince her I needed a change from my natural ashy-blonde locks. Originally I wanted to go balls to the wall and make my whole head purple, but I wasn't sure if this school had any restrictions on appearance for their students and figured silver was at least a more "natural" color.

"Do you like?" I loop my arm with hers and let her guide me toward the food to select our lunch.

"It's amazing. It's very Savvy King, if that makes sense."

I bounce my gaze around those closest to us as Carter's paranoid warning rings in my ear—again—but it doesn't look like they are paying us much mind.

"Yeah...about that..." I wait until we each have a ceramic bowl filled with a delicious-smelling chicken and vegetable stir fry on our trays before continuing. "You should probably get used to calling me Samantha or some variation of that at school."

A small V forms between Tinsley's brows. "Samantha?"

I nod. "It's my name."

The furrow only deepens, going from what looked like a lowercase letter to an uppercase one. "Savvy isn't short for Savannah?"

I shake my head with a smile. It's an easy assumption. I've been Savvy for so long, and those who didn't know me before I was given the nickname always have this reaction when they learn my real legal name. Natalie *loathes* the reasoning behind the moniker, which is why she refuses to use it.

Me? I love it.

CHAPTER 3

UNDER THE TABLE and out of sight, my hand forms a fist on top of my thigh, knuckles popping under the pressure. *Who the fuck is she?* The question has been on repeat any time I've seen her, followed quickly by *Why the fuck do I care?*

What's most annoying is the nagging sense that I *know* her from somewhere, but like it's stuck on the tip of my tongue, I can't quite grasp it. It's frustrating as fuck.

Control is what I need, what I *crave*. I've put in the time and the work to become the top dog at BA, and it shows. News of the new girl made its way to my boys and me before I got my first glimpse of long silver hair. Gossip is one of the foundations holding up the prestigious walls of Blackwell Academy. Information is the currency here, and when you're the king of this castle, your peasants make sure to pay up and keep you in the know.

BA isn't your typical high school. The bar you set for yourself here can easily carry into the next stage in life. When the bulk of the student body is made up of the spawn of the country's millionaire and billionaire facet as well as significant players in the political sector, establishing yourself as a cut above the rest *means* something here. And for me? I can have any student—or teacher, for that matter—do my bidding with a snap of my fingers. This bitch won't be any different. I'll have her on her knees and choking on my cock before the end of the week.

"She's got total DSLs, man," Duke muses. He's my best friend so I probably shouldn't want to hit him for commenting about what I have to agree, given where my own thoughts went, are the definition of *dick-sucking lips*—yet the urge to lay him out is there.

What. The. Fuck?

Duke has been my partner in crime since we moved into the dorms freshman year. My loyalty lies with him, not some chick who is essentially a random.

"Have you seen her ass?" Banks balances on his chair's back legs as if it can help him get a better view. Spoiler alert: it can't. Her back isn't facing us.

Brad still agrees. "Fuck yeah."

"I bet I can convince her to bend over Headmaster Wood-bridge's desk too—"

"Arabella." I crook a finger and cut off Midas's comment before he risks being impaled with a utensil.

With the confidence that's born from being the reigning Queen B, Arabella's hips sway as she struts over to our table and makes herself at home on my lap. "Jasper," she coos, her arms looping around my neck possessively.

I should stand up and dump her entitled ass on the floor. Since the hockey team won state last year, her sense of propriety when it comes to me has been an issue. Just because I let her suck my dick and banged her in the locker room a few times doesn't mean she owns me. Even so, playing into her power-couple dreams for five minutes is a small price to pay to gather the information I seek.

"What's the deal with the new chick?" I jerk a chin in her

direction, keeping my eyes locked on Arabella to prevent her from picking up on how interested I am. "Saw Woodbridge tapped you to play tour guide." I slide a palm over the thigh exposed by the hem of her short uniform skirt.

"Ugh, not much." She pouts her collagen-injected lips. "Her name is Samantha St. James."

"Like Mitchell St. James?" Duke asks, referring to the hotel magnate who also happens to be his father's longtime friend and campaign donor.

"Yup." Arabella twists around to face him, intentionally grinding over my dick as she does. "His marriage a few weeks ago wasn't the only surprise. Seems he's also inherited a stepdaughter with his new trophy wife."

"What's her real last name?"

"No idea." This time I get a shoulder shrug, one that rubs her breasts against my chest, in addition to another one of those pouts.

I need to cancel this bitch before she becomes a stage-five clinger.

I finally allow myself another glance and see her hugging Tinsley Warren. *Interesting.* If they know each other, Samantha must be relatively local since Tinsley is one of the few students who are residents of New Jersey that BA has awarded a scholarship.

With a pat on the ass, I send Arabella on her way, waiting until she takes her place with her minions at the girls' table.

I lean back in my seat and fold my arms over my chest. A perk of being in charge is knowing Tinsley and her new friend will be passing by our table as soon as they have their lunch. I also know Banks will stop them when they do. He has a fascination that borders on obsession with Little Miss Scholarship.

On cue, the harsh sound of wood scraping against marble hits my ear as he backs his chair into their path, a frown forming on Tinsley's pretty face when she has to pull up short or risk falling over Banks with her ass in the air. Not that my boy would complain. I would put money on him flipping her skirt up to spank her for the whole school to see if that happened—exhibitionist bastard.

"What do you want, Banks?" Tinsley asks with a heavy sigh.

Banks blatantly checks her out, his gaze lazily running over her body, stopping to linger on the exposed cleavage in the deep V of her uniform shirt and vest, then the expanse of leg between her uniform shorts and knee-high socks.

I can't blame my buddy for his interest in her; Tinsley is a smokeshow. She has smooth light brown skin and these eyes that are brown but aren't. She reminds me of that chick who played the witch on that vampire show people were obsessed with years ago.

Unfortunately for her and Banks's dick, the Unholy Trinity (Arabella and her posse) have deemed her unworthy of our circle due to her lack of net worth.

Like now, though, it hasn't stopped Banks from looking his fill. Tinsley bristles more the longer he does, the speed of her breathing increasing at the same time she drops her gaze to watch him run a thumb along his bottom lip.

"Aren't you going to introduce us to your friend, Tinsley?" Banks skims his fingertips up the back of one of her thighs, and she gasps.

With eyes narrowed on where Banks is touching Tinsley, Samantha steps in close. "If you want to keep your hand, I suggest you remove it from my friend *immediately*."

The cafeteria goes deathly silent. Not even the sound of cutlery moving against plates is heard as everything and everyone comes to a screeching halt. It's not like she shouted. In fact, the volume of her voice was relatively low and eerily calm. The shift in the atmosphere comes from her challenging the rulers. That *doesn't* happen—ever.

Oh, I'm going to have fun breaking this one in. It's always more enjoyable when there's a little fight in them.

Banks flips his gaze to me as if to ask *How should I handle this?* and I give him an *I got this* nod.

"Listen, sweetheart…" Her shoulders hit her ears at the endearment. *Ooo, someone doesn't like that.* "You're new here, so we'll forgive the indiscretion, but you"—I bounce my gaze over her body quickly, forcing myself not to get distracted by all the things the guys were pointing out—"don't tell *us* what to do."

I don't care how tight your pussy might be, baby. I'll be damned if you think you can undermine my control.

One of her blonde brows rises, and her lips purse as she does her own slower inspection of me. Up close, I can see her eyes are this crazy shade of purple.

I level her with a glare that gets defensemen on the ice shaking in their skates, but not her. Those DSLs of hers tilt up at the corners as if she sees it as a challenge.

I rule this school with an iron fist. No one dares to even pull a prank on BP without running it past me first. This…*girl* thinks she can step to me? I don't think so.

"Sa—" Tinsley coughs. "Sam, just forget about it."

Samantha keeps her body facing mine, angling her chin to glance over her shoulder at Tinsley, some of her silver hair falling forward and obscuring her face from my view. I'm hit with another one of those waves of familiarity. "Tins"—there's a hint of warning none of the females in this place have ever pulled off quite like her—"tell me this isn't a common occurrence."

Tinsley looks down and to the left, her throat working to swallow down the lie anyone can see she wishes she could tell but can't.

"Fucking hell," Samantha mutters under her breath. It's then that she notices Banks still hasn't removed his hand, and she whirls on him. Lifting a leg, she braces a foot on the chair in the space between Banks's spread knees and shoves with enough force to have the chair plus two-hundred pounds of jockhole skittering across the floor.

"From now on"—Samantha looks to Banks then to me—"Tinsley is *off-limits*."

Outwardly, my only reaction is an arch of a brow followed by the slightest curl to my lips. Inwardly? My muscles seize and prepare themselves for battle. Disrespect, especially from someone in possession of a pussy, will not be tolerated.

It's been a while since we really needed to exercise our control.

Somebody needs to be taught a lesson. What better place for her to learn from than on her knees?

This should be fun.

CHAPTER 4

SURPRISINGLY, the rest of the day passes by uneventfully, with the added bonus of Tinsley being in a handful of my classes. Yay for small class sizes. *waves one of Tessa's nonexistent pom-poms*

Being the new girl, I expected to hear whispers and catch the occasional side glance, but after that little scene in the lunchroom, those seem to have multiplied since this morning.

"So…" Tinsley leans a shoulder on the locker next to mine as I switch out the textbooks for the ones I need to take home. Homework on the first day—who the hell does that? "You survived your first day at BA." The tiny quirk of amusement on her lips tells me all I need to know about how she became friends with Tessa.

"Yup." I use a little more force than necessary when closing my locker. "Only one hundred and seventy-nine to go."

Tinsley snorts. "But who's counting."

"Me." I spin on my heel, and we fall into step as we make our way to the exit. "I'm most *definitely* counting."

I'm not saying I loved school when I attended BP, but I had my friends, my crew, *plans* for how this year would go. Now? Not so much.

I was supposed to carpool in every day with Tessa, not be driven in by a driver. We were going to joke as we walked the halls, pass notes old-school style throughout the day during the classes we weren't in together, and bullshit at lunch.

Our Fridays were supposed to be spent attending BP's football games—yes, I know I can still do that, but it's not the same. I'll miss out on the antics of the players wearing their jerseys to school and hyping themselves up.

The large entrance doors are propped open thanks to the steady stream of students pushing through them. However, the temperature change from the air conditioning to the lingering summer heat of early September is still jarring. Instantly I feel sweat bead on the back of my neck.

Movement flashes in my peripheral vision, and as I dip my chin to look back over my shoulder, I see the assmonkey and his *boys* loitering at the top of the stone stairs.

My breath hitches in my lungs, and it has nothing to do with my asthma and everything to do with the way those pearlescent eyes bore into me.

Arabella and her minions are also there, but he pays them no mind as he watches me, one hand hanging from the pocket of his pants by a thumb, the other wrapped around the strap of the book bag slung over one shoulder.

I stop, my foot hovering in the air for a second before I spin to face his glare head-on.

If they think I'm going to fall in line and do what they say just because they run this school, they have another thing coming. They may not know my real last name is King, but they'll learn soon enough this Royal doesn't bend the knee.

I bring my hands up to my own bag's strap where it

bisects my boobs, curling my fingers in a strangling hold until my blunt nails dig into the pads of my palms.

Others have started to notice our stare down, and one of his dark brows arches higher the longer it goes on.

His lips are *way* more shapely than should be fair on a guy; the perfect teardrop in the upper one's center only emphasizes the square cut of his jaw and the small dimple in his chin.

His body is fit, his broad shoulders stretching the limits of his uniform blazer, the cut of his tailored shirt showing off the way his torso tapers in that sexy inverted V-shape way.

He shifts his weight, the strength in his thighs unable to be disguised by the fine wool covering them as they ripple with the movement. Tinsley mentioned he was a jock, and it shows. It's a shame he's such a jerk because he's fuck-hot.

The blare of a car horn cuts in sharply. When I look toward the offending sound, the flash of light purple has my frown instantly morphing into a grin.

"Bitchy!" Tessa stands in the driver's seat, draping her upper body over the windshield, high ponytail falling over her left shoulder, a happy-go-lucky smile on her pretty face.

"T!" I squeal and hotfoot it as much as my body physically allows me to. When it comes to my best friend, there are times I feel like I have a personality disorder with the way she pulls a different side out of me that no one else can.

As I run my hand over the eyelashes surrounding the headlights, I pause, my fingers spreading, the purple color of the hood peeking through as I take note of the music blasting from the Jeep's speakers.

"You are such a smartass, Tessa Taylor."

"What can I say?" She pushes back, hitting the button on the steering wheel to increase the song's volume, and starts to swing her arms across her body before snapping them down to her side, imitating the choreography that goes along with the chorus of "...Baby One More Time" by Britney Spears. "My sister taught me well."

"For not actually being blood-related, you two are *scarily* alike." Like their fathers, the next generation of Taylors (Tessa and JT) and Dennings (Eric and Kay, or PF to Tessa) have also formed that ultimate level of friendship.

To most, it's complicated as fuck, but after years of knowing them, you kind of get used to it.

"Thanks." Tessa curtsies with a flourish then tosses a drawstring bag, which I barely manage to catch. "Tinsley? Oh my god, I forgot you go here." She jumps down from the Jeep, places a passing but still smacking kiss on my cheek, and rushes to her teammate in a jumping-around hug.

There are many ways Tessa and I are different, but we both have an I-don't-give-a-fuck side. T not caring that she is causing a scene with her over-the-top-I'm-so-excited-and-I-can't-hide-it greetings is one way she shows hers.

Knowing it's best to let Tessa be Tessa *and* ignoring the hairs standing on end on the back of my neck, I work my fingers into the cinched top of the bag and pull the sides apart until it opens. Inside I find a pair of cutoff shorts and an *If karma doesn't smack you, I will* slouchy off-the-shoulder tee. Guess smartassery wasn't the only thing Tessa was channeling when it came to her sister today. Looks like we are letting Kay influence our wardrobe, too—though I am a fan of her affinity for funny shirts.

"You brought me clothes?" I ask, already slipping the denim up my legs and under my skirt.

"Didn't think you wanted to walk around looking like Britney's music video extra longer than you had to." It is scary how much we can think alike.

Catcalls and whistles sound from the steps as I lower the zipper of my skirt. I crane my neck and narrow my eyes as I shimmy my hips and let it fall to the ground. There wasn't anything for them to see, and if they think I'll be embarrassed by them whooping and shouting "Take it off" and "Give us a show, baby," they will be disappointed. Instead, I give them my back and shrug out of my jacket.

"Umm…" Tessa's questioning voice has me glancing her way again and catching sight of Jasper's narrow-eyed glare boring into my back. *As if I had any doubt that was the case.* "Did you remember the thing about the bathrooms today?" I more or less have to read her lips since she cautiously drops her voice to a whisper.

Again I flick my gaze up the steps, rolling my lips between my teeth to restrain a smile at the simple yet brilliant prank BP pulled off.

"I feel like I should be surprised you were involved, but I'm not," Tinsley admits. I give her a simple shrug, neither confirming nor denying participating in the addition of vinyl decals so all the men's restrooms looked like they were ladies'. It was a minor prank, one that would only confuse freshmen…but I dare you to try to tell me that's not funny. Keeping a straight face any time I passed one while Arabella gave her tour was a challenge for sure.

Instead, I pull the tee over my uniform shirt, my head popping through at the same time I hear Daniel say, "Miss St. James." I finish maneuvering my arms through the short sleeves and snake my hands underneath to start working on my uniform's buttons.

"Oh no, Daniel"—Tessa jumps to greet him before I get a chance—"I *completely* forgot to tell Natalie I was picking our girl up today." Lies. T would never clear anything with the Momster. "I feel *terrible*." She places a hand on Daniel's arm and the other over her heart, playing up her nonexistent guilt.

Daniel blinks down at her, eyes wide, expression slack, disarmed and caught off guard by the full force of the Tessa Taylor charm. I have to work to restrain another smile at the spectacle. Tess could charm an Eskimo out of their snow gear and have them smiling through their hypothermia and frost-bite. This poor man never stood a chance.

"Now you went and wasted your time that I'm sure is valuable, all because my excitement to see my bestie had me forgetting common courtesy." Her hand goes to her forehead, ponytail swinging to and fro as she shakes her head. The girl is good at laying it on thick.

"It's okay, Miss Taylor." Daniel pats her hand, and I swear to Christ there's a tear in Tessa's eye.

"No, no, it's not." Yup, there she goes wiping under her lash line. "You know what?" Tessa perks up, bouncing on the balls of her feet. "There's a good chance I'll be picking her up a lot. Why don't the two of us exchange digits, and I'll text you on those days, so you don't waste a trip?" She holds a hand out to the side, pops a hip out, and tilts her head with the suggestion.

"Umm…" There's more blinking from Daniel, and now I'm swallowing down a laugh.

"Aww, don't be shy, Danny Boy." She pats his arm. "You don't mind if I call you Danny Boy, do you?" She doesn't wait for him to answer before she barrels on. "I do come from a firefighter family, and there are *a lot* of Irishmen at the house, and that was kinda my lullaby when I was a baby. Plus, nicknames are sort of a big deal in my family, and I figure since you and I will be becoming good friends with our mutual connection"—an arm flops out in my direction, but her words never slow—"we should probably have them with each other."

Daniel's mouth opens and closes, his impression of a fish spot on as he falls victim to the Tessa Taylor effect.

"T." This time, I do give in to both my laugh and my grin as I step toward them to save Daniel. "Take a breath and give the man a break." Grateful eyes blink at me as I tug on my friend's arm. "I think *maybe* you need to get decaf when we get to Espresso Patronum."

The tinkling sound of her musical laughter fills my ears and warms my soul. We head for her Jeep, but not before she successfully exchanges numbers with Daniel (no surprise there).

Espresso Patronum is the most unique coffee house I have ever frequented. The sign out front is done in old-school Broadway marquee bulb lights, with a lighted cartoon to-go cup brandishing a wizard's wand and adorned with the trademark Harry Potter glasses and lightning bolt scar.

The bright sign is only the start of the shop's awesomeness. The full glass front makes it easy to see inside the establishment, but that isn't enough to prepare you for the explosion of color that greets you once you step through the glass door.

I think the best way to describe EP would be if Harry Potter and the Mad Hatter had a baby and that baby's godparent was a unicorn.

The lights are all different colored upside-down coffee mugs, and the black chalkboard behind the counter is filled in with a rainbow array of chalks.

Tessa skips across the floor's diamond pattern, only stepping in the black squares and avoiding the whites on her way to the counter.

I let her do her thing, knowing she and Lyle, the owner, will spend a few minutes catching up before we'll be able to order.

"If we could bottle her energy to sell, we'd be rich," Tinsley whispers, causing me to laugh.

"You're preaching to the choir on that one." I step aside and hold the door for a pretty redhead carrying two coffee carriers before entering, watching her cross the street to enter The Steele Maker, a local MMA gym. There's a decent-sized crowd thanks to the after-school rush, and I scan for a space with enough available seating for us.

The barstools at the long mosaic counter are full, from the long-legged giraffe down to the thong-wearing bare ass stool that is my favorite to claim when we come.

"Let's grab seats while they're free," I suggest to Tinsley as another flood of patrons enter behind us. "We can text T our orders."

We weave through the occupied tables, skirting around a chair pushed out a bit too far, and are able to snag a large Marauder's Map-printed couch and the mini Hedwig and Deathly Hallows oversized armchairs across the table from it. Not one seat inside this place matches, but it's all part of its charm.

Tinsley and I fall into the same kind of easy conversation we've had all day, and I'm happy we were able to convince her to join us.

The couch dips, and I'm lifted an inch before resettling as a large body flops down beside me only to see Wesley Prince's handsome face smiling down at me. One of his muscular arms drapes across the back of the couch behind me, and I hit him with a gentle elbow to gain back some of my personal space. "*Ma reine.*" He winks, only adding to the swoon factor by how he rolls the French pronunciation of *my queen*.

"Wes," my brother growls as he takes the chair next to a stunned-silent Tinsley. Her eyes are so wide there's a whole ring of white showing around her dark irises. It's obvious she knows who my brother is since she's aware of the real name I go by, but knowing Carter King—*the* Carter King—is related to me and meeting him are two very different things.

The ends of my hair brush along the skin of my upper arm as Wes starts to twirl them around a finger. One would think he had a death wish with how he openly flirts with me in front of Carter. Still, as both my brother's best friend and number two in all things Royal-related, the level of trust affords him some leeway.

"Tinsley, meet my brother and Wes." I point to one then the other, snapping her out of her stupor. "Guys, this is Tinsley. She cheers with Tess at NJA and was my saving grace today at BA." A frown wrinkles Wes's brow as his gaze bounces between Tinsley and me. "What's wrong?" I ask.

"I thought you wore uniforms at the Blackwell Academy of Douchebaggery?"

Carter chokes on a laugh while Tinsley giggle-gasps an "Oh my god," and I hold out a fist for Wes to bump, living for his description of my new school.

"We do." I nod. "T brought me a change of clothes, and we swung by Tinsley's dorm to do the same and grab her cheer bag for later."

"Aw, man." Wes pouts. "And here I thought I would be able to live out all my schoolgirl fantasies with you—ouch!" He shifts forward to rub his leg. "The fuck, King?"

Across the table, my brother nonchalantly shrugs like he didn't kick his friend in the shin. Wes may get that leeway with me, but Carter puts him in his place from time to time.

"Rein it in, Prince."

Wes slumps back against the couch, and now I'm fighting the urge to roll my eyes. It's a damn miracle I was ever able to lose my virginity given how afraid others are of my brother.

"Aw, Carter," Tessa coos, pausing to kiss his cheek, "stop cockblocking your sister." She slides a carrier filled with coffees for the rest of us onto the top—Lyle must have done the boys' usuals—and cradles her paper cup in her hands as she takes the available cushion next to Wes with a "Hey, Charming."

"I wasn't cockblocking."

"You say potato." Tessa flops a hand forward. "I say vodka." She flips her hand back at herself.

"Isn't the saying 'potato, po-tah-to'?" Carter arches one of his blond brows.

"Pfft." Tessa rolls her eyes, a move she's picked up from her sister. "Lyle's always using this other one when Bette dyes his hair. He picked it up from one of the hockey players he's friends with, and I like it better." She gives Carter a *So there* head bobble. "Regardless of what you call it, *yes*, you were *cockblocking*. You know"—she taps her chin—"if it's because *you're* feeling backed up, I could always call PF and see what she and Em are doing—"

"Tessa," Carter warns in his deep, growly, I-am-the-king voice that has been known to have grown men peeing their pants—but not Tessa Taylor. Nope, she sees him as too much of a big brother to be afraid of him.

"What?" She blinks her big blue eyes in mock innocence then angles her face to wink at me without him being able to see. I give her a nod, agreeing with her wholeheartedly. It's been almost two years since Carter met Kay's roommate Emma, but he's never made a move.

"Don't you think it's about time you and Em did something about the sexual tension building between you?" Tessa goads.

"There's no sexual tension between Jackie O and me."

The entire table snorts. Even Tinsley, who doesn't know the backstory between Carter and the senator's daughter, is aware enough to read the room. I wonder if I should try to push that situation along. Maybe if Carter is focused on his own love life, he'll butt out of mine.

"Anyway…" Carter leans back in his chair, man-spreading his knees as he shifts into his leader-of-the-Royals persona. I *hate* when he tries to use it on me. "How'd today go? Any issues?"

He's probably asking because of whatever it is that has his panties in a bunch lately. Still, my gaze subconsciously moves to meet Tinsley's across the table, a move he certainly doesn't miss. *Damn observant bastard.*

"From a Savvy King angle"—I smash my lips together, barely resisting the urge to roll my eyes—"no."

"But…"

"But…" This time I shift to make full eye contact, knowing it's best not to show anything that could be taken as a sign of weakness. "BA is like living in a stereotype." I hold my hands up as if putting things on display. "Mean girls and douchebags abound."

Danger washes over Carter's features like a mask, and I adjust in my seat. Through the years, he's sheltered me from the bulk of his business dealings, but as hard as he tries, I'm not stupid; I know it's more than our family name that people fear.

The fact that three of the five members of the Royals are comprised of Blackwell founding families is what gave them the foundation they needed to assert their reign at BP years ago. It wasn't until Carter took over the street racing circuit and the underground poker ring that his reputation started to expand beyond town lines and into that gray area.

"Relax, Cart." He doesn't listen, his shoulders only hitching up more as he continues to glower. "It's not anything I can't handle."

"What happened to *flying under the radar*?" One of his brows arches until it hits the brim of his backward hat, his jaw kicking out to the side at my defiance.

I push up, leaning forward and bracing my elbows on the black lacquered table, canting my head, my hair falling around my shoulders like a waterfall. "Even though I'm going by St. James in that place, *you* are the one who raised me. Do you honestly think I'm going to let a bunch of bullies mess with my friend"—my eyes flit to Tinsley and back again—"and not say something?"

Violet eyes a few shades darker than my own stare at me,

not a blink in sight as the air around us grows charged. My spine lengthens, my arms falling to my lap, but I don't back down.

One breath, then two.

Finally…

A blink and the slightest of nods.

The breath I wasn't aware I was holding pushes from my lungs. With Natalie pretty much being an absentee parent, it's been Carter and me against the world. I may have said I wouldn't back down, but going against my brother is hard for me to do.

"Fine." This time he's the one blowing out a breath. "But if things escalate, you tell me."

JASPER NOBLE

CHAPTER 5

PRACTICES for high school hockey don't officially start until November, but that doesn't mean Coach isn't making sure we're working our asses off in the off-season. From the moment we move into the dorms, he makes sure we show up for morning workouts in the weight room, with the occasional ice time snuck in.

"What's the plan for the weekend?" Duke asks.

"When are we getting those BP pricks back for their little bathroom stunt?" someone, I'm not sure who, asks.

"Don't know," I say to both questions then finish doing up the buttons on my white uniform shirt and immediately start rolling the sleeves to my elbows, leaving my jacket in the locker. It's only seven a.m., and it's already too fucking hot to bother with it.

"You racing?" Banks calls out, slipping the strap of his bag onto his shoulder.

"I wish." Inside my veins, my blood pumps faster. Whether it's flying down the ice on my skates or racing on a highway in my Ferrari, nothing beats moving at top speeds.

"I haven't heard anything about there being one this weekend."

No one I encountered traveling this summer put up much of a challenge. The best competition I've faced since getting my license comes from a street racing circuit based right here in Blackwell. Unfortunately for me, it's run by Carter King and his crew. Though I can respect how they were able to evolve their power from the halls of BP when they attended a few years ago to extend to other parts of the state, I hate how the long-standing rivalry means those of us from BA can only participate when specifically invited.

I've won a race here and there, but I still haven't been able to beat the man himself or his right-hand man when they participate. It's frustrating as fuck too. My F8 should be able to take both the measly Corvette and the Camaro.

Banks leads the way out of the locker room while Midas and Duke work on figuring out what party we'll hit up after the school's football game later tonight.

With my boys distracted, I pull my phone from my pocket and continue to poke around on the internet to see what information I can come up with on one Samantha St. James.

So far, all I've figured out is she's local based on her friend picking her up yesterday. I also think it's probably safe to assume she attended BP. Logically, it's the only thing that makes sense because she's so fucking *familiar* to me.

In a wide line, the four of us walk down the hall, other students hustling to get out of our way, too scared to accidentally cross us.

"Now *that's* the way to start the day." Banks spots Tinsley at her locker and changes direction.

"Wonder where her new guard dog is," Midas muses before heading off to join Banks, eager to be a part of spreading any type of misery. It's an empty question. None of us give a fuck about Miss St. James's decree. She doesn't make the rules here—we do. Even so, it doesn't stop the blood from rushing to my dick at the mention of her.

Duke and I are too far away to make out what's being said, but Tinsley's startled gasp echoes down the hall, as does the clang of the locker when her back hits it. Banks cages her in, one arm bent over her head and braced on the locker door, his free hand gripping her at the hip.

Tinsley closes her eyes and drops her chin as Banks leans down to whisper in her ear. The color leaches from her fingers as Banks's grip tightens and pulls her tighter to his chest.

Midas just stands there, shoulders leaning against the lockers next to them, feet crossed at the ankles, buffing his nails on his stomach before lifting his hand to inspect them. The small quirk to his mouth is the only sign of how much he's enjoying the Banks and Tinsley show.

"Oh shit." Duke's curse is low but enough to have me whipping my head toward him only to follow the direction of his chin jerk when I do.

Fuck me.

In the same purple Chucks as yesterday, Samantha St. James strides over to her friend and mine, purpose in each one of her steps. We have some of the hottest, most put-together, and sometimes surgically enhanced women making up the BA student body, but *none* of them wear the uniform the way she does.

The short hem of the pleated skirt flaps as her hips sway, a swagger to them that would have Arabella selling both her firstborn and probably her second to be able to achieve.

Like me, she ditched our cashmere blazer, trading it out for the ladies' short-sleeved blouse and gray button-up vest option. Again her tie is loose, the knot resting between the open V of her shirt and the vest's top button.

She reaches our friends at the same time we do, but where Duke and I stop a few feet away, she slips in, ducking beneath

Banks's lifted arm and forcing him to put distance between himself and his prey.

"I'm sorry." She shakes her head, her long silver locks swaying with the movement. "Did I not make myself clear yesterday?" A hand comes up to cover her heart in feigned apology. "Keep your fucking hands"—she wraps one of her own around Banks's wrist and flings it off Tinsley's hip—"*off* my friend."

"What makes you think she doesn't *want* my hands on her?" Banks challenges, and Samantha straightens, her spine lengthening, her chin tilting up.

All she does is roll her eyes and shoulder-check him back two steps, just enough for her to link hands with Tinsley and pull her out into the center of the hallway, where students have stopped to watch the scene unfold.

This is the second time in as many days that this chick has openly challenged us. Same as yesterday in the cafeteria, the whispers pick up, and the questioning glances roll through those closest to us. As amusing as Banks's *What the fuck just happened* expression is, it's time to put a stop to it.

Before she can get too far, I reach out, grabbing Samantha's wrist, the delicate bones no match for the way my long fingers overlap around them. With my forceful tug, she stumbles back, her steps tripping over themselves until I slam her against the lockers with a loud *clang*.

One long stride is all it takes for me to cage her in much the same way Banks did to Tinsley.

Mint and the sweet scent of lime fill my senses as I position one foot on the outside of hers and the other between her tiny purple sneakers.

Eyes almost the same shade as the shoes glare at me with burning anger, and that earlier stirring in my groin surges again. Not wanting to give her the impression that she has any sort of effect on me, I angle my hips back as I push in closer, my chest pressing against hers.

I may be turned on by her defiance, but it needs to stop. Power and control hold more weight at BA than the number of zeros in our bank accounts. I will not allow someone who doesn't understand how things function here to come in and undermine all the work I've put in to claim the top spot because she doesn't respect the hierarchy. This is my world. She only gets to exist in it if I allow it.

"Jasper." The timidness in Tinsley's voice that almost breaks on the second syllable of my name is what we want.

There's a squeak, and when I glance back over my shoulder, Midas has a hand covering Tinsley's mouth, his other arm coiled tight around her middle, pinning her against him while she wiggles to get free to no avail.

My brows push together when Midas blows a few kisses, but when I catch sight of the death daggers Samantha is glaring at him, I know she's who he's taunting.

With a small growl, Samantha attempts to go after him, only to bounce off me, the soft press of her breasts pillowing against my hardness before she falls back with another echoing hit against the lockers.

Midas has a habit of pushing limits, but I know I don't have to worry about reining him in with Banks nearby. Instead, I can give one hundred percent of my attention to the task in front of me.

Samantha's glower is still focused on Midas, and I don't like it. Not one bit.

Pinching her chin between my thumb and forefinger, I lift until she's forced to bring those purple pools back to me.

Her dark mascara-coated lashes brush the top of her eyelids as she stares me down with that unabashed defiance.

"Listen here, Princess." The inner corners of her eyes constrict and her nostrils flare, the vibration of her jaw grinding felt in my fingers. "I don't know how things were over at BP…" The way she jerks in my hold confirms my suspicions about where she went to school. "But here at BA"

—I lift my thumb and run it along her plump lower lip, the skin soft and not covered by any of that sticky lip gloss—"my boys and I rule. It would be advantageous for you to learn it…live it…"

"Love it," Duke finishes.

She scoffs, and fuck me if it doesn't take my dick from half-mast to fully fledged. Why the fuck isn't she intimidated by me? Better yet, why do I like it so much?

"You're right." She nods, her lashes fanning across her cheeks with a long blink. "You're clueless about BP."

The tip of her tongue brushes along the skin of my thumb when it peeks out to lick her lips, and I barely manage to swallow down a moan.

"Because if you had *any* clue"—she shifts, her front brushing mine—"you would know that bullshit you're push-ing *won't* work on me."

Why does it sound like *she's* the one threatening *me*?

"You know…" She laughs, but there's no humor in it. "It's funny to me."

I get the feeling she's baiting me, but I can't resist. "What is?"

"Isn't your last name Noble?"

"Look at you doing your research." I bend further, my lips grazing the shell of her ear with my next words. "It's good you know my name." I give her a nip, a puff of air hitting my neck. "You'll be moaning it for me before long."

There's a snort, and the complete sense of disbelief has me pulling back only to see her roll her eyes again.

"I wouldn't hold your breath."

We'll see about that.

I lower my hand, my fingers wrapping around her nape, my thumb dragging down the line of her throat. She can front all she wants, but her hard swallow gives away that I do get to her, if only a little. She'll learn to bend to my will if she doesn't want to break.

"You're adorable, *truly*." Her word choice has me snapping out of my musings.

"That's the *wrong* kind of adjective to use when describing him, sweetheart," Duke singsongs.

"Uh-huh." Samantha tilts her head to the side as if we're boring her. "I just think it's ironic."

"What is?"

"That in a town founded by those with names like King, Prince, and Castle, you"—she pokes a finger to the center of my chest—"will *never* fit in."

She pushes harder, digging in hard enough for the gray of her nail polish to disappear into the white fabric of my shirt. My skin burns beneath her touch.

"But since you seem *so* concerned about the things I'm used to, and I'm feeling generous...I'll take the time to educate you a bit. Your name may sound royal, but you'll *never* be a nobleman...*or* Royalty."

She pauses as if waiting to see how I'll react to the mention of the well-known crew in town. I stiffen at the way her tempting lips curl at the corners. I don't know what the fuck she thinks she reads in me, but that added spark of confidence is *begging* to be snuffed out.

"What you seem to not understand is that the reason the Royalty Crew has power at BP—and in Blackwell in general —is because they are *respected* more than they are feared."

That breath she told me not to hold stills in my lungs as she reaches up to cup my cheek.

"You may have some *power* inside these halls at BA, but you'll never have it anywhere else...you'll never have that kind of respect." She taps my cheek in two quick slaps. "Because with your tactics, all you'll ever be is an ordinary bully."

I'm not sure if it's her words or the sudden way she shoves against my chest, but I stumble back, allowing her enough space to slip free.

Ordinary? Who the fuck is she calling ordinary? Where the hell does she get off insulting *me*? I'm Jasper fucking Noble. She's just some girl whose mom happened to marry a hotel magnate.

"I'll make you regret saying that, Princess," I warn as she frees Tinsley from a slack-jawed Midas.

"I dare you to try." She tosses the words over her shoulder, not bothering to turn around.

CHAPTER 6

"SAMANTHA," Natalie calls out the second I step inside the penthouse, and I'm beyond tempted to turn right back around and walk out.

After spending eight hours at school on edge, worried I gave my identity away somehow by bringing up Carter, I don't have the energy to deal with Momster drama. Thankfully, Jasper and his fellow douchemonkeys are too self-absorbed to see past their *You will bow down to me* mentality and view me as more than a transfer student from BP.

"Samantha!" I smirk at the haughty, put-out tone Natalie's voice takes on due to me ignoring her first greeting.

I follow the long hallway, past the massive kitchen island and into the living room, taking one last deep breath before stepping inside.

Dressed in the latest couture, one long leg crossed over the other at the knee, foot encased in a shoe-porn-perfection strappy Louboutin, the red sole winking at me with every bounce of her foot, Waterford Crystal martini glass balanced on the tips of her French manicured fingers, Natalie St. James is perched on an oversized velvet emerald armchair like it's her throne.

It's the beginning of September and seventy-five degrees outside, but that doesn't stop her from having the fireplace that takes up most of the wall behind her lit. Natalie is nothing if not dramatic. I swear she thinks our life is an actual telenovela.

"Mother," I greet when the flash of royal blue in my peripheral alerts me to Mitchell's presence as he too enters the room. He's the only reason I'll play nice…for now.

"How was school?" *It sucked*, I think, but I answer Mitchell's question with a shrug and an "It was fine."

Mitchell gives a *That's good* head nod as he moves to take the seat on the couch closest to my mother while her scarlet-painted mouth twists down into a frown.

"That's it? I would think after not coming home until late yesterday, you would have so much to say."

Ah, yes. Mother dearest did *not* like how I was able to spend most of the afternoon with my brother and avoided seeing her entirely. Sure, I spent more time with Tessa than Carter, having tagged along to her cheer practice, but she looks down on his "influence" over me. Guess she should have thought about that *before* she left him to raise me while she chased the next step in her social hierarchy.

I don't bother to dignify her passive aggressiveness with a response. I learned years ago it's best for my sanity to let it go and not engage. Instead, I pop a shoulder and continue toward the hallway that leads to my bedroom until an "Oh, Samantha" from Natalie brings me up short.

"Yes," I answer, eyeing her warily.

The smug *I won the game you didn't even know we were playing* grin that spreads across her perfectly made-up and contoured face sets my teeth on edge. I don't trust it…not one bit.

"I laid out a dress, as well as appropriate heels, for you to wear this evening."

Say what now?

That grin grows into a full-blown smile at the confusion clearly visible on my face.

"Dinner is at seven. Do make sure you're ready on time, dear."

Dear? Did she really just call me *dear*? And dinner? What the fuck is she talking about?

"If you had come home like you were supposed to yesterday, you would be aware of our plans for the evening," she states, answering my unasked question.

I close my eyes, using a long blink to compose myself before meeting her icy blue gaze. *I will not let her trigger me.* "I'm sorry our signals got crossed yesterday." I'm not, but I can pretend for appearance's sake. "It was my mistake for assuming you were aware I would still spend most of my afternoons with Tessa." Lies. All lies. "You know she helps push me to stay on top of things academically." *Or you would if you* actually *took an interest in my life.* I don't voice that last tidbit.

"Have you been assigned a lot of work already?" Mitchell asks, and unlike with my incubator, I get the impression he would actually like to know the answer.

"Nothing too terrible. But Tessa..." I hold my hand out, palm facing the ceiling as I wait for his acknowledgment that he remembers meeting my best friend. At his nod, I continue. "She'll be valedictorian, and with all her AP classes, she always has work to do. I've grown used to the strict study schedule she keeps."

"That's good." He swirls the amber liquid in a highball glass. "BA has rigorous academic standards. Establishing a system is important if you wish to not only meet but exceed them."

Yet another reason I *shouldn't* be at BA. I'm an average B

student at best. I was more than fine at BP. If anyone would fit in at my new school, it would be smarty-pants Tess.

That's not the point. Right now, I need to stress the fact that I have plans, and they *do not* include whatever dinner it is Natalie has planned.

The kickoff for the BP football game is at seven. Natalie laughs, but to me, it sounds more like a cackle when I inform her of this detail.

"Oh, sweetie." She waves her free hand like I'm being ridiculous. First dear, now sweetie? Did I step into *The Twilight Zone* instead of the penthouse when I got off the elevator? "You shouldn't bother with Blackwell Public social events anymore. It's beneath you."

Jesus fucking Christ. What in the *damn* hell?

"Listen, Mother." I move in closer, clasping my hands and letting them hang loose in front of me, concentrating on keeping my breathing steady and my blood pressure down. With great *painful* effort, I keep my voice even and calm, doing my damnedest not to sound patronizing when that's all I ache to do. "You wanted to enroll me at Blackwell Academy, and I didn't fight you on it"—*much*—"but this is my senior year. Just because I go to a new school doesn't mean my plans...my routine is going to change."

"Ah, yes, you do love going to your little football games. How could I forget? But, darling"—*oh my god, someone gag me over here, please*—"don't you think you should be going to the Blackwell Academy game instead?" Fat chance. "It'll be so much easier for you to make friends if you start socializing with your new classmates. Get to know the peers who are your equals."

Forget *The Twilight Zone*; I think I've straight-up gone back in time with this classist bullshit she's spewing. My equals? I need a drink. I wonder how she would react if I took her martini and threw it back.

"I have more than enough friends, thank you very

much." *Ones who aren't people I've grown up thinking were my rivals.*

Natalie bristles, the silk ruffle along the plunging neckline of her dress moving with what I would bet good money is her body vibrating with repressed anger.

I don't need her to voice it to know what she's thinking. How dare I challenge her? She's Natalie King. She's my mother. Too bad it's the first detail that holds more weight in this scenario. It's wrong, but it's a fact of life at this point.

"I just worry, sweetheart." It takes everything in me not to clap for her continued performance as a caring parent. My interactions with Mitchell have been limited, but I've always gotten a genuine vibe from him during them. He's pretty much the antithesis of Natalie. Guess that's why she plays this new role she's created for herself.

"I'm fine…Mom." Swallowing down the sarcasm on that word almost chokes me.

"You always are, baby." *Okay, I really think I'm going to throw up.* "I just really wanted you to attend this dinner so we can help introduce you to some of your new peers and ease your transition to BA."

I ask her who she has in mind, if only so I'll know who I should steer clear of. If they have the Natalie stamp of approval, I want to avoid them like the plague.

It's confirmed that my instincts are spot on when she lists Miss Queen B and the annoying assholes who won't leave me alone.

"How about a compromise?" Again Mitchell is the voice of reason without even being aware of the true dynamic between me and the woman who bore me.

I shift from one foot to the next. "What did you have in mind?"

He leans forward, placing his glass on a decorative coaster then curling a hand over Natalie's knee, his thumb moving across the joint. "You go to the football game tonight, and in the future, if there's an event we would like you to join us at, we'll give you at least two days' notice. Would that work?" He glances at his wife than at me.

It's subtle, but I can see the way Natalie grinds her jaw, not at all happy she's about to "lose" this battle. I wait for her to nod before I give my agreement.

"That's a wonderful idea, honey." Natalie covers Mitchell's hand that's still on her knee, and I give in to the urge to roll my eyes at her continued use of pet names. Who is this woman? "Besides—"

Ice slides down my spine at the triumphant smile that slithers across her face as she brings the full weight of her attention to me.

"—there should be plenty of opportunities for us all to connect." I'm not sure what that means, but I'll be damn sure to do everything in my power to avoid any and all situations that include Jasper Noble. "Tomorrow, the two of us can sync up our calendars."

Why does that sound more like a threat than a plan?

CHAPTER 7

TGIF IS REAL, people. I seriously have never been more excited
to see a Friday in my entire life.

All week I've been dealing with lame-ass hazing—people
stepping on the backs of my shoe to give "flat tires", lube on
the handle of my locker, cornering me in the bathroom to
"remind me of my place"—because I refuse to fall in line.
Really...it's laughable. If they want to get to me, they're going
to have to step up their game.

Plus, passing the recently pruned shrubs that bracket the
entrance gates has made arriving at this school all the more
enjoyable. What once read BA now is trimmed to boast BP.

The most tiring thing about the last seven days has been
trying to mollify Natalie and her desperate need to prove we
are the "perfect family". I haven't spent any time away from
the penthouse—outside of school—since the BP football game
last Friday.

I can't continue to go on this way. I need to find some sort
of middle ground. I've broached the subject with Mitchell—
he's the far more reasonable of the two—so my fingers are

crossed I shouldn't have an issue this weekend. He was the one to suggest we compromise about my social calendar.

Tinsley and I step outside the gilded doors of this over-the-top academy, and as always, the elite of the school are loitering about. Some lean against their luxury vehicles, others on the steps, all of them with a sense of entitlement I want to knock off their faces—with my fist.

I don't know if everyone at BP knowing who I ran with kept most guys respectful, or if the boys—I refuse to call them men because they don't act like it—at BA have more money than sense. Whatever it is, the shit I've put up with here is getting old. If they don't stop trying to touch me without my permission, someone is liable to lose a hand.

There's a buzz in the parking lot that hasn't been here before, but for once, their attention doesn't seem to be solely focused on me, so I let it go.

Then I spot him.

Even with the black helmet covering his face, I'd recognize that cocky lean anywhere, not to mention the sick Kawasaki Ninja he's leaning against.

Wes.

In two seconds flat, I double-step, my Chucks slapping against the stone, ignoring all the students checking out the badass with the motorcycle, and launch myself at him.

He catches me automatically, his hands cupping my ass, my legs wrapping around his waist, and my arms sliding around his neck. I place a kiss on the visor, right over where his mouth is.

"Ma reine." His voice is muffled behind his helmet as he lowers me to the ground, and I let my body slide along each bump and ridge of his muscles. He makes a noise in the back of his throat, and the first genuine smile I've felt in far too long spreads across my face at the simple joy of teasing him.

"What are you doing here?" I ask once my feet are back on

solid ground, the murmuring around us increasing in volume.

It's not that I'm not happy to see him—I'm ecstatic—but other than myself, Royalty doesn't step foot on BA grounds… ever. Sure, unless they know his bike, not many people would recognize Wes for who he is with the visor down, but this is unexpected.

"I've come to collect you for the weekend."

"The *weekend*?" My voice squeaks at the end from the pure, unadulterated excitement that possibility brings with it.

"Oh yeah." Even without seeing it, I know he's smirking at me. "Carter already cleared it with the Momster."

It's more likely he means Mitchell, but I don't really care. A whole weekend where I truly belong…nothing sounds better than that. Plus, it can only mean one thing—racing.

"Gotta say, Savs"—his hand goes to my hip, pulling me back against him, taking extra touchy-feely liberties without my brother around—"this is a good look on you."

Simple joy bubbles through my bloodstream. My favorite pastime is flirting with Wes, and when he's a willing participant in it, it's even more fun.

"Does it fulfill those schoolgirl fantasies you were talking about?" I arch a brow, daring him to make a move.

Like his smirk, his dark eyes are hidden, but it doesn't lessen the impact of them as he scans me from the top of my ponytail down to the tips of my Chucks.

"*Oh* yeah," he answers, dragging out the syllables.

Lust slams into me, and I'm instantly wet. Wes talks a big game and loves to tease me, but outside of a few make-out sessions with a side of dry humping—thanks to the rare occasion when alcohol lowers his guard and his concern about what Carter would say is lessened—I can't get him to go further than that. It's annoying as hell.

He scans the school behind me, chin jerking in greeting

when he spots Tinsley, and she gives a tentative wave, unsure of who he is.

A noise akin to a growl rumbles in Wes's chest, the vibration traveling through my hand that's placed in the center of it and up my arm as he takes in Jasper and company's blatant staring. We're yards away, but it doesn't take away from the burn Jasper's iridescent eyes have on the back of the hand I have on Wes.

"Jesus, you weren't kidding about this place." The sound of Wes's voice brings my attention back to him and off of my nemesis.

"Forget about it." I walk my fingers up the hard, sculpted muscles stretching the black cotton of his T-shirt.

"You tempt me, *ma reine*"—the rough callouses on his fingers set off a round of tingles as he lifts my hand, stopping its northern trajectory—"more than you know."

Too bad you only have balls of steel when it comes to fighting and not when it comes to giving in to your attraction to me.

"Now"—he pats the seat on the Ninja—"you going to be okay riding this in that skirt of yours?"

"You or the bike?" I press in closer, brushing the front of my body against his, hands falling to my hips and squeezing in a warning.

"*Savvy.*" The groaned use of my name tells me how much I'm challenging him.

I pop up onto my toes for another kiss to the visor. "Relax, Charming." I can't stop the smirk that forms when I use the nickname with which Tessa dubbed Mr. Prince. "I know it'll be a while before you grow a set and round a few more bases with me." *Because, of course, Carter has a say in who I'm with. Why on earth would I get to make that decision myself?*

Wes's hands curl around me more, the tips of his long fingers slipping beneath my silk uniform shirt and dipping into the hem of my skirt. My pulse picks up speed, hoping this will be one of the times he gives in to my teasing.

"Stop holding your breath," he cautions, and it's only then that I feel the tightness in my lungs I work hard to avoid.

I exhale with a rush and inhale with a slight wheeze. I bet if I were able to see them, his eyes would be narrowed. He and Carter have been friends my whole life. He's witnessed more than one hospital stay when my asthma isn't adequately managed.

"Good girl." This time the hitch to my breathing has nothing to do with my asthma and everything to do with the flush those two words uttered in his gravelly voice cause.

Wes releases his hold on me and steps back. "Now get your fine ass on the bike."

CHAPTER 8

"YEAH...THANKS." I end the call with my contact and step out into the common room that connects the bedrooms in our suite.

My boys are all spread out around the room, the U of J football game playing on the flat screen, beers cracked for those indulging.

"We set for the night?" Duke pulls three bottles of water from the mini-fridge and tosses the first one to Banks then another my way.

I make quick work of cracking the seal and chugging back half of the cool liquid. We haven't left yet, and already my adrenaline is spiking at the anticipation of racing tonight. To be fair, I think it's been sitting at a high simmer since school let out yesterday.

"Are you sure she's going to be there?" Duke asks, referring to Samantha St. James.

I pop a shoulder and finish off the last of the water. There's no guarantee, but after yesterday's realization of *where* I recognized her from, I'd say there's a good chance.

Samantha St. James is a race rat. She walks around these hallowed halls like she's a queen when she's really nothing more than a groupie for those who participate in Carter King's street races. Granted, I'll give her credit for getting with one of the top dogs on the circuit. The only way she could rank higher on the primo pussy scale would be if she were sleeping with the king himself instead of his number two.

The thin plastic of the bottle crumples between my palms until it's a flat disk as flashes of yesterday play through my memory.

He never took off his helmet, but there aren't that many Kawasaki Ninjas in Blackwell, let alone with that paint job. I knew right away it was Wesley Prince.

I eyed him, trying to figure out what the hell would bring him to BA. He graduated from BP years ago, so there's no way he would still be involved in the pranks our two schools trade back and forth. For as connected as the Royals are in town, they don't openly set foot on academy property. What changed? What brought him here? And why was he just standing outside?

Before I could come up with any of those answers, a flash of silver caught my eye, and the only woman I have been able to jerk my dick to since she told off our lunch table over a week ago jumped into *his* arms, long legs bared by her short uniform skirt wrapped around *his* waist, her DSLs placing a kiss to *his* motorcycle helmet.

Wesley Prince's hands cradled the ass my palm itches to spank. Every time Samantha openly defies me, the urge to put her over my knee or bend her over a table gets harder to ignore.

Then I had to endure watching them flirt while those around us whispered and speculated. The way she flipped the bottom of her skirt up at Prince with a pop of her ass nearly had me stomping down the stone steps in...

What?

A fit of possessive jealousy?

Fuck that.

This has nothing to do with jealousy.

No. Nope. This is about the way Samantha openly disregards every system put in place and how it risks more than rebelling against the status quo.

If others figure out she's even loosely connected to the Royals, it could lead to a headache I don't feel like dealing with.

Samantha needs to learn not to underestimate me. She may think being connected to the Royalty Crew will keep her protected when she's in "my house", but she'll learn I don't scare easily. I'm going to swagger onto her precious Royals' turf and prove no one, *especially her*, steps to me.

Crashing King's race tonight is about finding Samantha and reminding her who the real king of her new world is—me.

CHAPTER 9

ALL THE TENSION I've felt for the last week has been completely absent these last thirty plus hours. It doesn't matter that I haven't been subjected to many run-ins with Natalie; being forced to stay under her roof is enough to keep my cortisol levels in the red.

As much as Natalie likes to rewrite history as of late, the large colonial she sold when she married Mitchell hasn't been more than a house to us in years. After Dad died, Carter and I spent most of our time floating between our friends' houses and staying with our godfather, Anthony Falco, and various members of his family.

We still attend Sunday dinner with the Falcos, but our official home base became the industrial-esque warehouse I'm pulling the door shut on once Carter purchased it at eighteen. The three-story building sits toward the back of the two acres of paved asphalt, and its matte black walls are the perfect match to the four-bay auto garage beside it.

Carter's home also has an attached garage for his personal vehicles, but the bulk of the structure is split into a large gym and a loft-style residence, with bedrooms for not only Carter and me but also the four other guys who make up the Royalty Crew.

I wiggle the handle on the door, double-checking the locks have engaged before I move to weave my way through the crowd gathered outside.

Saturday night is party night, and Mr. Thinks-He's-Oh-So-Clever has deemed the parties that go hand in hand with his race nights Royal Balls—except there are no ball gowns, tuxedoes, or masquerade masks in sight. We're more a ripped jeans, T-shirts, and, when the weather cools, hoodies and leather jackets type crowd.

The bonfire that is a staple of these things is going strong; my brother, Wes, and the other three members of the Royals— Lance Bennett, Leo Castle, and Cisco Cruz—are holding court around it from their designated black camping chairs.

Closing in on race time has Wes busy doing his best to collect the last of the night's bets while Cisco prepares the GPS units with the race's route.

Typically the bonfire is a no-go area for me, the smoke one of the easiest triggers for my asthma. Instead, I hook a left and join the cluster of people Tessa and Tinsley are with.

"Hey." I tap Tessa with the cup I refilled for her as she seems to stare off into space. "You okay?"

"Huh?" She blinks in rapid succession and pulls her gaze away from a few of the jocks from BP, hitting me with one of her cheer-competition-worthy smiles. "Oh…yeah." She glances down at her cup. "Maybe I should have had you grab me a Red Bull instead."

I study her for a second longer before letting it go and fall back into the conversation happening around us, getting clued in on all things BP I've been missing out on and hearing all the details of BA's latest retaliation.

"Royals" by Lorde starts to play over the sound system, and I bite onto the plastic rim of my purple Solo cup, tipping it up to hide my smirk when Carter shoots me a knowing look.

Cuffing my brother on the shoulder, Wes pushes up out of his chair, all eyes in the vicinity turning to watch as he makes his way over to our group.

A muscular arm drapes itself around Tessa's shoulders, the other going around mine, his long fingers hanging and brushing along the back of my arm, the scent of fresh soap and motor oil filling my lungs as he brings his mouth to my ear to whisper, "You're such a smartass, *ma reine*."

"What?" I angle my head around, my nose brushing along the line of his jaw. "A little too on the nose? If Carter can be a corny motherfucker with his naming, why can't I?"

The throaty purr of an engine echoes through the night, and from over the curve of Wes's biceps, I watch a gorgeous taupe-colored Ferrari F8—the unconventional color only adding to the sexiness of the Italian sports car—and a silver G-Wagon find spaces in the area designated for parking.

All my senses go on alert. My heart starts to speed up, my lungs tighten, and the hairs on the back of my neck stand on end, the goose bumps now coating the skin visible on my lower belly and back having nothing to do with the cropped hem of my shirt.

"Um, Wes…" Tessa's voice is concerned, having reached the same conclusion as me.

I'm not sure if he answers her or not because I'm too focused on the half a million dollars' worth of automobiles that just pulled up and the people now stepping out of the open doors.

Like magnets, pearlescent eyes lock on me, the dark fringe of lashes surrounding them lowering as they narrow, seeing me wrapped in Wes's embrace.

What are they doing here? My fingers curl, pinching Wes's side, and it takes everything in me not to look my brother's way and ask. Yes, he opens some of these races to people from BA, but those are by special invitation, and never at the start of the school year when the prank war is in full swing. No. There's no way he would have done so tonight.

"You forget to tell us you're making friends at BA?" Wes asks, his body rigid in my hold, one eye on Jasper, another on Carter, waiting for his command.

"Hardly," I scoff, finally giving in and breaking my gaze from Jasper's tractor-beam-like hold to glance toward my brother. Both the shadows dancing from the bonfire and the shade created by the brim of his black ball cap make it impossible to get a read on him. It's the subtle way he shifts forward, his elbows bracing themselves on his knees, his black Solo cup—filled with seltzer like mine—dangling in feigned carelessness from the tips of his fingers that give away—to me—how alert he is.

"Let me handle this?" I voice it as a question even as I step free of Wes's embrace.

"Savs," he warns again, his eyes shifting back to Carter. I love this man—all of the Royals, really—but it's annoying as fuck how no matter how tough they are in life, they turn into pussies if I'm a part of the equation. It irks every one of my feminist tendencies.

"That"—I rock back on the rubber heel of my biker-style ankle boots and point a finger an inch in front of his nose—"is why it has to be me. His *Royal Highness* is all worried about these people knowing I'm Savvy King…" An overreaction. "How do you expect to stop them from hearing people saying my name if they get too close?"

Wes's chest expands as he inhales a deep breath. He hates that I have a point.

"Go to Carter." I tip my head at the bonfire. "I got this."

His jaw pops out to the side, his teeth grinding in frustration. Wes glances back to where Jasper and the rest of them have finally gathered, and I see he brought his entire court of douchebags with him. *Lovely.*

"Fine," Wes relents, his shoulders falling with a heavy exhalation. "But"—he reaches around to my back pocket—"put your gloves on before you head over there."

I do as he asks, wiggling my fingers through the fingerless leather gloves Carter purchased for me years ago. The black cowhide is supple from years of wear, the edge coming to a stop at the line where my bottom knuckles bend. There's a small cutout of the material over the back of my hand, the scalloped edging delicate, and when looked at closely enough, you can make out the subtle detailing that makes it resemble a crown.

I rotate my wrist, grasping the wide band that crosses over it and snaps closed underneath. I flex my fingers, stretching them out then forming a fist to make sure I have everything secured in the proper place. The thin metal hidden inside the leather sends a familiar rush of security through me before I repeat the process with my other hand.

Carter may have a few legitimate business ventures he's a part of—the body shop here as well as being a tattoo artist—but I'm not naive and know the bulk of his livelihood falls in the more...*questionable* category. These illegal street races are only one of those ventures.

When I was younger, he tried to shield me from most of his dealings, but in the same breath, he wanted to make sure I was always able to protect myself. Thanks to my physical limitations, I wouldn't last long in any kind of brawl. To combat that, Carter ensured the handful of punches I would be able to get in before needing my inhaler would have the most impact possible. Thus came the creation of my own modified and hidden version of brass knuckles.

Rolling my shoulders back, I wait for Wes to start to make his way over to Carter before I do the same toward our gate-crashers.

A pinky hooks with mine before I can get too far, and I

look down to see the delicate script of the word *Promise* on the inside of both digits linking together.

"You stay here too," I say to Tessa, giving her finger an extra squeeze before pulling away. She may be the definition of my ride or die, but that doesn't stop me from trying to shelter her from things when possible. She's too good, too light to allow these jerks to taint it with their hostility. Tinsley is subjected to it at school, but I'll be damned if they try to get to her when outside of it.

Jasper's gaze is hard, assessing and challenging as I travel through the maze of cars separating us. The tightness of his jaw only seems to emphasize the cleft in his chin, and I hate him a tiny bit more for thinking it increases his hotness factor. This guy is a grade-A jerkwad, and the effect he's having on my panties makes me question my sanity.

"Are you lost?" I plant my feet, pop a hip out, and cant my head to the side, reaching up to twirl the end of my high ponytail when the long strands fall over my shoulder. "I would think rich boys like you would be able to afford GPS in your fancy cars."

From their position bookending him, the peen gallery snickers, and I think I catch a whispered "Oh shit" in there somewhere too.

Jasper's expression never changes, and I tell myself I don't notice the way the muscles of his arms strain against the sleeves of his dove gray T-shirt when he crosses them. Or how the shade of his shirt emphasizes the lighter hues in his eyes.

No. Nope. I don't notice those things at all.

Liar.

"Are you judging our choice of automobiles, Princess?" Jasper drawls the words out like this is the south and not the northeast, the smooth cadence washing over me as my hackles rise at his continued use of that endearment.

I bite the corner of my bottom lip, my heart rate picking

up speed when his gaze falls to my mouth. With a shimmy of my shoulders, I shake off the tingles that glance evokes and instead say, "Just making an observation."

Silence stretches, growing more heated the longer it does. Excitement bubbles up inside me at how openly he challenges me, even without saying a word. *What the fuck is with that?*

As fun as this little showdown is, it needs to come to an end. A quick glance behind me confirms this as I see all five Royals are now on their feet, all their attention homed in on me. Watching. Waiting. Preparing for an attack.

It's probably wrong to be annoyed when they're only trying to make sure I'm safe. Their actions come from a place of love. I know this. *Really* I do, but the way they handle situations I'm involved in *feels* different. It doesn't feel like a *We have your back if needed*, but more like a *Be on guard, someone is messing with Savvy.* It rankles because these fools flipping nicknamed me Savage for how I can handle myself yet conveniently forget that fact in real-life situations.

It's too bad they're too far away to properly read the *Can you fools chill?* eye-widening I send them. With a shake of my head, I step to the left and let the SUV behind me block most of me from view. I can handle this on my own.

"Look." I blow out a breath, annoyed my stress-free weekend is being spoiled by those who shouldn't even be here. "I know you guys think you *rule the universe*"—my sarcasm couldn't be any thicker if I tried—"but this"—I point to the ground—"isn't your kingdom, so yous gots to go."

"Oh, *really*?" Jasper drops his arms, feet moving to widen his stance.

"Really." My nod is pure sass and one-hundred-percent confidence. No way, no how will I let this asshole try to pull his dominance bullshit on my turf. He may not be aware of that minor detail, but this *is* my turf, and he *will* do as I say.

"It's cute…" He takes a step in my direction, but I hold my ground and don't move.

"What is?" I flex my fingers at my sides.

"How you *still* think you can tell me what to do." Another step, then two more, and his designer sneakers' tips are touching the toes of my boots.

It's a good thing I moved out of view as Jasper steps again, finally forcing me back until I feel the metal of the SUV touch my skin. If the Royals saw him this close to me, they'd be over here in a heartbeat. I need them to trust I have the situation handled on my own; otherwise, it'll be open season for Jasper and his fellow douchecanoes when it comes to me.

"You know what's *not* cute?" I tilt my chin up to maintain eye contact.

"What's that, Princess?" Jasper shifts closer, his chest now touching mine, effectively pinning me to whoever's car is behind me.

It takes effort to swallow, and I force myself not to blink. "How long it's taking you to realize that I actually *can*. Are you a dumb jock? Is that it?" My ponytail brushes the forearm next to my face as I tilt my head with my taunt, ignoring how the sinew twitches as it does. "I'm sure we can get you a tutor," I add, just to be an asshole.

A vein pulses at his temple, and again his eyes fall to my mouth as he brings a hand to my face. "One of these days"— he drags a thumb along my bottom lip—"this mouth of yours is going to get you in trouble."

My nipples tighten into painful peaks, and my panties are officially drenched.

The scent of sandalwood grows stronger as he fully invades my personal space. "For so long"—his lips skim the rim of my ear as he speaks—"I've tried to figure out *why* you look so familiar to me."

Panic swift and strong slams into me, and I cough around the constriction it forms in my lungs. Lifelong experience with my asthma has taught me many ways to control my condition, but it's the emotional triggers I have the hardest time managing. *Goddamn Carter putting ideas in my head.*

"I asked myself what I was missing. What gave you the confidence—no matter how misguided—to *think* you could challenge me? I figured it was because you were just another BP prick, one of those who always thinks they can do what they want. And then…what do you know?" I feel more than see him shrug. "Wesley Prince picks you up from school yesterday."

"Fascinating story. Riveting…*really*." I turn my face, using my cheek to shove his away a scant inch or two. "But your obsession with me still doesn't give you the right to be here."

A humorless chuckle rumbles inside his chest, the sound vibrating against my greedy nipples.

"Oh…that's where you're wrong."

He touches the tip of one finger to the small black diamond hanging from a delicate silver chain that sits in the hollow of my throat, dragging it down my breastbone, between my now-heaving-in-an-effort-to-increase-airflow breasts, over the bare skin of my tummy, not stopping until it hooks into the buttoned waistband of my black skinny jeans.

"Just because you're a race rat for a Royal, that doesn't give you any actual power."

Relief that he didn't actually figure out my true connection to the Royals has my body sagging into the car, the unyielding metal frame digging into my shoulder blades. The band around my lungs loosens, but if I don't extract myself soon, I'm at risk of having to pull my inhaler out here. The *last* thing I want is for Jasper to know about my asthma.

Having asthma doesn't make me weak by any stretch of the imagination. Hell, all the treatments I've gone through prove I'm made of tougher stuff than most, but Jasper is the type that would exploit it to his advantage if he knew about it.

"The only power you have is your pussy's ability to make a dick wet, nothing more."

I lick my lips, my nostrils flaring with my next inhalation. "If that's what you want to think, who am I to tell you you're wrong?"

He swallows, and I watch how his Adam's apple bobs up then down with the action before flattening my palms against his chest, ignoring the hardness of it as I shove him back for space.

I manage to get three steps away before his deep voice has me spinning back to face him. "No need to be sad that you're nothing but a street slut to them." His expression is arrogant and annoyingly sexy. I want to punch it. My hands ball into fists to prevent myself from giving in to the urge.

"*Excuse* me?" I arch a brow.

"It's okay." Jasper holds his arms out as if to say, *Don't shoot the messenger.* "You rats serve a purpose. There's no better way to work off the adrenaline from a race than with one of you on your knees."

"You're so fucking off base it's laughable." I start toward the back of the SUV, only to spin back around before I clear it. "But like I said earlier, you should leave before you embarrass yourself." I wave a hand at his I'll-never-admit-how-panty-melting-it-is Ferrari. "No matter how much horsepower Mommy and Daddy buy you, you'll never beat a Royal in a race."

Jasper's features turn to stone, and in a blink, he's closed the distance I've managed to put between us. His grip is hard as he pinches my chin in his fingers. I refuse to give him the satisfaction of flinching.

"Wanna bet on it?" It's his turn to arch a brow.

"Isn't that kind of the whole point of all this?" I circle a finger in the air, indicating the Royal Ball as a whole.

"I'm talking about a little side wager just between us."

I do my best to swallow past my dry throat—another

symptom presenting itself. I need to go but instead say, "What did you have in mind?"

Victory shines in his gaze. "I do have a caveat, though."

"Isn't that the definition of a side bet?"

The pressure of his pinched hold increases until my lips separate and purse. "What did I say about this mouth?" His thumb stretches up, slipping inside the space he created, the taste of salt landing on my tongue.

I will the saliva to form to wash away the desert-like situation I have going on and the essence of *him* he's trying to imprint on *me*.

"If you really aren't just another race rat like you claim…it should be easy for you to have them switch the docket tonight."

Around us, the crackle from the bonfire, the seductive rasp of Kehlani playing from the speakers, and the low comments from his boys fade until all that's left is Jasper and me in this bubble of clashing wills.

Jerking my face to the right, I shake off his hold, arching my spine to create a few inches of precious space for my upper body. "Scared to face King?" I taunt, knowing my brother's undefeated record.

"No." Jasper's long fingers wrap around my nape, tugging me straight again until I'm forced to push onto my toes to ease the pressure on my neck.

My hands fall to his sides to steady myself, fingers curling and bunching the fabric of his T-shirt to keep from making direct contact with his hard body.

Those envious lips lower to mine, not quite kissing but skimming with his next words. "I want the added satisfaction of Prince knowing *he* was the one who lost to me before I claim my prize."

My breath hitches, but this time, it has nothing to do with the pending asthma attack I need to get under control ASAP.

Why? Why the hell does he affect me? Why do I give in to his taunts?

"Your prize?" His grip turns punishing, but I'm still able to manage to shift enough for his lips to land on my cheek instead of my mouth. "We don't race for pink slips. Here it's all about the Benjamins, bay-bee."

Against the curve of my cheekbone, his lips stretch into a smile. "The only pink slip I'm interested in racing for tonight is the one between your fine-ass legs."

CHAPTER 10

SAMANTHA TRIES TO HIDE IT, but it's impossible to not feel how she trembles in my arms. If I have my way, later I'll be feeling *all* the ways her body can shudder while her cunt milks my dick.

Crossing an arm over my body, I latch onto her opposite wrist, my fingers sliding across the leather encasing her hand as they overlap, emphasizing how easily I could break her. If she doesn't learn to toe the line, that's exactly what I'll do.

She thinks she can tell me what to do? Not happening.

She thinks I'm scared of her? That's cute.

She'll learn the error of her ways as soon as she realizes she's not the hunter but the prey in this story.

The silky strands of her hair hit the skin of my neck, and I whirl her around and tuck her tight to me, her back flush with my front. I bend the arm connected to the wrist I have manacled and shove it into the cleavage of her boatneck collar— fucking thanks, Mom, for me even knowing something like that. Using her own body against her, I secure her almost like a seat belt would.

When she tries to wiggle free, I bring my other hand around and flatten it to her belly. The softness of the pale skin exposed between the jeweled hue of her purple shirt and her black painted-on skinny jeans only increases the hardness in my pants.

I revel in the way her breathing is labored. She can deny it until she's blue in the face; I know she wants me.

I came here tonight to teach her a lesson. Like the puck bunnies at school, race rats get a certain type of consideration, but like Arabella, Samantha has made the mistake of thinking because she spreads her legs or opens her mouth for someone at the top of a social hierarchy, it gives her power. It doesn't. Hell, it doesn't even mean she falls into the *hands-off* category. I'll take great, ball-emptying pleasure in teaching Samantha what a grave miscalculation she made when it comes to me.

I may have zero intention of keeping her, but it won't stop me from taking her. Beating her precious Prince to do it will be an added bonus. And if I can knock her down a peg or two by proving she's just another hole to fill by doing precisely that, then fucking her on the hood of my Ferrari, well…

I give a quick check, but the Royals can't see me playing with their toy.

Burying my face in the curve of her neck, I trail my nose down it, inhaling the sweet lime on her skin. The vein visibly pulsing there is impossible to ignore, and I drag my tongue and the ring pierced through it along the vein and bite down. Her gasped moan and hip wiggle have me grinding my hard-on into her as a preview of what's to come.

"Now, why don't you be a good girl for once and go tell them the only Chevrolet we want to see in the race tonight is the Camaro, *not* the Corvette."

He may have beaten me the last time we were in a race together, but this time Wesley Prince will be the one seeing *my* taillights through his windshield. Then, because

I'm sure I'll be feeling generous after my win, I'll let him watch as I make Samantha scream in ways he never could.

Samantha stumbles as I release her, body swaying as I step away. After a beat, she whirls on me, hands encased in badass fingerless gloves going to her hips. She pauses instead of doing what she's told. "Listen, dickhead—"

"Now, now"—I tick my finger back and forth—"don't go talking dirty to me early." Her eyes narrow, and I slide in close again, swiping a finger over her bottom lip. "But if you do what you're told for once, I promise you'll get *very* acquainted with my dick's head." I love how that slight hitch to her breathing gives away how affected she is by me when I know it most likely *kills* her that she can't hide it. "*And*"—I bring my mouth to her ear—"if you're a *really* good girl, you'll get to meet the rest of my cock while you're choking on it."

She scoffs, an actual sound of disgust rolling around in that spot at the back of her throat my dick aches to ram against repeatedly.

"I'll arrange your *little*—"

Her eyes drop down to my belt, her lips kicking up at the corners as if she has X-ray vision and she's making a dig about what she sees behind my fly. *Sorry, baby. The only thing little going on there is the amount of free space in my boxer briefs.* A fact only emphasized by the blood flowing south.

"—bet." She flicks the cleft in my chin with her finger. "But I'm *only* doing it so that when *you* lose, I'll win my freedom from having to deal with you."

I give her a half nod, allowing her the illusion of control.

With one more of those death glares she seems to always have on hand for me, she puts a hand to her chest and walks away. Something catches my eye near her spine, but it's too dark to make it out. Instead, I focus on the way her ass swings with each purposeful stride.

"What's the plan, brother?" Duke steps up to my right, his own gaze on Samantha's retreating form.

"We wait and see *just* how special she is to them."

We put up a good front for Samantha's benefit, and yes, this isn't the first time we've come to Royal territory, but we know where the line is. Okay, so maybe we like to play jump rope with it when the mood suits us. I'm not looking to make an enemy out of the Royalty Crew, but that's not going to stop me—win or lose—from playing with their toy.

"Fuck me," I curse when Samantha bypasses the Royals and heads straight for Carter King's residence, pulling something from her back pocket and stepping inside. *Hmm, maybe she is as connected as she claims if she has a key.*

"Isn't that what you bet her to do?" Duke holds a fist out for me to bump.

As Wesley Prince *and* Carter King follow behind Samantha, a frown tugs at my lips, the latter pausing when a redhead runs to join them.

"Is it wrong that it doesn't surprise me to see Tinsley here?" Banks takes his place on my other side when she disappears with the redhead.

I think I answer him, but I'm not sure, all my focus on the building, wishing I was the one with X-ray vision to see what's happening inside.

It's a solid five minutes later when the door finally opens, and out steps Wesley Prince. He makes a quick detour to confer with the other Royals still outside then heads straight for us.

The partygoers have watched us since we pulled in, but with the exception of Samantha, none of them have approached until now.

Rolling my shoulders back, I stand up straighter, finding that perfect balance between *I don't give a fuck* and *I'm ready to throw down if needed.*

Dark eyes flit up and down my body, dismissing me as

quickly as it took to complete their inspection. That familiar flare of anger at the disrespect sparks to life. One would think after experiencing it every day with Samantha, I would be immune to it. Unlike my recently acquired pain in the ass, Wesley is one of those balancing acts with the line I was talking about earlier.

Keeping myself in check, I do my own slightly more thorough inspection of the number two of the Royalty Crew. He's what you'd expect: black T-shirt, ripped jeans, backward hat, ink running down his arms onto his hands and knuckles. The thing that sets my teeth on edge is his devil-may-care attitude and the taunting smirk that says he could take us despite being outnumbered five to one. I would never admit it out loud, but considering that his reputation in the underground fighting circles might be more revered than the one he has as the other Royal to drive in these races, it's a distinct possibility.

"You're a cocky motherfucker—I'll give you that," Wesley says, slipping his hands into his pockets, again taunting us by not holding himself at the ready for a fight.

"Does that mean you will or *won't* be altering the race roster for tonight?" I fold my arms over my chest, waiting for his answer.

"Don't you worry, rich boy. You'll get your shot at the Camaro tonight." It's not the Camaro I want. It's what's between Samantha's legs that I'm racing for.

I let my lips tug upward, matching his smirk with one of my own, wondering if Samantha told her precious Prince what is *really* on the line.

An hour later, I'm finally sitting behind the wheel of my Ferrari, the supple leather of the bucket seat cradling my body like a lover as we wait for the race to begin.

I drum my thumbs on the prancing horse emblem in the center of my steering wheel as Duke secures the GoPro camera to the dash. He waits until our view of the empty lot in front of us shows on the gigantic projection screen that hangs on half of Carter's residence. This is the draw of what King does. None of the quarter-mile races you can participate in at tracks around the state. Instead, his are usually a route, given through pre-programmed GPS units. They take about thirty minutes to complete, all while being broadcasted back to those at the party to watch.

With the change to the lineup, the race itself was pushed back an hour. Unlike what I thought, King wasn't on the docket for tonight. Increased buy-ins had to be collected, and the odds of the bets needed to be adjusted to reflect a Royal now being one of the racers.

The few grand I had to pay for entry is small potatoes compared to the bigger races those from BA are invited to participate in, but the purse isn't why I race. I do it for the adrenaline rush. Adding a little pocket change is only a bonus.

All through the paying, betting, breathalyzing for safety, license plate covering, and camera setup, I didn't once see Samantha again. The fact that I register this pisses me the fuck off. The only reason I know she didn't dip out is because when Cisco Cruz—the Royal in charge of the GPS units— passed us ours, he did so with a comment about how she'll have a front-row seat to my demise. I can only assume that means she's the one riding shotgun with Prince.

Engines rev, and the final-minute countdown starts to sound from the GPS.

Gripping the steering wheel, my knuckles turn white as I wrap my hands around the leather, turning my head to the matte black Camaro idling beside me. The damn tinting is too dark for me to see inside, but I can feel her eyes on me regardless.

At the thirty-second warning, I press the button to lower my window and blow two kisses in a promise of what is to come for the prize I'll be claiming.

Determined, I flick the button up. Glass back in place, I crank up the radio and stretch my fingers until they curve around the gear panels at the side of the steering wheel, readying myself for having to switch gears on a dime.

Ten. Nine. Eight.

A glance at Duke shows his nod that he's ready too.

Seven. Six. Five. Four.

The muscles on my right leg tense in preparation to lift off the brake.

Three. Two. One.

The throaty purr of the V8 engine in the back roars to life, and we take off with the other cars making up the half dozen participants.

The start of the course is like a typical drag race from the back of King's lot as drivers jockey for position to be the first one to pull out onto the road.

The torque and horsepower of my Ferrari are greater than the souped-up Camaro, and I manage to edge in front of Prince to be the first to pass the threshold free of other traffic thanks to King's Corvette blocking the road.

The navigation's mechanical voice guides me down a short straightaway before directing me to take the next right turn.

The skinny rectangles of the Camaro's headlights disappear as its front bumper inches closer to my rear one.

The suspension of my supercar hugs the road as I follow a series of curves and turns through Blackwell until I'm instructed to take the entrance ramp for the highway.

At midnight on a Saturday, the roads aren't packed, but they aren't anywhere close to being empty either. This is another thing that sets the Royals' races apart from the rest. Horsepower and spec-wise, only King's Corvette should be a match for my F8, but these races are more about the driver's skill versus if they have a NOS unit under their hood.

Periodically Duke calls out those in the closest position to us, with the Camaro and a Mustang the only two able to challenge me for the win. I ignore how my dick perks up thinking of all the ways we will use Samantha to celebrate when we do.

We're halfway done with the race, having completed a loop of an exit ramp followed by taking the next right onto the entrance ramp that will take us on the southbound side of the highway, when the flash of purple under-lighting becomes visible in my side mirror. *Prince.*

"Oh shit," Duke curses, and I drop a gear, swinging into the lane to my right and around a slow-moving SUV to maintain my lead.

I'm not fucking losing this race.

My back loses contact with the seat as I straighten, keeping one eye on the road and using the other to make sure I don't give him the opportunity to pass.

Long vertical strips of red taillights show we're coming up on a cluster of eighteen-wheelers.

With a press of the right pedal connected to the steering wheel, I swing into the right lane before gliding across the highway into the far left and around one of the Mack trucks.

The navigation calls out the mile warning for my upcoming exit, and I move back to the right lane, victory so close I can taste it like the burned rubber on the pavement when it happens.

In a move that is either suicidal or the most impressive stunt-driver-level skill ever depending on how you look at it, the Camaro squeezes between the eighteen-wheeler I just passed and the Toyota behind it, the sound of its tires kicking up the loose gravel on the shoulder of the road loud enough to be heard over my engine and my music as it skirts around the line of traffic for the exit. The opportunity to feel Samantha's cunt squeeze my cock slips away as the Camaro slips in front of me for the first time.

Sonofabitch.

Strobe lights in the taillights flash at me as we pull into King's lot, the bitter taste of second place instead of Samantha's pussy juices on my tongue.

I may have to accept the loss, but the little princess will have to come to terms with me not honoring the bet. Nah... you know what? I think it's time to kick things into a higher gear.

CHAPTER 11

ANOTHER YAWN BREAKS free as I make my way to my locker to switch out the books in my bag for what I'll need for first period, the deep exhaustion I haven't been able to shake since pushing myself too far this weekend still lingering. Not even Nonna Falco fussing over me at Sunday dinner was enough to banish it entirely.

I know it's my own fault that I ignored the signs of an asthma attack without treating it for too long, and now I'm suffering the consequences.

Reaching for the lock dial, the bruise-like, resistance-band feeling tightens around my chest, another yawn only intensifying the sensation. Careful to not spill and stain my white shirt, I bring the hand holding the paper to-go cup from Espresso Patronum to rub at my sternum to help alleviate the pressure.

Damn me for being such a stubborn bitch and not using my inhaler when I should have.

Yes, you should have. But nope, you pushed yourself into an asthma attack, and then you went and participated in the race with Wes when you should have taken it easy. Bet that *really helped, hmm?*

My head falls forward, my forehead touching the cold metal of my locker as I chuckle to myself at the shade I toss my own way. *It's no wonder Tessa nicknamed me Bitchy.* Can't say I regret pushing through the aftermath symptoms to witness the look on Jasper's face when Wes and I stepped out of the garage after parking the Camaro.

Jealous?

Thunderous?

My favorite was the murderous turn it took when I gave him a small finger wave and pressed a kiss to the underside of Wes's jaw.

It may be immature game playing, but I'm only seventeen years old; if ever there was a time to get away with childish behavior, it's now.

With another painful yawn, I spin the dial right, then left, and back to the right, slowing as I come to the last number of the combination. I pinch the lock handle between my fingers —grateful there's no lube coating it this time—and tug upward until it disengages.

Something small and white falls onto the white toe of my purple Chucks the second I pull the locker open, and it takes a few seconds for my sluggish reflexes to react to what I'm seeing.

"Oh shit!" I jump back and slam the door closed with a loud *clang*.

Is that a fucking mouse?

My knees crack as I bend and lower myself as slowly as possible, and sure enough, a two-inch rodent looks back at me with its beady black eyes. Even as it ping-pongs between my foot and the wall, I can't help but think it's actually kind of cute.

Continuing to keep my movements slow to not spook the thing, I set my coffee cup down and hold my hands out like I'm cradling a softball between them, hovering over my stow-away. On a silent count of three, I scoop up my furry friend.

Needle-like pricks scratch against the skin of my palms while the *twitch-twitch* of whiskers tickles me.

Not wanting to risk being bitten, I use my wrists to nudge the flap of my messenger bag up and carefully set the little guy in the free space available on top of my English lit textbook.

I shake out my hands, reclaiming my coffee, and rise to stand. I'll need to remember to thank Carter and his insistence on having a pet boa constrictor growing up. If I had never helped him feed Merlin this little dude's cousins through the years, I surely would have reacted like the jumpy, squeaky scaredy-cat those I suspect are responsible for my new buddy here expected me to be.

Way to welch on your end of the bet, fuckface.

With a slow, deep breath to calm myself before I trigger another asthma attack—I'm always more susceptible to one after experiencing one—I spin the dial and ease my locker open enough to peek inside.

Now that I'm paying attention, I hear the tiny chorus of squeaks before seeing the mischief of mice jockeying for position on my textbooks.

Before any more of them can pull a Michael Scofield and perform a prison break, I close the door and think of what would be the best course of action to take.

"If they want to play games with you, Savvy, show them how they're played." My brother's words and his innate confidence in me play through my memory and chase away the last of the negativity lingering from this latest juvenile bullying attempt.

The back of my neck prickles at the weight of expectant

eyes watching me. I don't turn around, refusing to give them even the briefest glimpse into my own thought process.

My foot taps, and I worry the strap on my bag with my hand as another piece of advice from Carter pushes to the forefront. *"A ruler is only as strong as the allies they curry."*

Mentally I roll my eyes thinking of all the times I've teased him about his *Game of Thrones* type thinking. Though…

I'm loath to admit it, but his monarchical principles always find a way to be relevant. It's why I find myself walking down the hall to the left toward where the custodial offices are located instead of to the right toward homeroom. Guess I'm going to be late.

Pulling my Ray-Bans out of my bag, I slip them on as soon as Tinsley and I step out onto the cafeteria's outdoor patio. Looking around, I see most of the tables are filled with students who, like us, are taking advantage of the warm weather while we still have it.

Personally, I'm not looking forward to when the temperatures drop and we are forced to sit inside where I can't escape the scrutiny of a particular set of pearly eyes.

Tinsley and I fall into our typical easy conversation, but if she thinks she's disguising her concern about how I'm feeling, she's most definitely failing. I don't call her out on it, though. If I were still attending Blackwell Public, Tessa would be sticking to me like I was Peter Pan and she was my shadow.

Plus…

It's nice to be cared about. And Tinsley? She's a blessing I wasn't even aware I needed. She's the perfect bridge between all the things I love about my old life at BP and the shark-infested waters I need to navigate through at BA.

"I still can't believe no one's talking about how you had *mice* in your *locker*." As if it wasn't evident enough in her tone, her full-body shiver gives away her disgust.

I bury a laugh with a long swallow of Pepsi Wild Cherry. "It's probably because I didn't react. I didn't scream or cry. I didn't run away or cause any kind of scene they could document." I pop a shoulder. "Who's gonna waste their time gossiping about something without drama?"

Tinsley gives me a *You've got a point* head bob as she munches on a bite of chicken marsala. I can find many, *many* faults with my new academic establishment, but their culinary selections are not one of them. At least Arabella was right about one thing in this pretentious place.

"What did you do with them anyway?"

I open my mouth to answer, but before I can speak, a bowl filled with tan pellets, sunflower seeds, pumpkin seeds, and dried corn is slid in front of me, and the metaphorical thorn takes his place in my side by dropping into the empty chair beside me.

An arm whose muscle definition displayed by a rolled-up sleeve I pointedly ignore drapes across the back of my seat, and knees connect with my thighs. I refuse to watch the strain of the wool of his dark trousers as he knocks into my leg and the chair scrapes then clangs against the stone.

I shift to angle my body around. Carter taught me you never give an enemy your back. You face them head-on and dare them to come at you.

My hands ball into fists as I resist the urge to smack that damn smirk off those stupidly tempting lips. Warm air caresses my cheek, and the breath I shouldn't be holding is held in self-defense as his sandalwood scent tries to invade my senses.

"Yeah, Samantha..." Calloused fingertips circle the jut of my kneecap, my legs snapping together to prevent their progress up my inner thigh. Unfortunately, there's nothing I can do about the way my muscles tremble under the touch I don't want but can't bring myself to hate. "What *did* you do with your new friends?"

If only shooting daggers out of one's eyes were a real thing. It would solve *so* many of my issues right now.

"They are taken care of, thank you for asking." I roll my shoulder back in indifference and to knock the fingers tracing figure eights on the back of it off.

Those pearly eyes bounce over the features of my face, that smirk slipping slightly at my stoic demeanor. The tick of Jasper's jaw is the only tell of his disappointment. It *kills* him that I don't react like he believes I should.

"Tell me, Samantha." The command in his tone has shivers shooting down my spine. Since the Royals dubbed me Savvy for short, I've hated my legal name, but the gravelly way it rolls off Jasper's tongue? Yeah, my issue now is that I *don't*.

"You know…" I lay my hand over the center of his chest, the muscles tensing under my touch, and toy with one of the buttons on his uniform shirt. I keep my gaze on where I pluck at the small plastic disk, lifting and pushing it around the buttonhole.

I wonder if he wears an undershirt. If I undo this button, I'll find out…

Shit! I shake my head to rid myself of those *highly* inappropriate thoughts. *What the hell?*

"You really should work on your retention skills, because if *I*"—I flatten my free hand over my heart—"recall correctly, *you*"—I push harder on his chest—"lost and are now *supposed* to leave. Me. Alone."

A vein pulses in his temple.

From beneath my lashes, I meet his gaze, only to find all his attention focused on where I've connected us. I swallow at the intensity in it, my teeth biting into the soft flesh of my lower lip, worrying over the small piece of chapped skin in the corner.

"Oh?" He arches a brow. "And are you saying if I had won, you would have willingly gotten on your knees for me?" He grips said knees. "That you would have eagerly opened your mouth?"

Behind my ribcage, my heart pounds, the steady *thump-thump-thump* increasing at his dirty words.

"That it wouldn't have taken my hand wrapped around your hair while I force-fed you my dick?"

The visual he paints has my nipples pebbling against the lace of my bra. When Jasper drops his eyes to them before sliding his gaze up to where I'm nibbling on my lip, my nostrils flare, and my eyes widen to hide a deep, steadying inhalation as I try to control my outward reaction to his close proximity. Why the hell does he affect me?

Determined to ignore the thoughts he inspires, I look for a redirection. I clear my throat and start to walk my fingers up the seam of his shirt. "Your pranks are as unimaginative as your driving skills." I lift my hand and fill the dimple in his chin with the pad of my forefinger before flicking it off, my nail catching his skin on the way down. "Must be why you lost to a Royal this weekend."

A hand clamps around my thigh, fingers digging into the space where the muscles connect to bone, his thumb spreading under the pleated hem of my skirt with authority, spinning me around until we're once again face-to-face.

My eyes cross in an effort to maintain eye contact, the tip of Jasper's nose bumping mine before dragging along the jut of my cheekbone and back to my ear. The world goes black as my eyelids close with his exhalation.

"When are you going to realize I'm not the type of man you want to play games with?" I jolt in my seat like I've been electrocuted when his teeth nip at my earlobe.

"I'm not playing at anything."

"The fuck you aren't." I'm tugged closer, the leg in his punishing grip pushed out into a wide V that straddles his knees, the drape of my skirt pleats the only thing keeping him from getting a panty shot of my pussy. Thank fuck for that because there would be no way to hide what I can feel is most definitely an embarrassing wet spot he is the direct cause of.

"No, *Noble*." My lips twist to the side, making sure to remind him just how much I think he lacks in living up to the title. "I don't play games. I set the rules." With his cheek still pressed to mine, all it takes is a dip of my chin to nip his razor-sharp jawline.

Whip fast, his free hand is in my hair, fisting the locks like in his earlier threat, pulling until my scalp stings and my neck is forced to arch back. His mouth falls to my exposed throat, lips brushing my skin as he murmurs, "I promise you this"— he licks the length of the vein pulsing double time, and the contact of his piercing has my panties officially soaked through—"you *will* learn the *only* one who makes the rules here is me."

Instinct urges me to argue, to assert my dominance the way I've been raised to do. I can't. Nothing happens. No words form. Instead, I have to concentrate on choking down the whimper of need that's trying to escape. *What the fuck is with that? Need? That's some shit right there.*

"I hope you enjoyed yourself this weekend—"

"*Immensely*," I say breathlessly.

"Fuck." With his face still buried against me, the growl he emits vibrates through me at the insinuation. The hand in my hair twists, and I cry out. Warm heat blankets my pulse point for a second before blinding suction transforms my bones to jelly.

I wiggle and squirm, slamming my hands against his pectorals, trying to get free. Nothing I do fazes Jasper; he just continues to suck. When he finally pulls back, he's not only smirking, he's full-on smiling, his thumb rubbing over my still damp skin.

This motherfucker better not have left a hickey.

"Keep pushing me, Samantha"—he presses down on the same spot, his eyes flashing open to me, the center of them a deep swirling gray, purple, and silver, the pupils dilated—"I dare you."

CHAPTER 12

MIRACLE OF MIRACLES today wasn't one of the days Natalie "required" my presence at the St. James. *Thank god for small favors on Mondays.*

Not gonna lie, it was a little strange having Daniel drop me off at Carter's, the Bentley seeming out of place in the vast lot of my brother's property. Still, I thanked him for the ride and promised I wouldn't need him any more for the day. Carter can more than handle taking me back to the St. James later.

Carter's Corvette is parked next to the Camaro as I make my way through the garage, but he's nowhere to be found when I call out "Party's here" à la Snookie.

Dumping my bag in the living room area, I make my way to my bedroom to change out of my uniform into a pair of dragon-printed leggings, the purple, gray, and black scales of the beast's large wings wrapping all the way around each of my legs. I pull on a black sports bra and complete the look with a cropped Blackwell Public wide-neck tee, the school's dragon mascot breathing fire from the center of my chest.

Across the room, the door leading from the gym that takes up a quarter of the residence opens, and my brother enters at the same time I step off the final stair.

"No." The word whips out quick as a bullet when he sees me dressed to work out.

"Cart," I argue, the purple fabric of my hand wrap hooked over my thumb and skimming the ground as it dangles from my finger.

"Not just no, it's a *fuck* no, Savvy." He slashes a hand through the air when I go to object again. "The only thing you're allowed to do this week is yoga. *Nothing* else."

I love yoga, but I really, *really* need to hit something. If it couldn't be Jasper earlier, I was okay with settling for the punching bag in the gym.

We both keep moving until we meet in the middle of the open-concept floor plan. "But—"

"Nope." I get a head shake for good measure. "*Maybe*— and that's a *big* fucking maybe"—a finger shakes inches from my nose—"I'll allow you to add swimming laps back in before the weekend." The harsh line of his mouth eases as it curls into a smile. "But I wouldn't hold your breath."

Hardy-har-har. Isn't my brother a regular comedian? I grind my teeth and fold my arms over my chest, putting every ounce of teenage angst I can muster into my actions, going as far as tapping my foot. I'm sure most girls my age would argue with the classic *You're not my father*, but I would never *ever* disrespect Carter that way. He may not be my father, but he actually gives a shit about me, unlike Natalie.

The triple beep of the lock from the garage disengaging sounds, and a second later, Tessa breezes into the room. As my gaze slides her way, a frown tugs down the corners of her lips and there's a lack of peppy bounce in her steps.

"Ooo…" The shadows fade from her blue eyes as a mischievous sparkle takes over while she studies the scene in front of her. "Did I walk in on a King duel? Should I get out the jousting sticks? Oh, wait!"

While she fumbles around in her pocket for her phone, I feel it's important to point out we do *not* have jousting sticks here. Carter may be obsessed with playing up all the royalty stuff, but he's not into the Renaissance.

Rhythmic bass pumps out of the speaker of Tessa's iPhone as Lin-Manuel Miranda and the cast of *Hamilton* start counting out the "Ten Duel Commandments".

"You're such a smartass," I say around a laugh.

"You love me anyway," she responds with a shoulder shrug, but again she's missing some of her familiar sparkle.

"Tess, you're in charge of making sure Savs takes it easy," Carter instructs, knowing full well she will keep me in line.

"As you wish, Your Majesty." Tessa slides her left leg behind her right and dips down into a curtsy, going as far as lifting the hem of her *I'm not a book worm, I'm a book dragon* tee like it's the skirt of a ball gown.

Carter shakes his head, and I think he mutters something like "Fucking Dennings" as he stalks to the fridge for a bottle of blue Gatorade.

Tessa preens, as she does any time someone compares her to Kay, and I leave the two of them to banter back and forth, walking over to the terrarium that houses Merlin King.

The dude lives like his surname, Carter having spared no expense when having the habitat designed for his ghost morph boa constrictor. The whole structure is about four feet tall and ten feet long. Carter spent a small fortune on top-of-the-line equipment to maintain proper temperature and humidity for his precious reptile. Personally, I think if MTV were to do a *Cribs: Pet Edition*, Merlin's digs would be at the top of the list.

Half of the base level is a water feature for Merlin to drink from or soak in, the landscaping sloping gradually until it reaches the deepest section of eight inches.

In the opposite back corner is one of the two hides—essentially cave-like structures Merlin can, you guessed it, hide in —this one a badass blackened skull. I always thought it looked a little like Skull Rock from *Peter Pan*, and if you look close enough, you can see a pirate's flag etched into the side. Honestly, I shouldn't have been surprised. Tessa pretty much confirmed that's what she was going for when she gifted it to Carter a few Christmases ago. Her mom loved the story of the boy who never wanted to grow up when she was alive.

There's a middle layer that hangs halfway over the base level that houses the second hide. Unlike the skull, this one looks more like a plain rock, but the hole in the top allows Merlin to make his exit that way should he choose, and my big dork of a brother likes to say it's like Excalibur being pulled free.

As aesthetically pleasing as all those features are, none of them have the reptile I'm searching for.

It isn't until I scan the giant replica of a T-rex skeleton that spans most of the terrarium's width and height that I find my query coiled around the bleached bones.

Snakes are both deaf and nocturnal by nature, but when my eyes meet his shiny black ovals, Merlin raises his head, his tongue popping out to scent the air.

After confirming with Carter he hasn't been fed too recently and is able to be handled without the risk of wearing his last meal—I've dealt with enough mice today, thank you very much—I unhook the latch and reach inside.

Sensing my body heat, Merlin slides his narrow white head over the flat of my palm I have open for him. I love how I can feel the slight bump of his scales while he remains smooth to the touch.

As he works his way up the length of my forearm, I reach in with my other arm, making sure to support the heft of his body with my free hand. At six years old, Merlin is considered an adult. He's five feet long and roughly seven pounds, definitely making handling him a two-handed job.

Calm instantly washes over me from holding Merlin. Leo once joked that he's my emotional support animal, which only spurred Cisco to add how I of course wouldn't have anything as stereotypical as a dog to calm my nerves—they did nickname me Savage, after all.

Once Merlin is comfortably coiled around my arm, his body wrapped above and below the bend of my elbow, head resting on the ball of my shoulder, tongue peeking out and tickling my jaw, I straighten and head for the couch.

"I swear he likes you more than me," Carter grumbles, cupping a hand under Merlin's head and letting him slither around the back of it before pulling away.

"Don't hate." The shoulder shimmy I do prompts Merlin to move across them and down my opposite arm, popping up to check out Tessa next to me.

"Maybe if you took a shower and washed the stink off from your workout, your snake might like you better," Tessa tosses out while lifting her phone for a selfie of the two of us and Merlin and posting it to her Instagram with #snakefie.

"This is true." Merlin goes from one hand to the other, continuing to travel along my body until he settles back into his original position coiled around my arm, this time with his head resting over the flat of my stomach. "They are sensory animals, Cart. You're just jelly he thinks I smell better."

"Brat," Carter teases with a kiss to the crown of my head, then he jogs up the staircase two steps at a time.

"I know *just* what to watch while we work on your calculus." A picture of Leonardo DiCaprio kissing Claire Danes fills the flat-screen, and Baz Luhrmann's version of *Romeo & Juliet* starts to play. My mouth twists to the side, and Tessa's booming laugh washes over me. "What?" She shrugs, trying to act all innocent when she's anything but. "This is your life now," she says with a hand extended toward the '90s version of the Capulets and Montagues battling at a gas station.

"You're ridiculous." It's meant to come out as a complaint, but I can't muster conviction behind it. Tessa is a dreamer, a hopeless romantic thanks in part to the romance novels she's addicted to. Plus, I'll deal with all the razzing in the world if the end result is the return of Tessa's normal perkiness.

"Fine"—she blows out a breath, the fringe of side bang covering her eye fluttering from the force—"I concede that it's not a familial feud, but what's new with your Romeo?"

I hit her with an eye roll, but the action doesn't have the impact it should given Kay's penchant for it. "Jasper is *sooo NOT* my Romeo, T."

"Mmmhmm." She rolls her lips over her teeth, utterly unimpressed by anything I have to say. "You know what they say? Famous las—"

In an instant, the atmosphere shifts, Tessa's words cutting off as she sucks in a breath that sounds like she's choking on them. It's the only warning I get before a finger pokes me in the jugular.

Tessa's touch and shout cause me to jolt and Merlin to startle, the muscles of his long body tightening around my arm and constricting the blood flow.

"Savannah! King!"

I smother a chuckle at Tessa full-naming me with *not* my full-name. A little thing like that, especially now when I'm forced to use the name I despise so often, is just one of the many reasons I love this chick so fiercely.

"Is. That. A. *Hickey*?" Her finger pokes the offending mark with each word. I choose to ignore her in favor of running a hand down the length of Merlin's white and gray scaled body in hopes of getting him to relax. It takes a bit, but eventually, I'm able to wiggle my fingers to help restore the circulation.

"I don't know what you're talking about." Deny, deny, deny. "I burned myself with the straightener this morning."

"Bullshit." Her deep midnight blue eyes sparkle, the couch bouncing as she pops around, tucking her feet beneath her body. "It's from *him*, isn't it?"

"Isn't *Not My Romeo* the name of a book you made me read?" I fall back to one of my earlier comments, hoping for a distraction.

"Yes, by Ilsa Madden-Mills, one of my one-click authors." Her hair goes flying with a sudden and vicious head shake. "Stop trying to distract me with fiction, Savannah King." She waggles a finger at me. "Answer the question."

There's no use avoiding it any longer. If anyone is capable of getting the truth out of me, it's Tessa Taylor. For one, we don't lie to each other. I may try to shield her from some of the more...*unsavory* dealings Carter is involved in, but we don't out-and-out lie. For another, she has one of those faces that make it impossible to lie to.

So I don't.

I spill all the details about my day, starting with the mice in my locker, continuing with the same petty bullshit I deal with daily inside the halls of Blackwell Academy, and finally ending with Jasper and his macho bully posturing. A part of me is tempted to admit that I didn't necessarily hate it, but if I give Tessa an inch, she'll take that story and send it to the sky in a basket toss.

"Ugh..." Tessa flops back against the couch, her arms folding over her face with a heavy sigh. "If I didn't love you so damn much, I'd hate you right now."

"What? Why?"

"You're living out my bully-romance-loving *dreams*, Sav." She leans forward, and a hand reaches out to cup my shoulder, giving me a small shake while the other comes up to cover her heart like she's about to say the Pledge of Allegiance.

"You read too much."

"Maybe." The casual way she snuggles back into her

corner and gives a sexy young Leo her full attention has my internal warning system blaring *Danger! Danger!* "Then again"—she slides me a sly grin—"PF said the same thing to me, and now look at her and Mase."

Fuck me that's not a good sign. If Tessa could see the writing on the wall when it came to I-prefer-to-live-out-of-the-spotlight Kay who is now shipped so hard with her hotshot football-playing boyfriend that their ship name is a constant viral hashtag, what the fuck does that mean for me?

CHAPTER 13

THE SIGHT of Tinsley standing on the stone entrance steps to BA, worrying the hem of her uniform skirt in her fingers, has my brow furrowing as I step out of the Bentley with a thank you to Daniel.

"Couldn't wait for your caffeine fix today?" I pull her caramel latte from the carrier and pass it off. Having a chauffeur take me may not have been how I thought I would be driven to school for my senior year, but the perk of having Daniel pick up Espresso Patronum before doing so is one I could get used to.

"Umm…" Tinsley glances back over her shoulder, but there's no one there.

"Tins?" My steps are cautious, hesitancy bleeding into my movements at her uncharacteristically waiting for me before school.

Is it Friday yet? For reals, how is it only Thursday? This week has been one thing after another. It started with the mice on Monday before they doubled down on that message, filling my locker with mouse feed on Tuesday.

Yesterday's attempt was probably their most creative. The pink papers printed as mock "pink slips" with the words *Samantha's Pussy* typed across in thick black bold lettering fluttered around me like oversized confetti the first time I swapped out my books, and Jasper and his cronies offering me pens throughout the day to sign them was a nice added touch.

Why won't Jasper just leave me alone? He acts like my being here, in "his" school, is a personal insult. It's not like I *want* to be here.

Ugh. What's today going to bring?

"Just"—another look backward—"come on." Tinsley hooks her arm through mine, sticking close to my side as we enter the building.

She ignores each of the side glances I send her way, her gaze locked resolutely ahead. The nibbling of her lower lip ticks my nerves up another level, as does the way I can see her lipstick is worn as if she's been doing so for a while.

When we turn the corner for the senior hallway, the small crowd gathered in front of the area where my locker is located has my chest tightening in a way that has me subconsciously checking my pocket for my inhaler.

Something is most definitely up. "Tins?" I ask again. I hate being blindsided.

"I sure hope your badassery extends to larger rodents, Savs." The use of the shorthand of my "real" name has my steps halting and my eyes cutting sharply to her. Since the first day of school weeks ago, Tinsley has never once let my Royal identity slip. This must be bad.

One of the onlookers spots us and elbows their neighbor, and shortly after, the full weight of the crowd's attention is on us. The volume of the whispering increases, and more than one phone is turned our way.

I ignore them. On a good day, I don't have the patience for petty bullshit. And today? It is *not* a good day.

Through a gap in the bodies, I can make out…something attached to the outside of my locker, but I'm still too far away to make out precisely what that something is.

"Tinsley?" My grip on her tightens, the exhaustion I've been dealing with all week washing over me in another wave.

"Let's just say I think the kings"—there's a tiny quirk to her lips at the use of that particular classification—"went with a more literal approach to the role Jasper thinks you play when it comes to the Royals."

Huh?

Guess there's only one way to find out what she's talking about.

Keeping my movements slow, I do my best to radiate an air of calm I certainly don't feel and free myself from my link to Tinsley. Head held high, chin tipped up, shoulders rolled back and away from my ears, I push through a set of gawking freshmen and don't stop until I'm the one directly in front of my locker.

Nailed to the metal door, the shiny flat heads visible through the pink of the tails where they're attached, are two rats. The one in the top corner has a miniature crown placed crookedly and secured by an ear on its head. The other, placed on a forty-five degree angle from it, has a checkered flag tied to one of its tiny pink feet.

An envelope with my name written in fancy calligraphy is stuck in the vents at the top. Without paying any mind to the dead rodents in my sightline, I step close and work the corner free. Beneath the pads of my fingers, I can feel the high quality of the fibers by the thickness of the paper.

Tuning out the questions now flying at me, I flip the envelope over, and I shit you not, there's a genuine wax seal stamped with the crest of BA securing the flap closed.

I'll give them an A-plus for presentation, that's for sure.

I break the seal with my thumbnail, the wax cracking with

a jagged line through the middle. Card stock embossed with gold foil rests inside. Unlike my name, this note is a hard black scrawl.

Careful, Princess.
You should know better. Race rats don't survive long.
Eventually, your tenure will come to an end...

He didn't sign it, but he didn't have to. The use of his preferred name for me gives him away. Plus, really...who else would go to as much trouble?

I don't have the patience for this bullshit. Tessa is back to acting weird, and when I reached out to our friends still at BP with her, it was like I was getting the runaround. I don't like it. I hate that having to come *here* every day makes everything about my old life feel like exactly that—like something in the past.

Tinsley shuffles her way closer, and I hold up the notecard for her to read. She sucks in a breath through her teeth, her not-really-brown eyes flaring as they trace over the words. "Oh my god," she whispers. "Should you call your brother about this?"

I'm shaking my head before she can finish asking. The only thing that would accomplish would be bringing the wrath of Natalie down on him when he inevitably did something stupid. And he *would* do something stupid. Why else do you think I haven't told him about what's been going on here? This isn't something I can't handle myself. Besides, veiled threats don't scare me. Losing my brother? Yeah, that does.

I make quick work of the dial, wanting to confirm nothing is waiting for me...*inside.*

CHAPTER 14

THE BUZZ from this morning's festivities still hums through my bloodstream as I take my seat in the cafeteria. Posture slouched, elbow hooked over the corner of my chair, knees spread wide, I observe my kingdom.

All around, students whisper and point at the screens of their phones. It's music to my ears. The soundtrack of my reign. Proof of my control over the sheep.

Pictures of selfies taken with the dead rats have already made the rounds on Snapchat, Instagram, and TikTok, all thanks to a trend started by yours truly. My only regret of the day? That I wasn't able to get one with Samantha before the rodents were removed.

I was positive *this* would be enough to pull a reaction from her, but nope.

Fuck! What does it take to push her over the edge?

The more maddening question is: Why do I care to know?

After almost a full school week focused on putting Samantha in her place by pushing her buttons, it might be time to change tactics. She has invaded my thoughts like a bad case of crabs, infecting each one with images of what she would look like when I fuck her.

Bent over, plump ass in the air.

Legs spread, wet-ass pussy on display.

Eyes streaming tears as she chokes on my dick.

Each one hits me with the force of a defenseman checking me into the boards, the pressure building behind my zipper enough to have me adjusting my junk and shifting in my seat.

A lazy, amused smirk plays on my lips as I keep my half-lidded gaze on the entrance to the cafeteria, anticipation pumping sure and strong.

"Gentlemen." The voice of one of the culinary technicians drags my attention off the ping-ponging table-to-doorway gazes of my classmates and to the female in the white chef's coat standing behind a rolling cart with silver domed dishes. "Can I interest you in today's chef's special?"

Where's Samantha when you need her? This would have been the perfect teachable moment. Because this—being served by the staff instead of needing to retrieve our lunch—is one example of *who* we are to this school.

"What's on the menu today?" Banks asks, already lifting one of the domes by its pointy handle.

"Ratatouille." She reveals the dish closest to her, waving a hand over the round white ceramic bowl filled with neat circular rows of white, red, and black sliced vegetables.

My earlier smirk blooms into a full-blown smile, and a deep bark of laughter escapes at the irony. I can't wait to offer some to Samantha and hold up two fingers.

Unlike me, the guys start to dig in immediately, only pausing when Samantha and Tinsley finally make their appearance.

From across the room, those purple eyes find mine, that dick-hardening defiance I itch to fuck out of her burning like a bright flame. That urge only pulses stronger when the end of her ponytail falls over her shoulder with a tilt of her head.

It's the first time all week she's worn her long silver locks up. I don't know if it's because the hickey I marked her with on Monday finally faded or not, but what I do know is it makes me want to wrap it around my fist as I drive into her from behind.

Figuring I have a few minutes to kill while the girls collect their food, I turn to Duke to discuss our game plan for after school.

The familiar scrape of wood against marble alerts me it's time to play as Banks pushes himself into Tinsley's path. Instead of stepping back like she usually would, her eyes drop to his partially eaten bowl of ratatouille then go back to Samantha.

The lips I'm counting down the moments until I get wrapped around my dick fold between Samantha's teeth and press into a line to restrain…a smile? Why the fuck is she amused? Since when does she take enjoyment from these little tête-à-têtes?

"Tell me something, Banks…" Tinsley slides a hand up his arm, my buddy's jaw falling open as she steps into his space for the first time…ever. "How's today's special taste?"

It takes Banks a few seconds to blink himself out of the daze having the tables turned on him put him in. "It-it's good." His eyes flash to her tray, then back to the cleavage directly in his sightline.

Again Tinsley glances back at Samantha.

"Not hungry, Noble?" One of Samantha's delicate eyebrows arches high at the untouched bowls sitting in front of me.

"Actually"—with my foot, I kick out the empty chair to my left as an invitation—"I was waiting for you, Princess."

"Were you?" Sarcasm drips from her words, and it's a struggle not to pull her over my knee and spank her.

The air grows thick with tension, snapping with volatile electricity. Then, shocking the shit out of me and everybody else in the room, she takes the chair. Her movements are graceful, her long, toned stems swinging around the wooden legs, hips swaying, back arching as she perches that delectable ass on the edge closest to me.

The fresh scents of cucumber and lime should be understated, but with my every molecule and hormone tuned to her, they easily overpower the spice of pepper and oregano wafting up from the dish.

Her body leans to the side, elbow sliding across the smooth surface of the table as she balances her head on the tips of her purple-painted fingers. "Not gonna lie—"

I'm disappointed when instead of moving to place my knee between the straddle of her legs, she crosses her feet at the ankles and tucks them off to the side.

"—I can't think of a single thing I've done to make you think I would *want* to share a meal with you. So this"—one of those purple-tipped fingers bounces between one of the bowls and me—"makes no sense."

"Play hard to get all you want..." I shift, placing my elbow an inch from hers to mirror her position. With my free arm, I hook it around her hip and tug her closer until our chests brush, and I drop my mouth to the shell of her ear, grinning when she shivers exactly the way I knew she would. *Such a pretty little liar.* "Because the more you fight me, the sweeter it will be when I have you screaming my name."

Our close proximity allows me to feel the vibration of her scoff and has me spreading my knees wider to make room for the full-blown erection I'm now sporting. There's a lot, and I mean *a lot* I can get away with at this school, but fucking Samantha in the middle of the lunch period? Yeah, that's a line even I can't cross.

Oh, how I want to...

She splays a hand on my chest, and I flex just to hear that tiny hitch to her breathing she can never hide from me. She pushes on me, but my size is too much for her to move, and she's forced to arch her back to create space.

Except it backfires. All it does is thrust her luscious tits at me, her budded nipples begging me to suck them into my mouth.

Want surges and precum leaks onto my boxer briefs.

Thanks to her preference for not tucking in her uniform shirt, I'm able to snake my fingers underneath the hem of it, the silkiness of her skin momentarily distracting me from my train of thought.

I clear my throat and push one of the bowls in her direction. "See...I thought given how you started the day..." Her eyes narrow, the long mascara-coated lashes shrouding them as they lock onto where my mouth is hitched to the left. Messing with her has easily become my favorite part of the day. "How could I resist offering you a serving of ratatouille?"

A shocked gasp sounds from across the table. A beat passes before Samantha shifts her attention to her friend with only her eyes, leaving the rest of her still trained my way. My gaze falls to her plump mouth, watching the way it curves upward in increments until a line of straight white teeth is visible.

The hand that never left my chest rises, stretching between us and picking up the fork resting on a folded cloth napkin. Her ponytail swings forward, the soft strands brushing across my jaw as she peers into the ceramic bowl and spears a bite of the savory dish on the metal prongs.

Bringing her purple gaze back to mine, she raises the fork to her mouth, and I have to adjust myself as her lips purse to blow on the food, my tongue running across my own in response.

Instead of opening her mouth to swallow, she reverses, holding out the food to feed me.

My nostrils flare, and I push in, meeting the challenge in

her eyes head-on and wrapping my lips around the rata-touille, pinching the metal prongs between my teeth. I'm so focused on *her* that I barely register the flavors dancing along my taste buds.

Slowly and with purpose, I chew, demonstrating how I savor the things in my mouth before swallowing.

There's no missing the way she watches my jaw work or the line of my throat when I swallow.

The fork clatters on the tabletop when she drops it, then she's curling her hand underneath my chin and using her thumb to wipe across my bottom lip.

I wrap my hand around her wrist, my fingers overlapping her small bones before she can pull away, and I suck the digit into my mouth. Another one of those hitched breaths escapes as I swirl my tongue and piercing over the tip and nip at it.

She visibly shakes her head to clear the haze in her eyes that she has no hope of hiding from me. Deny it all she likes— she *wants* me.

"You know"—again, she flicks her gaze to Tinsley and back—"it's funny you say that, Noble."

I resist the urge to growl at her continued refusal to say my name. One of these days, I'll get her to say it, and when I do, it'll be on a moan.

"Why's that, Princess?" She's not as successful at hiding her growl.

"Because"—she picks up the fork and stabs it so it's standing upright in the bowl—"while you spend your time *trying* to prove you're the king around here, playing your games by nailing rats to my locker, *you* are the one who ate the *rat*atouille." Her body sways closer to me as she stands while remaining bent close, her lips brushing mine as she adds, "Emphasis on...*rat*."

Does she mean...

My jaw unhinges, falling to the floor as her implication hits its intended target.

Samantha spins on her heel, rounding the table and taking Tinsley by the hand. "Hope none of you boys are vegetarians," she calls out, increasing the volume of her voice and garnering the attention of the tables around ours. "Last I checked, *rat* isn't a vegetable."

One by one, the guys do spit takes, dramatic gagging and sound effects included. My gut roils with nausea at the idea that I'm currently digesting rodent, but I'm too focused on a backward-walking Samantha and the little finger wave she's giving us before flipping us the bird to upchuck. The "special ingredient" she had served to us has nothing on the message she delivered.

CHAPTER 15

I MAY HAVE ENDED my day on a win—the shocked, disgusted expressions painted on Jasper's and his friends' faces permanently etched in my memory—but the events of the week are taking their toll on my body.

There's a bone-deep exhaustion I can't shake. My muscles are sore, and my lungs still have an edge of feeling bruised. While Lyle's pecan pie latte—his variation on a fall staple instead of a PSL—is delicious, the nutty aroma enough to have my mouth watering, I long to trade it out for a Red Bull. Unfortunately, due to my asthma, I have to be mindful of my caffeine intake. An energy drink is most likely to have adverse effects, so sticking to coffee it is.

After putting in some face time at the St. James with the Momster and playing along with the character she puts on for Mitchell, I was lucky enough to avoid getting shit about spending the rest of the evening with Tessa—though she did try to get me to change out of the leggings and purple plaid button-up into something more "appropriate". I have no *idea* what that means when I'll be spending the majority of my time watching Tessa's cheerleading practice.

I beat feet the second I was able. I'd choose dealing with Jasper and his bullshit over spending any more time in close proximity to Natalie than strictly necessary.

Coffee cup in hand, I thank Daniel for dropping me off, confirm I'll see him in the morning for school, and pull open the door to the NJA All-Star's gym, The Barracks, then make my way through the massive one hundred thousand square foot building.

Exchanging greetings with the cheer parents I know from years of being around during Tessa's cheer career, it takes me more than ten minutes to make it to the family viewing area upstairs, and then another fifteen before I can take my usual seat in the front corner.

By the time I fold my arms into a makeshift pillow, practice is already well underway for the teams filling the blue mats below. The Marshals—the large level six all-girl team Tessa is a base for—are on the mat directly under where I sit in the front corner. My best friend's red hair makes it easy for me to find her in the sea of high ponytails and bows.

The seven four-person stunt groups go through the stunt sequence, flipping and spinning their flyers around while moving into a perfect diagonal line.

After holding a move called a bow and arrow, the seven flyers do a military salute and spin-twist down into a textbook cradle. Even from up here, you can hear the sound of bodies hitting bodies, and I wince. I've seen the bruises Tessa sports after a brutal practice. Tossing and catching a human in the air over and over is no joke.

I let the rhythmic beat of claps and counts from the coaches drain the tension from my shoulders. For the next two hours, I enjoy the simple pleasure of these elite athletes lulling me into a sense of peace I lack when at school.

Practice comes to an end, and as twenty-something girls

cross the blue mats to the locker room, I settle back into my seat and scroll through my social media notifications.

"Can I tell you how much I love that you and T might be more codependent than JT and me?" I look to the left as Kay Dennings takes the free seat next to mine.

"Question…" I scroll back and hold my phone out so she can see the latest post from the U of J's gossip site on the screen. "Do your ears ring when UofJ411 posts about you and Casanova the same way they say they do when people talk about you?"

Kay is no stranger to scrutiny from internet trolls. If her life hadn't been severely affected by them, Tessa and I might find it amusing that she lives a real *Gossip Girl* existence. Thing is, when it comes to people you care about, it's not as fun as when it's fiction.

"No." Kay shakes her head and pokes a finger to her left eyebrow, wiggling it around. "But I get a twitch right here."

Not wanting to add to her stress, I lock my screen and pocket my phone. Bending a leg, I prop a foot on my chair and loop an arm over my knee. "I'm surprised to see you coaching tonight."

Kay is an NJA alum and one of the head coaches for the senior level six large co-ed team, the Admirals. As a multi-time National and World Champion flyer, Kay is a stunt specialist for NJA, and it's not uncommon for her to help the other teams, but usually that happens closer to the competitions.

"I decided to swing through so I could see you."

That piques my interest, and I readjust to sit cross-legged, giving Kay my full attention. "Go on."

"JT called me earlier—"

That's not surprising. I'm sure getting a phone call from Tessa's older brother is a daily occurrence for her. I make a rolling motion with my hand.

"—and mentioned that T sounded"—her head tilts back

and forth as if working out the best way to explain—"*off* in her texts this week."

Automatically, I nod in understanding. I may not have been prying as hard as I typically would due to all the bullshit I've been dealing with this week, but I've picked up a similar vibe from my bestie, and I say as much.

Kay stands, bracing her hands on the ledge I rested on earlier, and does a scan of the gym floor before spinning around to face me again, this time with her arms crossed over her *Fix your ponytail and try again* tank. Not even her trash-talking funny shirt can cut the tension pulsing off her. There are many people who would look at Kay and assume the four-foot-eleven beauty isn't anything to worry about. For the most part, that may be true…until you mess with her family.

"She hasn't said anything officially, but I get the impression things have been…*difficult* at BP without you there."

Damn! I hate that my suspicions were correct.

Most would suspect with Tessa being both beautiful and a cheerleader, not to mention sweet as apple pie, she would be the most popular girl at Blackwell Public. Unfortunately, for the stereotypical high school hierarchy, that is not the case. For one, my best friend is brilliant—future valedictorian, remember? The other, and probably bigger issue: there is this weird, almost rival-like tension between the BP cheerleading squad and any of the students who cheer for NJA. I don't need Kay to say it to know this is precisely what's been going on.

I was afraid this might happen, and even more so I hate that when I started asking around about Tessa, I wasn't able to suss out a straight answer. Because. I'm. Not. There. Nope, instead, I'm wasting my time dealing with bullshit at BA.

"I'm surprised you didn't go to Carter with this." Kay herself had a similar issue back in the day before my brother helped shut it down.

Kay pulls a face. "I'm trying to limit the amount of contact

Mase has with your brother. Brainstorming revenge plots that could negatively impact his future career..." She rolls her eyes. "The last thing I need is for those two idiots to find themselves alone together and getting...*ideas* to use against that insignificant pencil dick."

I snort, hiding a smile behind my fist. Carter may be more JT's friend than Kay's, but that didn't stop Mason from seeking him out in dealing with Kay's ex-boyfriend.

"To be fair..." I hold up a finger. "Carter *may not* be the King you have to worry about influencing Mr. Tight End."

There's no missing the way Kay's lips twitch at the pun about Mason's position on the U of J Hawks. I may be the Royal, but as her aforementioned shirt helps demonstrate, she is the queen of puns.

"Oh, I heard *all* about your fingernail-ripping suggestion, *Savvy*." She levels me with a look that says *Thanks for that.*

I shrug, keeping my hands out in front of me, shoulders hunched up to my ears. "I guess it doesn't help if I say that's not the *only* appendage I could suggest removing?"

"I don't doubt that for a second, Savage." I beam at the use of my full nickname and shoot her a wink, which earns me another one of her famous eye rolls. She can't blame me for my mutilating thoughts. Liam Parker could inspire *Tessa* to maim—he sucks *that* much.

"Before we get too distracted by *your* creative revenge plots"—she blows out a breath, her entire tiny frame deflating under the weight of her sisterly worry—"do you think you can find out what's been going on with T?"

"I've already been doing some digging."

"Okay, great." Kay nods. "I don't think it's anything like... what I went through, but something is definitely up."

This is true, and it's honestly the only reason I haven't lost all control of my emotions.

Carter and the Royals established that bullying, in any

capacity, would not be tolerated. It's a cardinal rule. Guess without a Royal walking the halls at BP, it's been all out of sight, out of mind.

That's not going to work for me. It's time to put my plan into motion and give a little refresher on the Royalty way to those who need it.

CHAPTER 16

TOWELS SNAP and shoes squeak as the athletes filling our designated locker room make their way through various stages of showering and getting ready for the school day to start. We may not begin official on-ice practices until next month, but Coach makes sure to have us in the weight room with the football team bright and early every day.

Fucking Samantha.

My muscles protest and long for an ice bath after the punishment they took from the supersets I did trying to work out my frustration with the silver-haired vixen. Thank fuck it's Friday and I'll have the weekend to recover.

I ate rat because of her.

She. Fed. Us. Mother*fucking*. Rats!

I have to have a screw loose or something because the memory of her retaliation shouldn't make me hard—but it does.

Adjusting my semi so my belt helps hold it down, I finish dressing and wait for the rest of the guys to do the same. Having an athletes-only locker room makes it easy for Duke,

Banks, and me to meet up with the others despite them playing a different sport.

"What's today's lesson for your little race slut?" Midas asks as we make our way down the senior corridor, barking at the few underclassmen we happen to pass, causing them to flinch.

I rub at my jaw and debate the best response. The answer is nothing. For as much as I loathe to admit it, Samantha had a point when she called us out for following a predictable script. I thought it best for us to hit pause and take a few days to regroup.

We're nearing the section of lockers where the topic of our discussion is located, and I shake my head.

"Bruh…" Brad rounds in front of me and stops me with a hand to the center of my chest. I glance at it then at his face. The tick of his jaw tells me he's past the point where I could intimidate him. *That's a mistake.* "We can't let what that bitch did slide."

"Someone's salty he pretty much finished his meal before the special ingredient was revealed," Duke singsongs, and Banks reaches out a fist for him to bump.

"You're saying you're okay with having been fed rodent?" Brad challenges. I push a palm to his forearm when he still doesn't make any move to take his hand off me and resume walking without waiting.

"Fuck no," Duke calls back over his shoulder, automatically falling back into step beside me. "I gifted that shit directly to the porcelain gods."

"How about *you* focus on tonight's game since BP is already at the top of our division." Bringing up the football team's current lackluster record is a low blow, but it serves as the misdirection I need. "We'll figure the rest out."

"What's there to figure out?" Midas comes to a stop halfway between our two homerooms. "Fucking bend the bitch over a desk, and we run a train on her ass until she learns who's really in charge here."

My hands ball into fists at my sides. The only person who will be sticking their dick inside any of Samantha's holes will be me. We may all be members of the court that rules this place, but make no mistake, I'm the motherfucking top dog here.

"Listen to me, Abbot." I get in Midas' face, the tips of my Uptowns covering the winged ones of his Ferragamos. Dude is obsessed with his designer shoes, and it shows in the way he tries to murder me with his eyes. Too bad he doesn't intimidate me in the least. "The only person teaching the pretty little princess a lesson is me, so keep your dick *far* away from her." I step closer, forcing him to steady himself with a hand on the wall if he wants to remain upright thanks to his feet still being trapped under mine.

My silence dares him to challenge me, and I'm disappointed when he doesn't. Seconds later, Midas and Brad scurry off to their class while Duke, Banks, and I enter ours.

Tinsley is already seated at the table she shares with Samantha. Banks makes a beeline for her, bending over and bracing himself on his elbows in front of her. "Morning, baby."

Tinsley rolls her eyes at his greeting and mutters something about not being his baby.

Duke's gregarious laughter has the other earlier arrivals lifting their faces from their phones to check out what's happening. Without anything exciting going down to keep their attention, they quickly fall back into their own self-obsessed existences.

The Banks and Tinsley show is like an old rerun—fascinating to watch, but you've seen it because they play all the time. It's why I let the familiar weight of Duke's arm sling around my shoulders and guide us to our own table catty-corner to the girls'.

I feel her before I see her. Unlike Duke's antics that only got the briefest glance, every eye in the room turns to follow Samantha as she stalks inside.

Well, fuck me raw with my hockey stick.

Chick is feeling herself today. The only other time I've seen her look this…fierce was when we crashed the Royal Ball.

Instead of her typical rotation of purple, gray, or black Chucks to finish off her uniform, she has on a pair of black leather lace-up knee-high boots. There's a heel to them and a few buckles on the sides, but my favorite is the contrasting innocent-looking lace gray socks sticking out two inches above them to cover the base of her knee.

If the footwear weren't badass enough to have my fingers burning to grab hold of her, the long strides and confident sway of her hips would do it. Not once has Samantha St. James cowered to those of us at BA. This version? It's some next-level, dick-hardening stuff. Fuck Midas for only adding to the images of what she would look like bent over a desk for the taking. My control is dangerously close to snapping.

"Not today, Satan." Samantha knocks Banks's hand away from where it's hooked under Tinsley's chin. Except for a snort from Duke, the room sucks in a collective breath as she goes as far as to shove Banks, then shoves again when he doesn't move away fast enough.

My friend drops his chin, and his eyes go so wide that even with the distance between us, I can see a full ring of white around his irises. Me? I kick back and get ready to enjoy the show.

With a simple twist of her body, Samantha dismisses Banks by giving him her back. If it were anyone else, I'd say that was a tactical error.

Like an artistic photograph, everything surrounding Samantha goes blurry as she becomes the center of my focus. I notice every detail about her. How she switched out her nail polish to black—matte, like her precious Royals prefer—as she pushes a to-go coffee cup across the tabletop. Her makeup is heavier, again like that night, with that winged black liner at the corner of each eye the girls like to wear.

"How do you feel about a little lunchtime field trip?" Samantha asks Tinsley as I shamelessly eavesdrop.

"Having a craving the cafe doesn't serve?" Tinsley cradles the cup between her hands and cautiously takes a sip after blowing across the lid, Banks tracking her every move. "Rat du jour not tempting the palate today?"

"Oh shit." Duke coughs the words into a fist, and I throw an elbow back to shut him up so I don't miss anything. He shoots me a knowing look at the way Samantha's teeth bite into her lower lip.

"As...*appetizing* as that may be"—Samantha's nose twitches in amusement—"I need to roll through BP."

Tinsley sits up straighter, and I mirror her action. "Why?"

"Some people need reminding to not be assholes." Her eyes flit in my direction, and she flips her hair with an air of aloofness that shouldn't be able to go hand in hand with the threats she's clearly making.

"Bruh..." Duke nudges me between the ribs with an elbow. "Chick might have bigger balls than you do."

I cant my head in agreement, keeping my eyes on Samantha. The way she's leaning across the table has her back arching just so and causes the hem of her uniform skirt to barely hit the tops of the back of her thighs. In this position, it wouldn't take much to discover what type of panties she has on. Are they boy shorts? Those lacy, half-short things that show off the bottom curve of the ass cheeks? Or maybe it's a thong, the fabric minuscule. All it would take is a simple hook of a finger and I would have easy access...

"...figure out who can drive me." Lost in my musings on if her pussy would be wet when I touch it, I miss a chunk of their conversation.

"What about...?" Tinsley asks, and the two of them do that thing girls do where they finish their sentences with facial expressions. It's annoying as hell when you're trying to creep on a conversation.

"I didn't want to involve him." Samantha shakes her head with a sigh, finally rounding the table to claim her seat. "It's fine. I'll order an Uber or something."

The bell rings, signaling the start of class and an end to their discussion.

If asked, I couldn't tell you a thing about today's lesson. Instead of focusing on the teacher, I stewed in thoughts about Samantha. Tinsley had to have been referring to Wesley Prince. It's obvious Samantha spends a significant amount of time with the Royal—she's a race rat, for Christ's sake. Why does the thought of her calling him for a ride make me feel like punching a wall?

It doesn't make sense.

But *goddammit*, this is *my* time with her. If I couldn't get the alone time with her I wanted at the Royal Ball, who the fuck does he think he is trying to encroach on mine?

Yours? The bitch isn't yours. Stop getting territorial. You have more important things you should be focusing on this year anyway.

Fuck! I'm arguing with myself. What the hell is this girl doing to me?

Irrational or not, it doesn't matter. It's time to take control of the situation. The second the end-of-class bell rings, I'm out of my seat, stalking behind Samantha and caging her against the lockers across the hall.

Her back is pressed flush to the metal, her breasts grazing my chest as she sucks in a startled breath. I've learned it takes a lot to catch her off guard, and I relish the times I'm able to do so.

It doesn't last long. First, her eyes narrow, her makeup accenting the purple hue of them in a way that makes it seem like she's using a real-life Snapchat filter. Then that defiant chin tilt makes an appearance, followed closely by the I'm-not-impressed-by-your-shit-so-let's-get-on-with-it-already flat purse to her lips.

"What do you want, Noble?" She sighs as if I'm putting her out. When will she learn this school runs on my timetable?

Off to the side, Tinsley stops, watching, waiting, worrying the strap of her book bag.

I cup Samantha's jaw, running my thumb over her bottom lip and smearing the pale pink gloss coating it. "I heard our little princess's carriage turned back into a pumpkin."

"Aw, look at you using the cute fairy tale wordplay." She tries to knock my hand away from her face, but I only curl my fingers around her nape and press the pad of my thumb to the center of her lip.

"Samantha, Samantha, Samantha." I increase the pressure of my finger until her bottom lip pulls away from the upper. "When are you going to grasp that I'm the man of your dreams?"

"More like nightmares," she counters.

"So you admit you do dream about me." Using my grip on her, I tip her head to the side and bury my face in the exposed curve of her neck. She trembles as I run my nose along the vein protruding from her throat, the slight vibration of her body only distinguishable to me by touch. She fights me—and, as evidenced by this, herself—at every turn, but there's no way to disguise how responsive she is. I've fantasized more than I probably should about how she'll react when I finally get her under me.

"Was there a point to all this? Or did your morning coffee kick in, and you finally realized you forgot to do something to my locker, so you're just going to mess with me instead?"

First Brad and Midas, now she's the one pointing out my lack of action. What I'm about to offer might be insane—especially after what we did to the BP locker room last night—but knocking Samantha off balance with it will make it more than worth it.

"Careful, Princess." I latch onto the skin behind her ear and suck, re-marking her as mine. "That's no way to speak to your chariot."

"What the fuck are you talking about?" Hands braced on my stomach, fingers flexing around the abdominals hidden beneath my clothes, her words lack their usual bite. The breathy quality they take on makes my dick hard, and I grind my hips against her lower belly.

"You need someone to take you to your old kingdom"—she stiffens, but it's so slight I might have imagined it—"and I'm offering up my services."

"Why?"

Damn this girl. Here I am trying to do something nice for her—don't ask me why—and *still* she can't just say *thank you.*

Unable to handle the fire burning in her violet depths, I shift my gaze from her face to my hand braced against the locker beside it. The skin around my knuckles blanches, and I press into the last bit of space separating us until we're sharing carbon dioxide.

"Because I said so." I silence her protest before it happens by stretching my thumb up like a staple across her glossy lips. "And one of these days, Princess…you'll learn that what I say goes."

There's a permanent zipper imprint on my dick by the time the bell rings for lunch. Each death glare, scowl, and attitude-riddled hair flip from Samantha had me hardening another inch. I think having her know I was doing her a favor might have been more fun for me than any of the pranks we pulled this week.

Not willing to risk her wrongly defying me—again—I

post up at her locker. Back to the metal, ankles crossed, hands loosely shoved into the pockets of my trousers, I smirk at each person that genuflects as they pass. It doesn't matter how many people automatically fall in line with the status quo; I won't be satisfied until Samantha does as well.

Students move through the halls like salmon swimming upstream, but like a beacon, I spot Samantha the second she rounds the corner, my teeth snapping together when I see her phone in her hand. She better fucking not be ordering an Uber.

Lost in what she's doing, she doesn't notice me standing here until I pluck her phone from her fingers and shove it into my pocket.

"You were serious?" The disbelief in her voice has me lifting my gaze and rubbing my jaw to hide my amusement at her wide-eyed shock. Knocking her off balance is quickly turning into my new favorite hobby.

"I don't waste my time saying things I don't mean." Reaching into the pocket without her phone, I pull out the red key fob to my Ferrari and shuffle it over my fingers. "The real question is…are we doing this or not?"

Her mouth purses, once again drawing my attention to it, and her nose scrunches with an adorable little wrinkle. *Adorable? What the fuck is wrong with me?* She glances first to Tinsley at her side then back to me, her indecision clear as day.

Other than moving the fob across my knuckles, I don't move. I want her to come with me—to me—on her own. The mindfuck of knowing she *chose* me will be enough to worm my way deeper into her subconscious.

"*Fine.*" She sighs more than speaks the word. "I'm going to regret this," she mutters then holds out a hand to Tinsley for her phone. "If I'm not back in an hour, call this number and tell them where I went"—her eyes find and hold mine—"and *who* I went with."

I lay a hand over my heart, fingers splayed. "You don't trust me, Princess?"

She rolls her eyes and hip-checks me away from her locker. "Do I have *moron* written across my face?" She drags a finger across the smooth skin of her forehead while pulling a leather jacket out and slamming the metal door closed with a *clang*.

"Are you sure this is a good idea?" Tinsley asks, eyes shiny with worry, the corner of her lip swollen from her teeth biting into it.

Having started walking away without waiting for me to follow, Samantha doesn't stop but spins to speak to her friend while walking backward. "It's not," she confirms, adding to my personal enjoyment. "And if it were anyone *but* Tess prompting this, I wouldn't even consider it."

Tinsley doesn't look convinced but nods anyway. "Just be careful."

Samantha assures her she always is, but what I find most interesting about the whole exchange is that she holds this friend of hers in higher regard than her precious Royals. Based on their reputation around town and beyond, one would think they would take precedence for any of their faithful followers.

Yet another thing that makes Samantha St. James an enigma.

She makes it to the F8 before I do and shrugs out of her uniform jacket. "If you wanted car sex, all you had to do was ask."

I round the hood and beep the locks open. "You're delusional." The tilt to the bucket seat of the Ferrari causes the hem of her skirt to flip up, and my eyes instantly lock onto the extra two inches of exposed toned thigh.

She catches me leering but doesn't call me out on it. *Interesting.* Even more so is the fact that she doesn't take advantage of it. If it were Arabella or any of the other bobbleheads at this school, she would be lifting the hem the rest of the way to entice me into action.

Long silver hair obstructs my view as she leans forward and starts to rummage through her bag. I'm not quite sure what possesses me, but I reach out and tuck the strands behind her ear so I can see her face.

There's a whistling as she sucks in a breath; it's something I've noticed she does a lot around me.

The pink tip of her tongue peeks out to wet her lips, and I follow its path. The moment charges between us, but unlike earlier, she's not meeting my eyes, focusing on the space over my shoulder instead.

She fidgets, her body trembling slightly. *Good.* I want her off balance.

It isn't until she lifts her necktie over her head that my hand gets knocked off her. The black silk coils into a pile on her lap, bringing my attention back to the space between her legs.

"You sure you don't want me to fuck you? You keep taking clothes off."

Samantha moves away, twisting her torso and pressing back against the passenger side door. Mouth pinched, neck and heaving cleavage flushed pink, she glares at me with contempt rolling off her in waves. Whenever she's like this, my dick gets hard, which is pretty much *all* the time.

"Listen…" She flops a hand forward, palm facing up. "The only reason—and I mean the *only* reason—I'm in your car is because I need a ride, *and*"—she adds so much sarcasm to the word I'm shocked we're not drowning in it—"I *clearly* did something to piss off the man upstairs given *you* became my only option."

The laughter I've been restraining all morning finally breaks free, echoing inside the confined space. This chick…

"Aww…" I reach out and cuff her under the chin with a bent finger. "What about your Prince Charming?" Her eyes flare, lashes brushing her brows at the nickname for Wesley. "No white horse or black motorcycle to ride in on and save the day?"

Her arm snaps up, slapping mine away with a smack of skin on skin.

"You still don't get it." From her lap, she picks up one of those fingerless leather gloves she wore at the party and starts to work it onto her hand. "I don't need a man to save me."

"Yet here you are." I wave my hands over the dash like a game show host presenting the grand prize.

"You're *not* saving me." She scoffs. "All you are is a very fancy Uber. Now"—her mouth presses into a flat line—"are you going to use your subpar driving skills to take me to BP, or am I putting my mission on hold until you give me my phone back?"

Why doesn't it surprise me that she's *insulting* me when I'm doing her a favor?

Adjusting myself away from the painful teeth of my zipper, I push the ignition button, the throaty purr of the engine behind us sparking to life. "Don't get your panties in a bunch, Princess. We're going."

The vehicle rolls back as I shift out of neutral and into drive, peeling out of my parking spot with a squeal of the tires.

"Don't think about my panties."

It's my turn to scoff. "Oh, sweetheart, that's not even the first time they've been on my mind *today*. I can guarantee it won't be the last."

"Well...look at that," Samantha exclaims as I pull onto the Blackwell Public campus. "You may not have it in you to beat a Royal in a race, but I commend you on your ability to cut the travel time in half."

I bite my cheek to hold back a grin, following her directions around the back of one of the buildings and into the empty lot that separates the two school buildings. There's a large grassy knoll in front of the one at the back of the campus, and students are spread out in small clusters eating lunch.

"Park there." I arch a brow when Samantha points to a row of parking spaces, away from the curb in front of the knoll. "It's bad enough they know I go to BA. I don't need them seeing me getting out of a BAsshole's car."

There's a slight incline leading down to the knoll that will allow me to see down and prevent some from seeing the Ferrari, but not all. "That's why you did the partial wardrobe change?" I gotta say, between the boots and the leather jacket, the pleated skirt has never looked hotter. She's a walking, talking, snarking schoolgirl porn fantasy come to life. All I need is a desk and a ruler, and we could have some fun.

A cocky smirk is all I get before she's opening the door to get out. It isn't until she hears me move to do the same that she spins around, ducking back inside with a forceful "Don't."

"Excuse me?" Who does she think she is commanding?

"Stay. Here."

Again...what? "What if you need help?"

She bursts into laughter. Like straight-up laughs in my face, hand slapping the leather seat before banding her arm around her middle. The purple hue of her eyes is the brightest I've seen when she drags a finger beneath her lower lash line, miming wiping away a tear.

"Did you magically grow a conscience overnight?" She doesn't give me time to answer before she continues. "Because you *do* realize you've spent the better part of my tenure at BA fucking with me, right? *Now* you're concerned about my well-being?"

She has a point. I may not like that I can't control her, but

not being able to control a situation she's about to walk into
—*without* me—I absolutely fucking despise. I don't know
what that means, and now is *not* the time to analyze it.

I shoot out a hand and wrap my fingers around her wrist.
"You're not going down there without me."

She snorts, but a veil of steel forms behind her eyes. "If I
thought I needed backup to handle this, you *know* who I
would have called." She swivels her hand counterclockwise,
reversing our grips until she's the one in the position of
control. "Spoiler alert"—she pinches the soft spot between my
thumb and forefinger, pain radiating up the length of my arm
when she increases the pressure—"it's *not* you."

I shake out my arm, trying to rid it of the lingering spikes
stabbing at the nerve. "Samantha," I warn.

"Oh, come off it, Noble. You're just wasting my time."

I might be, but so be it. I grind my teeth, the engine
revving to life as my foot *tap-tap-taps* on the accelerator.

"I'll be fine." Is it my imagination, or has her tone soft-
ened? "I can take care of myself."

"You're fucking frustrating. You know that, right?" I
growl, but the answering smile that spreads across her face at
the accusation almost makes the heartburn shooting up my
esophagus worth it.

"So I've been told a time or two."

I arch a brow. "That's it?"

She pops a shoulder, nose twitching as she admits, "That
may be a daily total."

"Still sounds like a low estimate."

Tinkling bells sound, and I realize she's giggling. Hold the
phone—did the tough-as-nails Samantha St. James really just
giggle? In my presence? Holy shit, will wonders never cease?

"Look…" She glances toward the knoll and back at me,
running her fingers through her long hair, the silver strands
shining in the sunlight streaming through the front windshield. "There may be this rivalry between BP and BA, but

it's not like I'm about to walk into a scene out of *West Side Story*."

She's got jokes, but it doesn't do a thing to calm the roiling in my gut. *What the fuck?*

"Princess…"

"For fuck's sake." She kneels on the seat with one knee. I don't get a chance to appreciate the way the position shows off her thighs because she leans in close, the scent of lime enveloping me a second before she cups my cheek in her gloved hand. The affectionate gesture catches me off guard before she flips her hand around and digs her knuckles into me, hard enough to turn my head. "Feel that?"

I nod as something bites into my skin.

I cup her elbow, sliding my hand down her arm, watching the goose bumps spring up in the wake of my touch. I'm sure if I checked, her nipples would be peaked against her blouse, but I keep my attention on my current goal. Lowering her hand from my face, I cradle it in mine and run my thumb across the backs of her knuckles.

The leather is warm from her body heat and supple from years of wear. It's what I feel underneath the material that makes me pause: an elevated bump on top of a knuckle, then a dip into the crevice between the fingers before repeating the pattern three more times.

It feels like…

Brass knuckles?

She's gone before I can work out what it all means, the slam of the car door jolting me back to the present. Why the hell does she have brass knuckles hidden in her gloves? They must be a modified version because it's not obvious. It's brilliant to give her extra protection.

Wait…

Didn't she put them on when she came to me at the Royal Ball? Did she think she needed to protect herself from me? Why does that particular thought bother me so much?

By the time I break out of my mental musings, I've lost sight of Samantha. Nerves I'm not accustomed to feeling build beneath my skin, and I have to wait until she's crossed the halfway point of the knoll until she's back in my line of sight. I shift in my seat because not even the distance can take away from the natural swagger she possesses. I'm not the only one captivated by it. Like this morning, every eye in the vicinity is turned her way, and as a group, we watch her walk up to her redheaded friend.

The coppery gold of her hair makes her easy to spot among the crowd, and the widening of her eyes and O shape her mouth forms tells me she was not expecting Samantha to show up. *Interesting.*

Samantha doesn't stop to talk to her friend, only reaches out a hand, and the two link pinkies.

Hair fanning out from the intensity, Samantha turns on her heels and stalks toward a group of eight co-eds filling one of the few picnic tables I can see. Thanks to the uniforms and varsity jackets, I know they are jocks and cheerleaders. Another slap of...irrational worry smacks me with the *What if?* What if they see her as a target for retaliation for what our group did last night? The timing of this little field trip couldn't be worse.

Hip cocked, she perches her tempting ass on the corner of the table, one foot braced flat on the ground, the other balanced on the toe of her boot, her knee lifted, skirt inching up her thighs. I wrap my hands around the steering wheel, choking it the way I want to do to the asshat checking out the creamy skin on display. *Whoa.*

With a calm I'm certainly not feeling, Samantha folds her arms over her chest. I shift forward in my seat, wishing I could hear what's being said.

Number twenty-three attempts to interrupt Samantha, but she stops it with a slash of her hand. Unlike with me, though, there's an edge to her demeanor I'm not used to seeing. She's hostile. Radiating with intensity. Every person at the table watching with rapt attention.

Samantha hops down from her perch with zero fanfare and starts to make her way back to me. My spine straightens, and my back lifts away from the leather when I see Mister Twenty-Three follow behind.

When his hand reaches out to grip her bicep, my own go to the door handle, and I'm out of the car before I realize what I'm doing.

Mine.

Wait…

What?

The ludicrous thought has my actions stuttering long enough to take note of how Samantha reacts.

Rage I'm entirely unfamiliar with feeling in regards to a female runs through my veins, only paling in comparison to the possession that floods my system.

Samantha? She calmly glances from the vise-like hold on her arm up to the motherfucker with a death wish.

Again.

What.

The.

Fuck?

It takes a second maddening glance at his fingers before he releases her. As her arm falls, she steps in close, the sunlight no longer able to be seen between them. Her chin tips up ever so slightly, her torso angling in that much closer, and her hand…it goes to his junk.

One step is all I take before I notice how the douche's face is contorted in pain, lips twisted down, nose scrunched, a waxy pallor overtaking his features.

Fury builds until the high thread count of my shirt irritates my skin as if it's burlap. There's a roaring in my ears, and I slip two fingers into the knot tied at my throat and loosen it, but it does nothing to help with the restriction of my breathing.

What the hell is wrong with me?

Not even watching Samantha openly flirt with Prince in front of me affected me this way. This? There's obviously no enjoyment in this for her.

Relief floods me, and I have to catch myself on the open car door, arm falling over it, opposite elbow braced on the low roof as my knees go weak, finally seeing her cross the parking lot.

The closer Samantha gets, the easier it is to make out the vein pulsing at her temple and the grind of her jaw. At her sides, her hands clench and unclench.

When her eyes finally rise to see me standing outside the car, they are such a deep purple color it looks almost like someone took a purple marker and pressed it to paper, holding it there until all the color bled out. She pauses, foot hovering over the ground as she takes me in, trying to figure me out. *Good luck.* I don't even know what my deal is.

Neither of us says a word, the silent stare down stretching like we aren't in the middle of a parking lot. Finally, with a shake of her head, Samantha folds herself inside the vehicle with a slam of the door.

She's seething, inhaling a steady stream of air through her nose for a four-count, then puffing out her mouth for an eight-count that echoes inside the sports car as I take my spot beside her.

Hands braced on top of her thighs, her fingers flex open, her palms digging into her quads in a repetitive up and down motion. Up to her knees, down under her skirt, and back. The sight of her skin turning mottled and red steals my attention away from how the hem lifts and falls with each pass.

"Are you—"

"Don't," she snaps, cutting me off. "Just drive…please."

"Princess…" I try a different tactic.

"Noble"—she spins—"I said *don't*."

"Well fuck you very much, Samantha." Slowly her lips tip up at the corners, but I need to wrap my hands around the steering wheel again, or they'll be around her delicate neck. She's so damn frustrating I can't even handle it. "All I'm trying to ask is if you're okay."

"I'm fine." She starts to work the gloves free.

"Don't do that."

"Do what?" She throws the gloves at her bag.

Needing the distraction, I put the car in gear and reverse out of the spot. "Act like that assmonkey didn't just have his hands on you."

A humorless chuckle leaves her lips. "You act like having a jockhole put his hands on me without my permission isn't a daily occurrence." Point goes to Samantha with that one.

"Did he hurt you?" I mutter through gritted teeth instead of acknowledging her dig.

"I told you...I'm fine." She focuses on her phone, and as her fingers fly across the screen, I instantly regret giving it back since it's stealing her attention from me. "You may not realize it, but I'm tougher than I look."

Yes, I'm learning that is very much the truth.

"You certainly do seem to have a beast hidden inside the beauty."

Thank fuck we're stopped at a red light because the bold, genuine smile my comment gets knocks me on my ass. If I were driving, I surely would have crashed.

"*Now* he gets it."

CHAPTER 17

I'VE BEEN off balance all day. Actually...all week. At first, I thought the jittery feeling humming beneath my skin was because Tessa was dealing with something I couldn't control from a distance, but it's only gotten worse since Jasper and I returned from BP.

That's the true crux of my problem, isn't it?

I'm still having a hard time computing the fact that Jasper Noble offered—insisted, coerced—his way into being my ride to BP. Don't get me started on the fact that I actually let it happen, that I willingly went *anywhere* with *him*.

The irony of the guy who has spearheaded my own bullying being the one to aid me in stopping someone else's isn't lost on me. There's also how he was ready to jump in and be all *Defend the helpless damsel*, and, for the life of me, I can't figure out what to do about it.

If only he knew how much I'm *not* seen as a damsel to those at BP. At this point, I'm not sure it would make much of a difference if he knew me as Savvy King, seeing as how he didn't give a shit about not being invited to Carter's race last weekend.

Why? Why do I like that so much?

Tessa has been blowing up my phone since I left BP too. After the dozen or so thank yous and bestie GIFs, followed by an inquiry or two asking me how I found out what had been going on in my absence, the texts quickly morphed into question after question about *who* drove me. The hearts that maintain permanent residence in her eyes have her blinded to how *not* a match Jasper is for me. I swear I'm going to have to clear out her Kindle of the bully romances she loves to read. I can blame Laura Lee, Siobhan Davis, Meagan Brandy, and Penelope Douglas for her insistence that Jasper and I are *so going to happen*.

Needless to say, my brain is a befuddled mess. It's probably because of these countless distractions and my muddled thoughts that I don't stop to notice the different energy when we step outside.

"Huh?" I ask, blinking out of my self-imposed dazed when Tinsley smacks my arm repeatedly. The increased murmurs and activity of our classmates finally register.

"Umm..." Tinsley folds her lips between her teeth and points.

Following the line of her outstretched arm, I curse at the sight of my brother's matte black Corvette idling at the base of the stone steps.

Nearby, Arabella and her followers are trying their best— hips cocked out, hair twirled around fingers, glossed lips pursed in exaggerated duck fashion—to garner his attention. BA may technically be outside of his reign, but the distinct paint job, the etched crown detailing in the tint of his back windshield, and his reputation are enough to give away who is parked out front.

I can't tell you for certain thanks to the black-out tint on the windows, but I can almost guarantee Carter's not paying them any mind, more than likely texting one of the other Royals instead.

"I'll call you later." I cheek-kiss Tinsley and trudge my way down the steps. The back of my neck burns as I curl my fingers underneath the door handle. Straightening, I glance over my shoulder to meet Jasper's hard glare. A chill like someone walked over my grave dashes down my spine at the way his jaw pops at seeing me about to get in another Royal vehicle.

A lump of unexplainable emotion forms in my throat, and I struggle to swallow it down. Jasper looks…hurt? Betrayed? *Why does it matter?*

It doesn't stop me from holding his stare, a hand rising to worry the black diamond along the chain around my neck. *What the hell is going on with me?*

I open the door with efficient movements, slide inside, and slam it closed, shutting out the outside world. Taking a moment to gather myself after…whatever *that* was, I pull on my seat belt and click it home before I lift my gaze to my brother, only to find him watching me with one dark blond eyebrow raised to the edge of his black backward ball cap. I hate that with one barely-there facial expression, he can make me feel like a chastised child.

"Cart." I greet him with a smile, hoping to ease some of the tension crackling like Rice Krispies.

"Savs." He uses the same dad voice Pops Taylor is known for. *Shit!* When did he perfect that?

"*Someone* is a *little* bit"—I pinch my thumb and forefinger closed until the slightest space is between them—"too broody for a Friday."

His eyes narrow further at my attempt at levity. *Geez, what has his panties in a bunch?*

"Is your phone broken? Because that's the only reasonable explanation I can think of why you wouldn't call one of us to take you on your little field trip." His gaze falls to my hands as the traitor chimes, proving it is, in fact, not broken.

I sigh and slouch until my back is resting against the door behind me. I hate shit like this. Sure he taught me how to take care of myself, taught me the best ways to defend myself, showed me my inner strength and how to stand on my own, but when he gets like this, it always makes me feel…less than.

"*Sure…*" I inject a healthy dose of sarcasm, dragging out the word. "That makes sense. It's not like the five of you have your own lives—school, practices, work, whatever. It makes *total* sense to interrupt your days when I could have someone I go to school with take me."

Carter growls and levels me with a glare that has me squirming in my seat. *What the hell?*

"My problem is that that *someone*—"

It's no secret Tinsley is the only person I consider a friend at this place. The way he stresses *someone* tells me he picks up on the fact that I didn't use her name.

"—wasn't Tinsley." He throws a hand in the air, folding three fingers down to point close enough to my face that my eyes cross. "And don't even *think* about trying to tell me it was."

I wasn't planning on telling him *anything*.

"You were going to keep it a secret, weren't you?" he asks, his voice losing steam.

I nod. *Do you think it would earn you any points if you told him you tried to have Tinsley drive you?*

A frustrated growl rolls around in the back of his throat, and the way his jaw pops out to the side has my hands fisting the fabric of my skirt, a sense of foreboding coating my skin.

"What's with all the secrets lately, Savs?"

My throat goes tight, and it takes Herculean effort not to cough and reveal a symptom trying to present itself.

He can't know. He can't know. He can't know.

I've purposely kept Natalie's threats from him because I

have no clue how he would react if I told him. I can't lose him. I just can't.

Everything he's ever done has been with me and my well-being in mind. He never planned on being the "king" of Blackwell. His motivations to delve into the more questionable aspects of his business ventures never stemmed from power. No. He did everything he did for one simple reason—me.

I've lived with the guilt of knowing my brother gave up any semblance of a normal life, stuck living in that murky gray world that straddles that line of legality so I would be able to live. Without Carter stepping up and taking on adult solutions when he was virtually a child himself, the probability of me not being alive is high. Very high.

Uh-huh...sure. It's not like the Falcos didn't help and don't still take care of you.

Ugh. Dad would be so disappointed if he heard me thinking like this, and my stomach rolls with a fresh wave of guilt.

Acknowledging that there are others who love and care for us doesn't take away from how much Carter has put his life on the line to spare mine. For that reason, and that reason alone, I will *always* choose any path that protects *him*. It's why I'm enrolled at BA, why I allowed myself to be yanked from the life I knew, why I subject myself to living under Natalie's toxic roof.

Because if I didn't...

Nope, not thinking about *that* either. Natalie takes up enough of my brain space with her threats looming like a boogeyman in the shadows. I refuse to let her have more.

"Show me." The command in his voice has my gaze jerking to his as he snaps me back into the present. I hate, *hate* when he goes all *Carter King* on me.

"Show you what?" The blunt edges of my nails dig into

my palms as I resist the compulsion to follow the order, even if I have no idea what he wants me to show him.

"Show me who played chauffeur for you today." He points to all the students filling the stone steps and watching his car like they can see inside. "I want to put a face to the Ferrari."

I grip my skirt harder. Why I'm not serving Jasper Noble to my brother on a silver platter, I have no clue.

"It was the guy from the race, wasn't it?" Damn him and his elephant-like memory when it comes to motor vehicles. "You don't want me to know who was ballsy enough to use you to get into a race not open to a BAsshole?" He hums as he taps his chin. "Or better yet"—every hair on my body stands on end at the danger bleeding into his tone—"is he the same douche that's been fucking with your locker all week?"

Carter chuckles when my hair whips him in the face as my head jerks around. He knows about the bullshit bullying? "How?"

"I'm offended you believed I would let you enter this viper pit without having a way to make sure you're safe."

That's not it at all. He's Carter King—he has connections everywhere. It's the fact that he hasn't chosen to put a stop to what has been going on that surprises me. Most people would call Carter overprotective, but I think he defies the typical definition.

"I would have stepped in if you needed it." See what I mean? If he was truly overprotective, he wouldn't give me such courtesy, right? "Did you really feed them rat?"

I cringe-smile, the muscles in my neck straining. "Would you have preferred me to channel Marie Antoinette and let them eat cake instead?"

Rumbling laughter fills the car, and any lingering tension I was harboring melts away with the crack of my brother's hardened shell. One well-placed royal pun or reference can have that effect.

"Nope." He shakes his head, running his tongue over his teeth. "The Savage Queen method is *much* more effective."

I beam, my proud smile as bright as LED high beams.

Turning up the volume on the Thirty Seconds To Mars song playing from the upgraded sound system, Carter shifts the car into gear and merges into the flow of traffic exiting the Blackwell Academy campus. I glance at him then out the window, confused when I'm not pressed further on the topic at hand.

Jasper Noble lives to see another day. I snort at my somewhat ridiculous, somewhat accurate thought.

"Where are we going?" I ask when he takes the entrance ramp to the highway a few minutes later.

"BTU," Carter answers, seamlessly weaving his way around traffic and into the left lane, pedal pressed to the floorboards.

"You don't have class today." With everything Carter is involved in, it baffles me how he is able to be in his final year at Brighton Tynes University. I'm convinced he doesn't sleep.

"I need to meet up with Lance, and he has practice." Lance Bennett is the only member of the Royals not originally from Blackwell. He stumbled upon Carter squaring off against three dudes on campus at BTU, and the automatic way he had my brother's back without even knowing him was proof enough he belonged in the Royals.

"*And...*" I drag it out into multiple syllables. "What's so important it couldn't wait until tonight?"

His gaze flits to me for a second before refocusing on the road with a new surge of tension, his hands now choking the life out of his steering wheel. "Just...stuff."

Ugh. He's doing it again. He's keeping something from me...again. I hate it.

I drape my arms over one of the lane dividers, the hard plastic yellow and blue discs digging into my armpits as I let my body hang limp in the water as I bring my breathing back under control. Since I was younger, swimming has been one of the treatment methods used to control my asthma and is easily my favorite form of exercise.

Elbow balanced on one of the disk's flat edges, I drag a hand over my head, removing my purple goggles and black swim cap. Dipping my head back, I let the weight of the cool water untangle the knotted ball I twisted my hair into, thinking of the way Carter ruffled it earlier. After my attack last weekend, I was stunned when he dropped me off at the BTU Aquatic Center. I wasn't dumb enough to question it, though. Yoga just doesn't cut it when you need an outlet to work out your frustration in a physical manner.

"What's up, Mini Royal?" The loud echo of Lance's hockey gear bag hitting the ground with a heavy plop follows his greeting, and I see him and Carter settling onto the bleachers spectators sit in for swim meets.

"Hey, Lancelot." With a deep breath, I pull myself over the lane line and use my upper body strength to hoist myself out of the pool before wringing the water from my hair.

"What happened here?" Lance taps the bruise circling my bicep with my towel.

I don't answer right away, taking the towel to dry off instead. I was really hoping Scott's manhandling wouldn't have resulted in a bruise, but I guess I'm not that lucky.

"Tell me that's not from Gunderson?" My eyes fall shut, and I let out a sigh at the return of the *Carter King* voice. Again I choose not to answer. "Savvy."

My lips twist to the side, still silent.

"*Savvy.*" Nope, I look away, pretending he can't see me if I don't make eye contact. "Samantha," Carter snarls, my spine automatically straightening to attention. *Dammit.*

"*Oooh.*" Lance whistles into his fist, failing to hide his amused grin. "Droppin' the government name. Not good."

The singsong in Lance's tone has my own lips twitching to mirror his, but that impulse dies the second I meet my brother's narrow-eyed glare.

"It's nothing, Cart." I wrap the towel around my body and tuck the ends between my breasts to secure it while we continue to have a silent staring contest. "It was a misunderstanding."

"Get the fuck out of here with that shit."

I grab hold of the knot I created with my towel, using it to anchor myself in the moment and prevent me from snapping and making this whole situation worse.

"It was. It's done. Time to move on."

"Why were you even at BP today?"

I inhale deep and slow. It's really freaking annoying that I have to constantly account for my actions. Natalie, who spent years not giving a damn what I was up to, is suddenly concerned about my comings and goings, though more importantly, she cares *who* I'm coming and going with. She *will not* be hearing about my time spent with Jasper Noble.

Carter asking is different, but it almost seems like he feels I betrayed him by leaving him out of the loop when he shouldn't. Tessa is my friend. Having her back is *my* responsibility.

"I didn't think I needed *permission* to see my bestie." My tone of voice slips, some of my teenage attitude slipping through.

"It's not that." Carter palms the back of his neck. "It's *why* you needed to see her that I take issue with."

"Oh my god, Carter." I pinch the bridge of my nose and breathe. "All I did was have a simple conversation with a few people who needed reminding of the golden rule. That's all."

"Conversations don't result in bruises," he snaps through gritted teeth.

"I don't think it was intentional. I was walking away, and he wanted me to stop." Besides, I showed Scott the error of his ways.

"I'm gonna kill him." Carter jumps to his feet, stalking in the space between the bleachers like a lion in a cage. Lance's gaze and mine go from each other to the way Carter's hands shake and clench into fists.

"Carter." I channel every ounce of *namaste* yogi calm I've practiced and apply it to the tone of my voice. While I'm *pretty sure* my brother hasn't *actually* killed anyone before, I can't say with complete confidence that it's not something he's *capable* of.

I'm ignored as he continues to pace.

Stomp, stomp, stomp up the row.

Stomp, stomp, stomp down it.

All the tension I worked out with laps in the pool comes back with a vengeance with each one of Carter's footfalls. Knots form between my shoulder blades, and I swallow down the chemical taste of chlorine as I suck my lower lip into my mouth, worrying the chapped flap of skin in the corner.

"King"—Lance stands, finally forcing Carter to come to a stop by putting himself directly in his path—"relax, man."

I take in a breath when Carter's eyes meet mine. Typically we both tend toward the violet hue, with his more on the grayscale than mine. But right now? Here in this moment? His are practically charcoal, and it has me falling back a step, my foot slipping an inch on the slick surface. *Shit!* This is the Carter King hurt locker.

"It's fine." He scowls hard enough to force creases in his forehead no twenty-two-year-old should have.

Time for another tactic.

"I'm fine."

Uh-oh. That didn't work either. I don't think that steam is from the heated pool. I think it's coming from his ears.

"It's handled." Maybe if he knows there's no outstanding Royal business, he'll calm down. His focus should be on this weekend's race and not getting…justice or whatever for me.

"You should have called me," Carter argues. "Or at the very least, Wes."

I blow out an audible puff of air and bury my hands in my wet hair, tugging on the strands until my scalp burns. This. This right here is why I think of myself as a Royal only by association. Yes, they are a crew. If one of them needs backup, any one of them would be there, no questions asked.

But…

And it's a *big* but…

If they handled things on their own, that would be it. There wouldn't be a question of a round two being needed. Only when *I'm* the handler.

"Whatever." Done with this familiar cycle, I snatch my bag from the bleachers and turn for the locker room. "I know I'm only Royalty in name. I get it. Do whatever you want." As much as it goes against my nature to give up, this isn't a fight I'll ever win. It's best to avoid unnecessary stress altogether.

"Savs." The hurt in Carter's voice has my head falling forward, my shoulders rising and falling in defeat. "How many times do I have to tell you to knock that shit off?"

Keeping my back to him, I ask, "What shit?"

The smack of skin on denim tells me he's slapping his thighs in frustration. *Yeah, well, join the club.* "You. *Are*. A. *Real*. Royal."

Water droplets cut a path across my temple and down the bridge of my nose, dangling at the tip before falling with a *plop-plop* on the ground between my bare feet.

Clearing my throat, I do my best to rid myself of the messy ball of emotion clogging it. "If that were true, you would trust me."

Trust me to handle this.

Trust me enough to tell me why he thinks it's best for people to not know I'm a King at BA.

Trust me enough to stop leaving me in the dark on...whatever it is he's keeping from me.

"I *do* trust you." Sneakers squeak, and two strong arms wrap around my middle.

I scoff. "You have a funny way of showing it."

Paying no mind to how the cotton of his shirt soaks up the lingering moisture on my damp skin, Carter tightens his embrace, resting his chin on the ball of my shoulder. "Me wanting to rearrange Gunderson's face has *nothing* to do with you not being Royalty enough and *everything* to do with the fact that *you*. Are. My. Sister."

I slump against him and nod. I can accept that. "Well, don't worry." I pat his forearm so he'll release me and turn to face him. "Scott will be singing soprano in the shower for the next week or so."

"Oh shit." Lance coughs into his fist.

Twisted glee sparkles brightly in Carter's eyes. "What did you do?"

I pop a shoulder. "Twisted his balls like a light bulb."

The automatic way they both cover their crotches fills my belly with satisfaction. The mood officially lightened, I'm almost free, my hand on the handle to the women's locker room when Carter calls out, "Oh, Savs?"

That earlier sense of foreboding brings a fresh layer of goose bumps to my skin. "What?"

"I'll let the Gunderson thing go"—he taps the side of his nose then points at me—"but don't think I'll be that easy about your mystery chauffeur."

CHAPTER 18

I'M TEXTING with the Royals, fingers flying across the screen of my phone to keep up with the trash talk currently happening in the group chat, laughing at a particularly witty clapback from Tessa when the elevator doors open and I step into the penthouse suite at the St. James and directly into a brick wall.

"Oh shit!" I stumble back, my phone clattering on the marble floor, my feet scrambling for purchase as I try my best not to end up next to it on the ground.

Strong hands wrap around my arms and tug until I'm flush against a hard chest, the clean scent of soap and menthol infusing my senses as I suck in a startled breath.

"If you wanted me, all you had to do was say something. No need to throw yourself at me, sweetheart."

The cocky connotation grounds me back into reality, and I look up into the blue eyes of Duke Delacourte, palm itching to smack the smirk off his handsome face the same way it does when I'm around his best friend.

With a full-body jolt, I jerk myself out of his hold and

jump back about five paces. The right side of his mouth only hitches up higher, and with a grace I wouldn't have expected from a person of his size, he bends to scoop my phone off the floor. As his thumb glides over the thankfully not cracked screen, a stream of GIFs from *The Princess Bride*, *Game of Thrones*, and *Robin Hood: Men in Tights* scrolls past. I snatch it out of Duke's hand before he can read anything incriminating.

"Do you and Noble compare notes? Because you share the same delusions."

As if to prove my point, Duke takes one long stride closer, then another when I move away so we aren't sharing oxygen, and finally one more until my back is pressed to the wall. I'm really starting to suspect that when BA hands out student handbooks at the start of the school year, they also distribute a guide on *How to be a Douchebag*. Their merry band of morons all seem to use the same cage-a-female-against-something intimidation tactic.

Newsflash! It doesn't work on me.

Duke chuckles, our bodies now close enough for his to shake mine with the vibrations. "You know it drives him insane that you call him that, right?"

I shrug. That's why I do it. It's the little things in life.

Fingers curl under my chin, tilting my face up and holding it firmly in their grip. I swallow and caution myself to wait and see how this plays out before reacting. I don't necessarily feel threatened, but this is the first time any of Jasper's guys have gotten handsy with me.

Eyes that bring to mind the bright blue waters of the Caribbean bore into mine, studying me with a calculating intensity. It's uncomfortable. Unlike when his friend does the same, my body doesn't come alive under the attention. No, the way Duke studies me is more like I'm a bug underneath a microscope and not like he's trying to strip the clothes from my body with just his eyes.

The tension is thick. It's heavy and cloying, but worst of all, this entire situation is confusing and throwing me off balance. My shields are raised and my defenses fortified, prepared for an attack when at school. Now? Here? In a place that is supposed to be a home base for me, I feel ill-equipped.

I've never been a damsel, but being caught off guard doesn't sit well with me either.

The distinctive ring of a FaceTime call blares from my phone, and I jump like it's the sudden noise during a horror film. As if choreographed, both Duke and I look down toward my hand, Tessa's squinting, tongue-out goofy face staring back at us from the screen.

I'm about to hit the button to ignore the call when my hand is smacked from underneath, the phone popping out of it like a game of Perfection, and Duke snatches it in midair. I scramble, hands pawing for it back, but it's no use.

"Bitchy!" The excited greeting of my bestie rings out. "Can you *please* tell Charm—" Her words cut off before she can finish the nickname she bestowed on Wes. I don't have to see her to know her midnight blue eyes are Disney princess-wide and her jaw unhinged like Merlin about to devour his latest meal. "Uhh…"

A wolfish grin blooms across Duke's face as he takes in my best friend, interest sparking in his gaze. "Well, *hello*, beautiful."

I don't fucking think so.

Thankfully Duke's dick has him distracted enough at the prospect of a new conquest that it's easy for me to reclaim my phone before he can get too deep into hitting on Tessa.

"We didn't do it," two male voices I recognize as Wes and Leo's call from somewhere off-screen.

"Lucy, you've got some 'splaining to do," Tessa scolds in a poor attempt at an accent.

"Whatever you say, Ricky," I reply, pandering to her Ricky Ricardo impression. The way her teeth flash between her glossed lips tells me I better charge my battery because I'm in for a lengthy discussion tonight.

"What *didn't* they do?" I ask, seeking a subject change, but then I hold a hand up instead. "You know what…never mind. I'm sure you can charm one of the others into handling it for you. I gotta go. Love you. *Bye!*" I rush to hang up before things can spiral more.

"Hmm…" Duke strokes his chin in contemplation as I shove my phone into my back pocket.

"Spit it out, Delacourte," I snap, done with the conversation already. After spending the weekend at my brother's and Sunday dinner at the Falco's, I wasn't looking forward to having to come back here to begin with. Finding Duke Delacourte here when I arrive is the cherry on top of a shit sundae.

"It's nothing really." He curls a hand around my hip, holding me in place when I try to step away. "I just figured out how you can pay me back is all."

Pay him back? And why is he still touching me?

"What the hell are you talking about? I don't owe you a thing."

He chuckles and brushes away the hair hanging in front of my shoulder, skimming his fingers down the back of my arm. Again I notice how, unlike with Jasper, no tingles are trailing in their wake. *What the hell does that mean?*

"That's where you're wrong, *Princess*." I grind my teeth at both the use of and emphasis on Jasper's preferred endearment for me. "*All* weekend I've had to listen to my boy bitch about you riding off with one of your precious Royals."

My association—though incorrect—with the Royals is common knowledge at BA. It's been weeks. It's old news. "And it matters who picks me up from school…why?" I make a rolling motion with my hand. Am I the only one who feels like he's speaking in riddles?

"It's one thing when it's one of the others you're spreading your legs for." I ignore the misogynistic double standard and the thumb tracing over the jut of my hip bone. "But when it's the King Royal himself, it's a horse of a different color."

I fold my lips between my teeth so as not to smile at his *Wizard of Oz* reference while simultaneously trying to not throw up in my mouth at the insinuation that I'm fucking my brother. *Gross.*

"I don't see how it's *either* of your business…" I want so badly to play into the misconception, but I can't. It's one thing when it's Wes I'm using to tease, but the thought of even insinuating the same about Carter gives me the heebie-jeebies. Cersei and Jamie Lannister we are not.

"Haven't you learned by now?" Duke cups my face, and my nostrils flare at the casual way he strokes the clenched line of my jaw. "*You* are our business."

Ugh. The sense of entitlement and propriety is annoying as fuck. I choose to ignore it to hasten an end to this entire exchange.

"Anyway…" I puff out a breath. "Fear not—you can go back to your leader with a guaran-fucking-tee that I'm not *now* nor will I *ever* be spreading my legs for Carter King." The effort it takes to repress a full-body shiver at the prospect makes my muscles fatigued.

Something akin to relief flashes across Duke's features, and I can't help but add, "Though the same can't be said about Wes."

Momentary shock has Duke's grip on me slackening the slightest bit, and I use the opportunity to free myself and duck underneath his arm. I make it a few steps into the penthouse before a hand wraps around my wrist and tugs me to a stop.

Planting my feet, I swivel my head around, only to be knocked off balance by the return of Duke's cocksure grin. Why does the thought of me with Carter bother them more than me being with Wes?

Voices sound from down the hall before I get the chance to ask. If I expected the threat of an audience to force Duke into releasing me, I'm sorely disappointed. Instead, he lowers his hand from my wrist and threads his fingers with mine.

"Oh, good—Samantha, you're home." The pleased tone of Natalie's voice has my attention snapping from the confusing joining of hands to where she's leading the charge in our direction.

"Hi"—I swallow back a choking amount of sarcasm, indifferent to the audience—"Mom."

"I hope you weren't too bored waiting for us, sweetheart," the beautiful sandy-haired woman Natalie has her arm linked with says to Duke. Upon closer inspection, it's obvious how closely she resembles him, which can only mean…

"Not at all, Mom." He gives her the softest, most genuine smile I've ever seen grace his face.

Holy shit, I was right. That's Mrs. Delacourte. Which means one of the men with their heads angled down speaking softly with Mitchell behind our mothers is the governor of New Jersey.

What are they doing here? Who is the other guy?

Maternal affection radiates from Mrs. Delacourte as she gazes at her spawn, one of her perfectly sculpted brows rising as she takes in our linked hands. "Yes, I can *see* you found a way to entertain yourself."

I try to shake my hand free, but it only causes Duke to pinch my knuckles tighter between his.

Natalie eyes Duke's hold on me as well, but unlike Mrs. Delacourte, hers are filled with pure calculation. What she's calculating, I have no idea, but if the way the hairs on the back of my neck rise is any indication, it can't be anything good.

"Samantha, you didn't tell me Duke Delacourte was one of your new friends from school." To an outsider, Natalie's statement could be taken as a parental tease. I know better.

"Friends," I scoff. Duke, the only one close enough to hear me, gives my hand a warning squeeze. He was at the top of her list of *Friends Samantha Should Make*.

"Don't be cross with her, Mrs. St. James. She did it for me." My jaw unhinges at the charm oozing from Duke. Who is this guy? "I have a hard time letting people in, given who my father is." Duke lifts his free hand in the governor's direction, the man giving him a subtle nod when he does. "She probably didn't want me to think she was namedropping or anything."

"Oh, no. That's not our Samantha at all," Natalie confirms. How the hell would she know? She barely knows a thing about me. "Though this development makes me beyond happy." Natalie claps her hands, clutching them in front of her black heart.

The other man with my stepfather lifts his gaze to my hand still being held in Duke's. I choke on a startled breath as eyes so closely resembling those that haunt my nightmares rise to meet mine. His voice is pitched too low to hear him when he speaks to Mitchell, but I'm able to read his lips and wonder what the hell he means by "It could work."

"Afraid I wasn't making friends, Mother?" This time the sarcasm manages to sneak out.

"Pfft." She waves the question off as if I'm being ridiculous. "I was concerned about you having a good time at the gala next weekend, but now that I know you are"—again, her gaze flits down to mine and Duke's hands—"*friends* with Duke, I don't have to worry." She turns around to face Mitchell, snuggling up to my stepfather's side. "Sweetheart" —she places a hand on his chest, slipping a manicured fingernail under the seam of his dress shirt, running it down the line of buttons securing it—"do you think it's still possible to rearrange the seating chart to have the Delacourtes sit with us?"

"Frank?" Mitchell directs his inquiry to Governor Delacourte.

"I don't see why not." The governor slips an arm around his beaming wife as he answers. "Though I would suggest keeping the Nobles nearby if you do." He jerks a chin at the other man, confirming my suspicion that he's Jasper's father.

Mitchell chuckles and rubs at his jaw. "Should I be worried you would feel excluded, Walter?"

"We'll make it work," Mr. Noble confirms.

The camaraderie between the men is clear to see in the easy way they fall into an air of joking. How is it I wasn't aware my new family was linked with those related to my new nemesis?

Easy…

With the shotgun-esque style of their union, we were never given the opportunity to learn the details of our new stepfather. Though, in his defense, given our turbulent relationship with our mother, Carter and I feel no desire to entangle ourselves in her life more than is explicitly required.

The little I do know about Mitchell St. James is thanks to being forced to live under his roof by his wife's threats.

For the sake of keeping the peace, I agreed to toe the line. Shockingly, Natalie has let me spend most of my weekends at Carter's. This upcoming gala—for what, I'm still not completely clear on; such is the theme of my life now—is the first event she has insisted on my presence for.

That being said, I wasn't necessarily looking forward to it, and even less so now.

CHAPTER 19

I HATE HAVING to admit it, but I spent the bulk of the weekend stewing over Samantha St. James—again.

The increased frequency with which she has overtaken my thoughts is both concerning and frustrating as fuck. The fact that I can't simply excise her from my mind is a complication I neither want nor need.

There was a small part of me that thought maybe we turned a corner, that perhaps by helping her with her friend, things would…

Fuck! I don't know.

I've lost sleep and countless hours trying to wrap my brain around how she could be so set against calling Wesley Prince to be her ride for her little field trip but then goes and gets picked up from school by Carter King.

His reputation may bely his age: only in his early twenties and more respected than most men three times his age. To the best of my knowledge, he's never once—openly and in the daylight hours—set foot on the BA campus, but his reputation precedes him.

What's Samantha's deal with the Royals? What's her angle?

Duke had enough of my brooding and abandoned me to spend the weekend with his parents. When he did return to the dorms, he had a shit-eating grin I was close to knocking off his face with a well-placed punch until he relayed a particular piece of information—Samantha and Carter King aren't an item. I'm curious why she felt inclined to make the distinction. Any time I've seen her with Prince, it seems like she purposely rubs their connection in my face. Why wouldn't she do it with the leader of the Royals?

Why is it the mere thought of her with King had me spiraling when witnessing her lips on Prince only drove me to challenge her more?

Needing to silence the incessant questions from my internal voice, I kept my Beats headphones on throughout the team's morning workout, even going as far as pulling them back over my ears after my shower.

Now I'm the only one still in the locker room; the others have already gone to give me space.

Blackbear's "do re mi" is the perfect soundtrack for my mood as I stalk the emptying halls of BA. Most students are already in their homerooms, making it easy to spot the small cluster of bodies gathered against the lockers.

I approach, tugging the headphones down until they hang wrapped around my neck, the bass of the track loud enough to be heard by all now that they aren't pressed against my ears. Casually I lean a shoulder against the metal of the lockers, crossing my feet at the ankles, and settle in to watch Midas lord over whatever freshman has the misfortune of being his target this Monday morning.

"Noble." Midas acknowledges my presence.

"Abbot." I buff my nails on my shirt as I return the greeting, already bored with the situation.

Metal clangs from a body jerking against the lockers, and

when I look up, deep purple eyes find me over the arm Midas is using to hold her in place. *Samantha.* A surge of protectiveness floods my system as I reassess the scene in front of me.

Oh fuck no.

"I don't recall issuing any orders against the princess this morning." It's an effort to remain in my casual stance as I wait for Midas to turn his attention from Samantha to me.

"Fuck off, Jasper. I don't have to listen to you."

I nod. As a member of the court that reigns supreme, there's truth to Midas' statement.

A feminine snort escapes Samantha, and when I glance her way, she's attempting to hide her amusement behind the back of her hand. "Discord in the kingdom, Noble?" Why am I not surprised she's giving me shit when I'm trying to help her?

"What did I tell you about that mouth of yours?" It takes everything in me not to audibly groan when her teeth bite into the flesh of her lower lip. Chubbing up while in the midst of a pissing contest will not do me any favors.

"How about I catch up with you later?" Midas attempts to dismiss me, and Samantha tries to take advantage of his attention being on me to slip away. Before she can, he pushes her back into place by the shoulder. I see red. *Somebody* is about to lose a hand.

"How about *you* fuck off and take your hands off what's mine?" I challenge, encroaching into his space until my chest is pushing against his outstretched arm.

"She's not yours. You never called dibs."

It's my turn to snort, and I'm seriously starting to question the effectiveness of the football team's helmets because there's *no way* after four years at this school that Midas is this dense on how things work around here. What is with everyone challenging my authority? I blame Samantha for this shit.

"I may not have said the words, but *anyone* with eyes can

tell I did. Now…" I straighten from my lean and make a shooing motion with my hands. "Run along."

"And if I don't?" Midas growls.

Ooo, I'm shaking in my metaphorical boots—but not really. Instead, I lift a shoulder and say, "It's your funeral."

My eyes remain locked on Midas, waiting to see what he'll do. I rise to my full height, my muscles coiled tight and prepared for a fight. With the exception of the woman currently ping-ponging her gaze between the two of us squaring off, disobedience doesn't go unpunished.

"Whatever, man." Midas finally drops his arm and jerks his chin at Brad standing nearby. "Let's go. She's not worth it."

My teeth snap together at the insinuation, but I bite my tongue and wait for them to turn the corner.

"Thanks," Samantha says, bending for the strap of the messenger bag at her feet.

I can't help but grin at how the word feels like it is being forced from her. This is twice now I've come to her aid. I bet it's eating her up inside.

"No need to thank me. I was never good at sharing my toys. Guess that hasn't changed much."

Samantha's back snaps straight, and her shoulders pull together. With a squeak of sneaker on marble, she whirls around to face me, fire blazing bright in her eyes. "I am neither your *toy*. Or. *Yours*."

Oh, how wrong she is. She is mine, and I will play with her however I like.

Quick as a whip, I reach out and grab her by the back of her neck, hand squeezing her nape as I pull her close. The white tips of her gray Chucks overlap the rounded toes of my Cole Haan Original Grand Plain Toe Oxfords, the black leather inverting as she's forced to press up onto her toes as I increase the pressure of my grip until each time I inhale, I breathe in her exhalation.

My forefinger and thumb find the two hard bumps at the base of her skull and press, holding her head at the perfect angle. "Make no mistake, Samantha St. James—" My lips skim hers with each word, the minty hint of toothpaste and sweet coffee tickling my senses as I anchor her to me tighter with an arm banding around her middle.

Not even the Holy Ghost himself could fit between us. Her breasts are pillowed against my chest, the hard buds of her nipples as clear as my erection finding purchase in the V of her legs.

"—you. Are. Mine." The way she trembles in my hold is magic, and one day—soon, if I have anything to say about it —I'll get to feel it while she's naked beneath me.

I wait for her next objection, my eyes bouncing between hers as I do, but none comes. *Huh?*

Small hands snake their way between us, the muscles of my abdominals going concave as her touch skims over them on the way to the center of my chest.

It's difficult to make out with us close enough that our vision crosses, but it sure seems like her eyes fall as if trying to look at my mouth.

Underneath the tips of my fingers, I feel her throat work with a swallow.

Breathing her in one last time, the temptation to shift the last fraction of an inch it would take to seal my mouth properly over hers pumping hot through my veins, I ease my grip enough for her to lower down.

Once her feet are once again flat on the ground, I expect her to step away, to put as much distance between us as she can as quickly as possible.

She doesn't.

Samantha stands there, one of my hands curled around her nape, the other still anchored at her hip, her brow furrowed as she meets my gaze head-on.

We're in a battle of wills, the core of our beings like identical magnets forced together, only able to succumb and repel each other when too close, despite the cocoon of sexual tension that constantly wraps us in its grasp.

I want her, and I'll have her.

But...

It's her obedience I crave more than anything else. Even if it means I have to fuck it out of her—I'll. Have. It.

One thing does stick out and prickles at the back of my mind. "I am curious about one thing."

Released from my hold, Samantha is finally able to pull the strap of her bag over her head until it settles between her breasts, slung in a crossbody fashion. "What's that?" Her hands remain wrapped around the strap, thumbs twitching back and forth, worrying the edges.

"If you're so hell-bent on not *admitting* you're mine, why did you make sure to clarify you *aren't* with Carter King?"

Her mouth opens slightly, and as my gaze drops to her tempting lips again, I can make out the shadow of her tongue running over the backs of her teeth as she mulls my question over. Her wit is so quick; her pausing to contemplate what to say only makes me more curious about the answer.

Time ticks between us, only the faint strains of the next song on my playlist filling the silence. The longer our stare down continues, the more the urge to have my hands on her again increases.

Blowing out a breath strong enough to puff out her cheeks like a chipmunk, she straightens her shoulders, and the intensity in her stare grows. "Because contrary to what you believe about me, I'm not just some race rat who's happy to hop from one bed to another."

I need to lock my knees against the relief the confirmation levels me with. *What the hell?*

"I'm still trying to figure out your angle, and though your *methods* leave a lot to be desired, you did me a solid on Friday." The warning bell rings for homeroom, and she starts to walk away backward. "For some reason *I* can't explain, I don't want that tainted by some misguided alpha-hole possessiveness."

The left side of my mouth hitches up in the smirk that causes her eyes to narrow. She wants to smack me for it; I can tell. "I know the reason, Princess."

Her steps continue, the distance growing until we need to shout to be heard. "And what's that, Noble?"

One day I swear I'll get her to say my name. The final bell rings, and I jog to catch up, slinging an arm around her shoulders and making her huff when I do. "You and me?" I chuck her under the chin, my black mood from this weekend completely gone. "We're becoming friends."

She rolls her eyes and shrugs out from under my arm. "I think *someone* forgot to set their alarm this morning because *clearly*, you're still dreaming if you think that is true."

CHAPTER 20

A WOLF WHISTLE FOLLOWED by a "*Dayum*, Bitchy!" has my shoulders shaking as I lower my phone from the overhead angle I held it in to show off the back—or more accurately, lack of one—of my dress.

For as…weird as this week has been and as much as I'm *not* looking forward to this evening, getting to have my own movie montage Cinderella moment while shopping was definitely the highlight. Natalie's motivations for giving me carte blanche with Mitchell's black card may be steeped in some kind of hidden agenda, but I'm not going to complain about the end result.

"I take it you approve?" I make my way over to the vanity and settle on the padded stool, fiddling with the back of my stiletto until it lies flat against my heel, and I take a moment to appreciate the shoe-porn perfection gracing my feet.

The four-inch, pointy-toe high heels have a see-through fabric that encases the majority of my foot and a Swarovski crystal overlay grouped in a cluster over the toe, fanning up the side until it covers the spiky heel. When you look at them, the overall impression is that of a glass slipper, keeping with the Cinderella feel of the night.

"*Approve?*" The octave of Tessa's voice rises along with an eyebrow. "*Shiiiit*, talk about an understatement, Savs." She waves me off and rolls her eyes. "That dress is so damn lethal. I'm tempted to ask you to keep it on for tonight to help give me an edge." Her pretty face screws up, brows bunching, nose scrunching before she says, "You know what? Nope, don't do that. When I say it's lethal, I mean it's enough to distract even *me* later."

"Aww…" I flip my hair behind my shoulder and lay a hand over my heart. "You'd go gay for me, T?"

"Dressed like that?" Her blue eyes do another quick scan as if checking out my whole body when she can only make out the upper half. "Hell yeah I would." She shifts forward on the couch, elbows braced on her knees as she attempts to get closer to the camera mounted under the television at Kay's place. "Just think of how Charming's or any of the other guys' heads would explode"—she mimes the actions, hands opening in a burst by her temples—"if I started to tongue you down in the middle of a hand of poker?"

I choke-laugh at her insanity, thumping my chest to clear the saliva that managed to find its way down my windpipe.

"Alas." Tessa dramatically sighs like a heroine in one of her historical romances, back of the hand to the forehead, body melting back into the cushions of the leather couch and all. "We are homo-ly challenged." Another one of those full-face scrunches makes an appearance. "No, wait, that makes us sound homophobic. We are heterosexually…umm…that's wrong too. Shit! Why am I making it harder for us? We are strictly dick-ly."

This chick is over the top and out of her mind, but damn if I don't love the shit out of her.

"Samantha." Natalie calls my name, the *click-clack* of her own stilettos serving as a warning she's on her way to me.

"Oh, good—" Her eyes rake over me from the top of my professionally-styled curls down to the crystal tips of my shoes peeking out from the long hem of my evening gown. Unlike with Tessa, there's more calculation in the appraisal than anything else. "—you're ready."

I arch a brow, choosing to remain silent though a sarcastic comment about having been able to dress myself for years itches to burst free. Natalie hired a team of hairstylists and makeup artists to get us ready for tonight's Blackwell Academy Alumni Gala. All that was left to do was get dressed after having my long silver locks sculpted into big barrel curls and pinned back on the left side with crystal hair-pins, followed by the full-face glam treatment. I can't complain because my makeup is on point. I did allow myself a tiny streak of rebellion and finished the look off with a killer black lip.

Spinning around on the stool, I reach for the matching crystal clutch, double-checking I have everything I need. My shoulders tense, and I bite down on my molars at the hissed whistle I hear from Natalie sucking her teeth. *What now?*

"I really wish you would have allowed the makeup artists to cover that *monstrosity* on your back for the night." She makes a noise of disgust in the back of her throat. "I still can't believe you let your *brother*"—she spits out Carter's relation to me like he's not her own son—"mark you permanently. Tattoos are so uncouth."

Again I bite my tongue instead of giving her a response. If being overdramatic burned calories, Natalie wouldn't have to diet a day in her life. Tattoos are far from the taboo no-no they used to be. The tire tread running from the base of my skull to the top of my tailbone is both tastefully and artfully done in white ink. Hell, it's barely visible unless you get up close and personal with it.

"Remember our deal?"

I nod. While our beauty treatments should have been a

relaxing few hours, I spent them getting a crash course in what's expected of me tonight. Who I should associate with. How I'm expected to act. How essential it is that I make a good impression on the Delacourtes. Honestly, most of it went in one ear and out the other.

Smoothing down the stretchy jersey-style material of my gown, I click my heels together and say, "Ready?"

The sooner we get there, the quicker it'll be over.

Wrapping the good humor from my phone call with Tessa around me like a cloak, I thank the attendant holding the door to the largest ballroom at the St. James and step inside, opulence and grandeur smacking me in the face as soon as I do.

Candelabras and tall vases topped with elegant floral arrangements are the focal points at each of the ten-person tables. I can't count the number of crystal flutes and wine glasses set around silver charging plates and stacked bone china stamped with the Blackwell Academy crest.

Each of the large three-story square white pillars bracketing the archways that make up the massive space's perimeter has silver uplighting that ends with a twinkle-light effect. There's a sleek black lacquered stage at the opposite end of the room where a twelve-piece orchestra plays a medley of Sinatra's greatest hits.

It's kind of like a fairy tale. Guess that's what happens when the cost per plate is upward of four figures.

The bite of Natalie's nails pinches my skin through the long sleeve of my dress as she grabs me by the elbow. To anyone looking, all they would see is a mother guiding her daughter through a crowded room, but the way she discreetly twists her fingers is both a reminder and a warning to play along.

I slip on my congenial daughter smile, puff out a breath, and dutifully fall into step. A few hours of servitude, and then I'm free to spend the rest of the weekend at my brother's.

I follow along as Mitchell and Natalie make the rounds, stopping to speak and introduce me to more people than I'd ever care to know.

I'm not sure how long we've been at this, but it's long enough for the balls of my feet to beg for a reprieve from all the standing around I've been doing while the *parental units*— oh, you heard that sarcasm did you?—make idle chitchat.

Bored and in desperate need of something that will allow me to excuse myself, I start to scan the room. Unfortunately, I know Tinsley won't be here—none of the scholarship students are—but I seek out *anything* I can use as an escape.

I'm halfway through my survey of the massive space when all the hairs on the back of my neck stand on end, the familiar feeling of being watched washing over me.

It's him.

Changing my tactic from a cursory glance to a more detailed inspection, I search out the set of pearly eyes I know are on me.

The breath in my defective lungs hitches, and my nipples tighten painfully against the adhesive of my bra cups when I find them. *Holy shit!*

Dressed in a graphite gray tuxedo, a tumbler of amber liquid lazily held in one hand, ankles crossed, one shiny patent leather dress shoe draped over the other, Jasper Noble leans against the mahogany bar, braced on one elbow.

For years Wes has been the only guy I've consciously been attracted to. However, I think as I've gotten older, it's been more of a way to mess with my brother by flirting with his friend than deep-seated feelings. Besides, I get the impression the prince has more of a sweet tooth than he lets on.

Still…

None of that past flirting or my own personal experiences

seem to be enough preparation against the least noble man of all. I've admitted, albeit reluctantly, to being attracted—though it seems like such a mild word for what courses through me whenever I see, hear, smell, or hell, *sense* him near me—to Jasper.

Add in how he's been trying to "play nice" all week, and I have no idea what I'm supposed to do when it comes to him.

CHAPTER 21

THE BLACKWELL ACADEMY Alumni Gala is an annual event steeped in wealth. While the majority of the school's yearly fundraising quota is reached tonight, it primarily serves as a platform for boasting that eventually turns into the rich man's equivalent of a dick-measuring contest.

Freshman year, Duke and I spent the night fending off our mothers' attempts at matchmaking. Who would have thought the two of us would end up being grateful for our fathers' workaholic tendencies? When Walter Noble realized he now had a personal connection he could leverage to access the governor of our state, he jumped at the chance to exploit it. Since then, Duke and I have learned if we stick together at these types of events, our parents will mostly allow us to hang back while they work the room.

"Ho. Lee. Shit." The drawn-out way Duke whispers and enunciates the curse has me glancing his way. He must sense my attention because his eyes don't flit to me. Instead, he jerks his chin up and waits for me to follow his line of sight with a raised brow.

Scanning the sea of jewels, evening gowns, and tuxedos, it takes a moment to spot what, or more accurately, *who* elicited such a reaction…

Her.

Holy shit is right.

Are exorcisms a real thing? Is witch doctor a real profession? Asking for a friend.

Fucking Samantha St. James…

What the hell is it about her that has me and pretty much every person in possession of a penis—and some without—under her spell.

I don't like her. *Liar.*

Fine…I don't trust her. *Better?*

The problem is I barely know her. Hell, it's only been about a week that we've managed to have any semblance of civil conversation, and *that* might be a stretch.

The things I *do* know about her don't necessarily bode well for our coexistence.

She openly flirts with other guys and taunts me with them.

She pisses me off and pushes my buttons. Challenges me every step of the way, refusing to yield to the status quo.

She's bad for my sense of control.

So why the hell is her unwavering loyalty to Tinsley and her redheaded friend one of the things that draws me to her most? She is a living, breathing, dick-hardening paradox.

Despite the bored expression on her face as Mitchell St. James and who I can only assume is her mother given the arm looped through his speak to the Vanderwaals, Arabella's parents, she looks sexy as all fuck in a body-hugging black—no, wait, dark plum—evening gown.

The neckline is modest, running from one collarbone to the other, but the practically-a-second-skin fit of the dress shows off the plump swells of her breasts to perfection.

It isn't until another person between us shifts that

I *fully* understand why Duke has suddenly started to fiddle with the buttons of his tuxedo jacket.

Where the fuck is the back of her dress?

Every single inch of creamy skin from the nape of her neck to what I swear is millimeters above the crack of her ass is on display for anyone to see. The long line of her spine seems exaggerated, but that probably stems from fighting the urge to blind every person in the room to keep them from looking at what's mine. *Shit!* There I go with the possessive thoughts again.

Wanna know the fucked-up part? It's not the increased frequency with which those thoughts occur. No, it's how my dick is at risk of busting through the zipper of my tailored tuxedo pants from the way she doesn't shy away from my stare. She dares me.

"You're so fucked, brother." Duke snickers like a little girl behind his rocks glass, and I hate, *hate* that he's going to end up being right. Samantha tempts me in a way that means I would be more likely to stop touching my dick than stop touching her.

"Fuck off." I finally concede the stare down to glare at him.

I toss back the rest of the Macallan 25, relishing the smoky taste and thanking the loose morals of the privileged elite who don't give a damn about legal drinking ages, and I bull-shit with Duke, forcibly shoving all thoughts of Samantha from my mind.

My palm aches thanks to the intricate detailing etched into my rocks glass digging into it for the last hour. The constant barrage of comments from Duke and the other guys as they floated in and out of our conversation bubble had me clutching the crystal in an almost crushing grip.

"Look at that body."

"I wonder if she's commando."

"Do you think we can get the air conditioner lowered until we can see her nipples? There's no way she's wearing a bra."

"How hard do you think I'd have to fuck her mouth before that black lipstick smeared on my dick?"

Never in my life have I been more grateful for the master of ceremonies to announce the start of dinner than I am in this moment. Not even the knowledge that the Delacourtes aren't seated with my family like they have been the last two years since Dad took over as the governor's campaign strategist is enough to put a damper on my relief. Luckily our tables are situated side by side, and we'll be able to sit backed up against each other.

Having not taken his seat yet, Dad is speaking with Head-master Woodbridge and another man as we make our approach, and he gestures for Duke and me to join.

"Dad." I move aside for another diner to settle into their chair and step into the small circle they've created in the diamond-shaped gap between the circular tables.

Handshakes and greetings are exchanged all around. "Jasper. Duke." He waves a hand from us to the unknown yet familiar male of the bunch. "Have either of you had the privi-lege of meeting Mayor Chuck Falco?" Ah, that's why I had the hint of recognition. He's the mayor of Blackwell. Unsur-prisingly, Duke nods his head yes while I shake mine no.

"Walter, sweetheart"—Mom steps up to the left of Dad's shoulder, her eyes brightening when she catches sight of me —"oh, Jasper, honey." Whatever else she was going to say to my father is cut off as she pushes past him to kiss my cheek, the sweet scent of her Coco Mademoiselle perfume following in her wake.

"Hi, Mom." I return her embrace. I may be an asshole to most everybody, but not to her.

"Did you need something, Buffy?" Dad asks, bringing

Mom's attention back to him. And yes, before you ask, Buffy really is her name. She may have a stereotypical trophy wife name, but that's the only thing about Buffy Rockwell-Noble that fits that mold.

Duke loves to rag on me about how a shrink would have a field day trying to figure out the reasons why I am the way I am. Compared to most of my peers, I grew up in an idealistic environment with parents who seem to genuinely love each other and support their child's endeavors—except the weight of that support can become overwhelmingly crushing if you try to stray from the path laid out since before you were born.

"Yes. It's time to stop talking shop and eat the meal I tapped into my monthly Louboutin budget for."

A snort draws the group's attention to the left, the flash of silver shining under the twinkle lights alerting me to who it came from. Mom perks up at the sight of her, and I'm sure the matchmaking gene in her DNA is hard at work now that there's an appropriately aged female in a vicinity.

"These men...they just don't get it, do they, dear?" Mom's question must catch Samantha off guard if the deer-in-head-lights expression on her face is any indication as Duke shifts to allow her further access to us.

"Umm..." Those mesmerizing eyes of hers blink rapidly before falling to the red-soled high heel visible on Mom's foot thanks to the slit of her gown. Shaking herself out of her stupor, she answers, "No, they don't. Though I have to say"—there's another glance down—"your taste in them is exquisite."

Mom beams ear to ear. Complimenting her fashion sense is the quickest way to her heart. "Why thank you, dear. Aren't you the sweetest?" She lays a hand over her heart. "I must extend a similar compliment based on the ones I spotted you wearing earlier." It's no surprise she noticed Samantha's shoes from a distance, but the color staining Samantha's cheeks at the compliment certainly is.

"Thank you." Her blush only deepens as Mom gushes over them more when she lifts the hem of her gown to expose a sparkly heel.

"Oh, I *need* to add those to my wish list. Beautiful shoes for a beautiful girl." The tips of Mom's eyelash extensions fan as she glances back at me, her slender fingers reaching out and wrapping around my wrist. "What is your name, sweetheart? And have you met my son Jasper?"

The smile on Samantha's face loses some of its wattage when she realizes this charming woman is connected to me. White teeth bite the corner of her lip, eyes once again locking onto mine as she works out the best way to answer. I force myself not to blink as I hold her gaze, an unfamiliar churning in my gut brewing. *What the hell is with that?*

It's like…I'm worried or some shit about her blowing up my spot. Whereas Headmaster Woodbridge is more a figurehead when it comes to authority at BA, Mom would whoop my ass if she found out the games I've been playing with Miss Samantha here.

There's a shifting of weight and a clearing of a throat before Mayor Falco steps forward with an outstretched hand. "This is—"

The edges of his mouth pull to the side, and I get hit with another one of those waves of possession. I think I'm legitimately losing my mind.

"—Samantha." I swear his mouth hitches even higher as he finishes her name after a short pause, his hands cradling one of hers, lifting it to place a kiss to the back of her knuckles.

The familiarity of the move has me at risk of cracking a tooth, and that's *before* Samantha practically purrs a "Mr. Mayor" in response.

Are they *flirting* with each other? Openly? In public? With countless witnesses? Fuck me that can't be right. Yes, the mayor of Blackwell is younger than most who hold such a position, but he still *is* in his thirties.

"I didn't think you attended events for BA," Samantha muses.

"Typically I don't." Falco shakes his head, running a hand over the side of his carefully styled hair, not a bald spot in sight. "But when one of my favorite constituents makes the switch over from BP, I feel it prudent to involve myself in matters that could affect them."

"Laying it on a little thick for someone not of age to vote yet."

A ripple of amusement makes its way through the circle, but laughing is the *last* thing I feel like doing at the moment. I've been teased and tempted by glimpses of Samantha from a distance all night. I hate that as soon as she's close, she's so easily able to designate me as insignificant when I can't seem to do the same to her.

CHAPTER 22

TO SAY this evening has not been playing out how I would have expected is a gross understatement. The sheer amount of praise and gushing pouring out of Natalie in regards to me has me seriously questioning if a hallucinogen was slipped into one of my club sodas. Who is this woman, and what has she done with my Momster?

All night my gut has been screaming at me that she's working an angle, but for the life of me, I can't figure out what game she's playing. It doesn't help that the constant and unrelenting attention from one person in particular has frayed my nerves beyond repair.

I've lost count of the number of times I've had to lay my hand over my erratic heartbeat or grip my side to massage the area over my ever-tightening lungs, not to mention the trip I took to the bathroom just to use my inhaler.

Can I phone a friend to help me figure out what I did to piss off karma enough that the first person I enjoyed engaging in conversation with is the one responsible for birthing the demon spawn who has haunted my life this last month?

Then again, it might have something to do with the unfiltered burst of joy I felt from Jasper's reaction to what he mistakenly took as flirtation between Mayor Falco, aka Uncle Chuck, and myself. Yeah, the constant immature goading attempts probably aren't earning me karmic brownie points. Oh well.

I wasn't lying, though. Seeing Uncle Chuck at a BA event is not something I expected. From all the stories I've heard around the Falco dinner table on Sundays, I don't think any mayor of Blackwell has been involved in the happenings of the prestigious academy that calls our town home. I can't imagine a scenario where the first one would be a person who has participated in some of the more notorious past pranks.

There've been loads of speculation about the mayoral snub being one reason the rivalry between BP and BA has lived on for generations.

For centuries, the core value and foundation of Blackwell has been rooted in its residents and whatever is best to help them flourish. With the exception of whatever financial gain the town received from the construction of a private academic establishment back in the day, they haven't contributed much, keeping things mostly contained to themselves.

"Samantha, it's time to take our seats." The arching of one of Chuck's eyebrows tells me I'm not the only one to hear the snap of command hidden in Natalie's words. "And Charles…" There's a weighted sigh of disappointment as she turns her attention his way. "Maybe if you stopped flirting with people like my daughter, you would be able to find a date for things like these and we wouldn't have an empty seat at our table."

I barely manage to restrain a bark of laughter by folding my lips between my teeth and pressing down with force. Despite the slight age gap between them, Natalie has never liked Chuck. Carter once theorized that it stems from Natalie only marrying into a founding family whereas Chuck is a direct descendant of one like Dad was, but *none* of the Falcos have any warm feelings toward her. Guess that's what happens when you suck as a parent and another family has to help pick up the slack.

"I hate that she calls me *Charles*," he mutters under his breath so only I can hear.

"Oh, and I just *love* being *Samantha*." I nudge him in the ribs, causing him to chuckle. When I glance over his shoulder, it's a miracle I'm not bleeding out on the floor with the glare Jasper flays us with.

"Samantha, why don't you take the seat next to Duke, and Charles, you can take the one next to Headmaster Wood-bridge." Neither of us misses the fact that this particular seating arrangement keeps the one empty chair at the table between us.

Again keeping with the theme of not actively trying to piss her off, I do as I'm told. Too bad the less-than-two-foot gap is easy to lean across to continue our conversation. It feels like any number of Sunday evenings I can recall, except...you know...with suckier dinner companions.

It isn't until the chair is jerked away from the table and a seething Jasper makes himself at home in it that we break apart. The laughter dancing in Chuck's dark eyes is exactly the same as when one of the Royals messes with me at poker nights.

"I hope it's alright that I join you, seeing as you have a free seat?" Jasper directs the question to Natalie, who eventually acquiesces with a slight nod.

Duke stretches a fist in front of me, and everyone watches as the two of them bump knuckles while Mrs. Delacourte explains how the families typically sit together at these events.

I ignore my annoying bookends, wishing not for the first time and certainly not the last that Tinsley were here with me while we're served the first course of organic field greens topped with feta cheese, dried cranberries, walnuts, and a drizzle of raspberry vinaigrette.

Conversation flows around the table, politics being the majority of what is discussed, and I tune it out.

"So, Samantha…" Mrs. Delacourte turns her attention my way when there's a lull. "Tell us about yourself."

"Umm…" I stutter, not at all prepared to become the focus of the evening.

Mrs. Delacourte giggles, swirling the wine in her glass and taking a dainty sip while Natalie bores holes in my skull with a *Careful with what you say* glare. "Did you leave behind a boyfriend when you transferred to Blackwell Academy?"

It's my turn to chuckle. To have a boyfriend, I would first have to find a guy not afraid of my brother. I don't say that, though. Lord knows that would raise all kinds of questions Natalie wouldn't want to be asked. I don't even think she's said anything about having another child.

"No boyfriend."

"Really?" Her baby blues light up with interest and flit to her son. "A beautiful girl such as yourself—I would have figured you'd be beating them off with a stick."

Murder and warning blazes in Natalie's eyes as she stares down Chuck, who is choke-laughing. Under the guise of gathering my hair so it falls down my back, I pray he can see the middle finger I have raised against my skull. He's well aware I don't need a stick when a King plays the keeper of the castle.

"Samantha hasn't met anyone who has been worthy of her yet." Natalie beams as if she's the proudest parent in existence when instead she sounds like an entitled brat. Worthy? Really?

"We should all get together for dinner next time Francis and I are in town." Mrs. Delacourte bounces around in her seat, hands clasped in front of her like the excited best friend in the rom-coms Tessa and I devour on our movie nights. "Lord knows my son is perpetually single."

It's Duke's turn to choke as he sputters liquid back into his water glass. Are our parents suggesting what I think they are?

I jolt in my chair when a large hand grips my thigh under the table. I attempt to remove it, but that only causes Jasper to squeeze until the tips of his fingers turn white against the dark plum of my gown. It's supremely messed up that my core pulses at the proprietary touch.

From beneath my lashes, I chance a glance at him, and if the pop of his jaw is any indication, he's not the biggest fan of what's being suggested by the matriarchs. For once, we're on the same page.

Still…

It doesn't stop me from saying, "As long as I have enough notice, I can be there."

Tension builds, and an itch forms underneath my skin with the need to break it, regardless of being responsible for creating it. On top of my thigh, Jasper's thumb starts to trace lazy figure eights. It's such a contradiction to his agitation that I jump when a white gloved-hand cuts between us to deliver the chateaubriand dished for dinner.

The rumbly sound of amusement that rolls around in the back of his throat shouldn't be sexy when it's made at my expense, but like everything else when it comes to Jasper Noble, it is. At least the arrival of our meal forces him to remove his hand from my body.

I do my best to shake off the conflicting and straight-up confusing feelings he evokes in me and concentrate instead on the sweet demi-glace. The savory flavors burst along my taste buds as the cooked-to-perfection meat melts like butter as I chew.

Talk turns to college, with the Delacourtes debating the pros and cons of Duke either attending the governor's Ivy

League alma mater, Princeton, or continuing to pursue hockey at BTU.

After they share another one of their knuckle bumps at the idea of playing together in college, Jasper drapes his arm along the back of my chair as if it's the most natural thing in the world.

I hate it. *No, you don't.*

I huff, mentally cursing myself.

Fine! Wanna know what I *do* hate? How I can't knock his arm away like I would do any other time. The damn hitch I spot on his delectable mouth from the corner of my eyes tells me that smirk has made an appearance. He probably read my thoughts. Duke, too, based on the way he's trying to hide a smile in his wine glass. Fucking jerks.

Fingertips skim along my spine, absentmindedly tracing the detailing on my tattoo. I do my best to straighten from my slouch and create distance, but Jasper's fingers are long enough to close the gap without much effort.

Back and forth, the delicious drag of callouses between my bare shoulder blades causes me to shiver, and once again my nipples bud painfully against the adhesive sticking the silicone cups to my breasts.

"Aren't you considering BTU as well, Samantha?" Mitchell asks, startling me.

"Uh…" It takes me a second to recalibrate from the Jasper-induced haze I found myself falling into again.

"They don't have a competitive cheer program," Chuck blurts, and I swallow down a yelp when Jasper pinches me.

My eyes flare so wide the air conditioner starts to dry them out, and tears prickle at the backs of them as they begin to water.

"You cheer?" There are all sorts of accusations threaded in Jasper's tone.

"They don't," I answer Chuck, cautioning him with a *Will you chill?* glare. Natalie will freak if our personal connection reveals my—and *her*—connection to Carter. It's a slippery slope, never knowing what might be the thing that could end up pushing her into carrying out her threats.

"I don't," I say to Jasper, and I finally turn to my stepfather with a question of my own. "I might apply as a backup since they're local, but what would make you think BTU is my school of choice?"

I should probably explain my comment on BTU being a backup school. It's actually pretty hard to get accepted there, but as Chuck pointed out, there is no competitive cheer program. Not to sound like a codependent wienie—even though I totally am—but I've only been applying to colleges that have been recruiting Tessa for cheerleading.

"You've been spending a lot of time there the last few weeks. I figured you were doing campus tours or whatnot," Mitchell explains, and it doesn't escape my notice how *he* is the one aware of my comings and goings and not Natalie.

The truth is simple enough, but again…we have that slipperiness that would piss off his bride.

"I have permission to use the pool at their aquatic center and swim laps there a few days a week."

"Mitchell," Mrs. Delacourte scolds, playfully slapping him on the forearm with a girlish giggle I wouldn't have expected from a politician's wife. "Do you not let your own stepdaughter use the pool here?"

"He does," I rush to his defense, which earns me a grin.

Fingers slip under the edge of my dress, and I roll my shoulder back to warn them away from the ticklish skin near my armpit. "You make your poor driver wait around while you swim laps instead of letting him have the afternoon free?" Those fingers push deeper and curl around my ribcage while he leans in to whisper, "That's not very nice, Princess."

I dip my chin and cant my head like we're two friends sharing secrets but speak loud enough that the others at the table can still hear. "No, Daniel just drops me off, and a friend takes me home once *he's*"—I enunciate the particular sex of my friend, knowing what it does to him—"done with practice."

I purposely leave out what kind of practice it is given the company at the table. Plus, Natalie will flip her lid if I start to openly discuss anything that alludes to my connection to the Royals. She's not aware that Jasper and Duke know about it, and that's a bridge I'm not looking forward to crossing when it comes to it.

My phone starts to vibrate inside my small clutch, causing the crystals to rattle against the silver charger plate left over after dinner was cleared. Making my excuses, I reach inside and see a text from Tessa, thanking whoever is listening for her fortuitous timing.

CHAPTER 23

DINNER WAS a master class in restraint. The feel of Samantha's body close to mine, the wafting of her sweet lime scent, the tempting line of her neck, and the vein fluttering down the side of it exposed by the way her hair is pinned back had me wanting to sink my teeth into her the way I did my chateaubriand. I'm sure not even the premium cut of beef could live up to what she must taste like.

Eating a meal and making polite conversation is exponentially more difficult when all the blood in your body is relegated below the belt and you're sporting an erection to end all erections.

The sass, the defiance, the motherfucking *flirting* had me close to tossing her on this table to prove to her, Duke, her mother, Mrs. Delacourte, and *especially* the *god. Damned. Mayor* that she belongs to me and no one else.

It bugs the fuck out of me that this perv to my left knows intimate details about Samantha's life. *Shit!* I can't think of things like *intimate details* because all that will do is make me spiral into wondering how *intimately* he might know her.

If it weren't for her damn phone going off, I might have been able to glean more of an insight into her, and I shamelessly glance down to read the messages on her screen. All it is is a stream of different waiting GIFs ranging from the Little Rascal drumming his fingers to Judge Judy tapping at her watch.

It's nothing overly funny, but that doesn't stop pure happiness from radiating from Samantha. The change in her demeanor is so drastic it makes me do a double take. *Who the hell texted her?*

The live orchestra retakes the stage, the acoustic guitar player plucking the first few cords of Ed Sheeran's "Dive" while the MC announces the dance floor is reopened. This prompts Mrs. Delacourte to suggest that Duke escort Samantha out for a dance, and to my horror, she accepts.

Lord help me, will this night ever end?

Duke may act like a dick most of the time, but when he feels like it, he can turn on the charm like no one else. When it comes to roles, I'm the broody bastard of our duo, and he's the charming playboy.

One arm raised, Duke holds a perfect frame, developed through the years of classical ballroom training his mother made him take for the numerous events he attends for his father.

Samantha eyes it skeptically but eventually places her hand on his and lays an arm over the top of Duke's opposite arm, her hand curling over the slope of his shoulder.

In a move that is most certainly *not* proper frame, Duke splays a hand over her lower back, his palm and fingers in full contact with her naked skin.

They're stiff at first, their movements almost robotic as they start to move across the floor. It isn't until halfway through the song, after Duke's lips move, that it's clear he's flipped that switch with Samantha. His comment makes her expression break, her pink tongue running across the front of her teeth, the tip pausing on one of her canines in a restrained smile.

Mom turns in her seat, leaning to stretch across the small aisle separating our tables. "Why don't *you* ask someone to dance?" She never gives up.

The last thing I want to do is take her up on her suggestion, but I do, knowing it'll get me closer to Samantha as one song rolls into two.

Arabella is more than happy to accompany me.

Muscle memory has my feet moving appropriately, and I barely notice the way her talons dig into the back of my neck, my focus solely on the up and down motion of Duke's thumb along Samantha's tattoo.

Fuck me, that *tattoo*.

I thought her spine looked exaggerated as I stalked her like the prey she is. Up close? Damn, I'm going to need *hours* to fully appreciate the understated yet intricate detailing.

It was impossible to resist tracing the skinny tread lines during dinner. It doesn't escape my notice that it represents something iconic to the Royalty Crew. It's one thing for her to be loyal to them, but it's another entirely to mark her body—permanently—with a symbol others can easily associate with them.

Now that we're no longer sitting down, I'm able to see how extensive the piece of artwork is. Honestly, I can't believe I haven't noticed it before tonight. When she gathered her long hair earlier, I was able to see it begins just below her hairline, which is something you would think I would have picked up on the few times I've seen her with her hair up. I guess the collar on our uniform is high enough to disguise it.

The impressive part is how it runs down the entire length of her spine, and given the plunge of the back of her gown, I wonder exactly how far it extends down her body.

An annoyed huff sounds from in front of me then sharp

nails scratch my jaw as Arabella forcibly turns my face until I have no choice but to meet her narrowed eyes. "Will you just fuck her already?" She clicks her pointy nails at Samantha and Duke dancing nearby.

"I didn't realize you were so invested in my sex life," I say dryly.

She rolls her eyes, pursing her lips in that pout she thinks is sexy but only manages to make her look like a tantruming toddler. "I'm not."

"Sure," I drawl, which only causes her to pout until she looks like she's doing that Kylie Jenner lip challenge from years ago.

"Puh-lease, Jasper." She steps to the right, spinning us, so now my back is to the other duo. "You boys are all the same. You see something shiny and new, and you have to have it. We *all* know once you've had a taste of the Royals' party favor, you'll come back to where you belong."

Does she mean her? Bitch is more delusional than I thought. It's my own damn fault. She had all the signs of being a potential stage-five clinger before I stuck my dick in her.

"Arabella." I drop my arm and grab the hand heading for my belt buckle. "Regardless of if I'm fucking Samantha St. James—or anyone else, for that matter—you and I?" I bounce a finger between us. "We're *over*. Fuck! We never even started. You were a warm hole to fill when I wanted my dick wet, nothing more."

Am I being a dick? No doubt. And if Arabella's soul wasn't as black as the strapless gown she's wearing, I might feel bad. What she doesn't realize is I see her for what she really is. She's nothing more than a social-climbing gold digger. She's made the rounds of every athlete at BA that has shown professional promise in her four years at the school. What makes her more dangerous than most is she has a trust fund to back her up, so you miss that side of her at first.

Arabella is fuming, but I don't give a shit. She is right about one thing, though: it's time for the games to end when it comes to Samantha. She's danced with Duke long enough. It's time I cut in and make sure she, and everybody else, understands exactly who she belongs to.

It takes far too long for me to extract myself from Arabella's clutches, and when I move to put my plan into motion, Samantha isn't there. In a panic, I scan the room. *Where the hell did she go?*

Arabella tries to corral me again, but I shrug her off with a roll of my shoulder.

Duke is already at the bar talking to his parents and Mr. and Mrs. St. James, but no Samantha.

If she's with the mayor, I might legitimately lose it.

No, he's still at the table with Headmaster Woodbridge.

Jewels sparkle, and bodies sway around me until…*finally*, a familiar shock of silver catches my eye, and I spot Samantha sneaking out a door at the back of the ballroom.

You can run, Princess, but you can't hide.

CHAPTER 24

DAMMIT.

I can't believe I lost track of time.

I can already hear all the shit Tessa will give me when she learns the circumstances that led to my tardiness.

All night my phone has been pinging with texts from her attempting to live vicariously through me. I didn't think it was possible, but we *might* have watched *Gossip Girl* one too many times with how she's been all champagne wishes and caviar dreams.

Never have I thought her romantic heart was a cause for concern. The rose-colored glasses currently causing my best friend to act like my life is an episode of *Lifestyles of the Rich and Famous* has me rethinking that.

I could downplay the night, brush everything off, and act like *nothing* of substance happened. Except...there was a witness to my...misery, or whatever less dramatic adjective is appropriate.

All it will take is one quirk of the lips or side-eye from dear ol' Uncle Chuck *Mister* Mayor—oh, you heard that sarcasm did you?—at the poker table, and Tessa will sniff out potential gossip better than UofJ411 does about her sister with their latest #Kaysonova post.

The prolonged heightened emotional state has wreaked havoc on my lungs, so the last thing I should be doing is weaving through the tables in a rush toward the staff doors at the back of the ballroom. The service elevators are closer, and I'll be able to avoid any potential crowds on my trip upstairs to change.

"Where you running off to, Princess? It's not midnight yet."

The *click-clack* of my heels cuts off as I come to a halt, my soles skidding with an ear-cringing screech. Jasper's dark voice wraps itself around me like smoke, licking up my spine like the hellfire I'm sure he wants to rain down on me.

What the hell is he doing back here? Did he follow me?

"Oh no." He clucks his tongue. "Did the sea witch steal your voice?"

If he wasn't being a dick, I'd give him props for his *The Little Mermaid* reference, but the only thing I feel like giving him at the moment is a swift kick to the balls.

Lies. You wanna give him more than that, Savvy.

I really need to reassess how much I hang out with Tessa because my own thoughts are starting to sound like her.

"Too scared to turn around and face me, Princess?"

Oh no he didn't.

Balling my hands into fists—you know, to keep from punching him, not in preparation—I spin on my heel, roll my shoulders back, and stare him down.

I want to say Jasper Noble is the definition of a sheep in wolf's clothing, but there's *nothing* sheepish about him. A more accurate description of him is the earlier reference to a demon's spawn. If anyone had doubts about the devil being able to convince Eve to take a bite of the forbidden fruit, all they would have to do is look at Jasper Noble to understand how it was possible.

The shoulders I've already declared are too broad for a man of his age look wider, stronger in the expertly tailored silk of his tuxedo jacket, the open buttons on it revealing the trimness of his waist. His wide-legged stance has his legs flexing in anticipation. Muscular thighs—one of which pressed against me the whole time we ate—strain the fabric of his trousers, emphasizing how they taper down to polished dress shoes.

He's so perfectly put together. The longer flop of his hair is styled back in that sleek way that only makes you want to muss him up, and the undercut at the sides adds a sharpness to the overall look.

No surprise, his jaw is clenched, that dimple more defined than ever, making it all that much more tempting to put my finger in it.

As always, it's his eyes that are the most devastating. Pupils dilated, the swirling gray, blue, and purple that make up his unique irises swarm together like a hurricane ready to set out on a path of destruction.

Hello, Lucifer. Oh, you wanted a soul? Here you go.

Stop being so fucking easy, I scold myself.

"What do you want, Noble?" I spit out his laughable last name. Jasper is the furthest thing from noble; he's not even in the same dictionary as the word.

"What do I want?" He stalks toward me, those ethereal eyes promising all kinds of retribution.

No matter how hard I've tried, I can't figure out his problem with me. He's had moments when he's come to my, dare I say, rescue, but then he goes all I-wanna-kill-you-and-dance-on-your-grave. It's enough to give a person whiplash.

He continues in my direction, and self-preservation has me backing up until I hit the wall. Fuck me, I'm trapped. *Yes! Yes! Fuck me.* God, even in my head, I sound easy.

I hiss, my back arching away from the cold wall, but the action only thrusts my now heavy breasts out at Jasper, his eyes automatically falling to them straining against my dress. He has a way of making it feel like my front is as bare as my back, stripping away every wall and defense I erect.

With one more step, he cages me in fully against the wall, flattening his hands on either side of my face, the scent of sandalwood—not sulfur like the devil should smell of—filling my nostrils as he presses further into my space.

I've lost count of the number of times I've found myself in this exact position with him, but this time feels different.

We're alone.

The risk of being caught is there, but in this moment, there's no one else. The acceleration of my heartbeat and the goose bumps rising on my skin are an eerie premonition.

I keep my gaze locked on him, my attention resolute, as is my resolve.

Lead.

Me.

Not.

Into.

Temptation.

The corners of his plump lips curl, not in happiness, but evilly, reminiscent of when the Grinch gets the idea to steal Christmas from Whoville—except it's not the merriest of days at risk. It's me.

Unlike Dr. Seuss's famous character, I get the impression Jasper wouldn't return me. No, he would rather see me stuffed and mounted on his wall.

He presses in closer, a section of hair flopping over his forehead, giving him a boyish quality he has no right to when he buries his face into my neck, his nose running along the shell of my ear, his hot breath on my skin.

I fight it. The urges. The temptation. It's…it's…it's…*wrong*.

He's a dick.

He's entitled.

He's a bully.

He's not for me.

Except…

He's not scared of me or my brother like so many others. Sure, he doesn't *know* my brother *is* my brother, but he's aware of at least a mild connection to the Royals, and still, he's there, constantly in my face, messing with me.

Try as I might, my eyes flutter closed.

I'm giving in.

I'm weak.

Thump-thump-thump.

My heart rate picks up more speed, my breaths growing choppy, shallow, the weight of his strong chest pushing against mine as he presses into the last tiny bit of space only making the situation worse. I need to make a conscious effort to get my breathing under control before my symptoms spiral into a full-scale asthma attack.

I've been on the verge of one all night. Emotional stressors are triggers I've always failed to control.

This is bad. Bad, bad, bad, so very bad.

And now I sound like a broken record.

Forgive me, I'm panicking.

Jasper Noble is the *last* person I want to be aware of my condition. My asthma isn't what makes me weak, but I'm not going to hand over information he could use against me.

"No-Noble," I stutter as the smooth acrylic ball of his tongue ring connects with my skin. He's such a broody bastard I forget he has the piercing most days.

"*Hmm?*" he hums against me, the questioning sound vibrating through me, a knot of need settling like a rock in my gut. What does it say about me that *this* man, someone who looks at me with such dangerous intent, can affect me this way? "You want to know what I want,

Princess?" Teeth nip my flesh. "Think I'm gonna come right out and say it when you *insist* on playing games with me?"

Shit!

"You act like it's my fault." I wiggle my hands between us and shove on his chest.

He barks out a laugh, the harsh sound echoing off the walls. "You think it's *mine*?" Incredulity coats his tone.

"Yu*p*." I pop the P, channeling all the pep contained inside the walls of The Barracks, and shove him again, dropping my hands as quick as I can to avoid the risk of prolonged contact. "*You* were the one who made me a pawn in *your* game. Now *you're* mad at *me* for choosing to play?"

The dark fringe lining his eyes compresses more with each word I utter.

"*Mmm.*" Another one of those noncommittal questioning sounds has a bolt of heat pinballing through my system.

I need to go. Need to put as much distance between us as physically possible.

This time when I go to shove him, I curl my hands around his side, my fingers falling into place in the ridges of his ribcage under my touch. Planting my feet and pushing back hard with my shoulders to the wall, I leverage my weight as best I can.

An inch is all I manage before one large hand manacles both my wrists and stretches my arms overhead. A foot kicks at the sensitive bumps on the sides of my ankles, keeping my legs separated with the strength of his.

I jerk around, attempting to break free as another invisible band coils around my chest.

Thump-thump-thump.

"No, no, no, Princess." God. Does he *have* to call me that? "You're not going anywhere until I say so."

Fuck you very much, asshat.

"Oh yeah?" I run my tongue along the backs of my teeth,

Jasper's eyes automatically falling to my mouth. "And when *exactly* would that be?" I tap my foot. "I have plans."

"You can go after you tell me what. The. *Fuck* you think you were doing with Duke." His tone is hard, harsh, skirting the line of volatile. Why the hell does it bring a rush of wetness between my legs?

"Umm…*dancing*?" I phrase it more as a question than a statement since I would have thought it was obvious.

"That's not what you were doing."

"I—" Inhale. "I don't know what you mean." Exhale. Each breath is labored and painful as I try to get my lungs under control and loosen the band tightening around them.

I flex my fingers for circulation as Jasper pins them harder to the wall, his free hand snaking around to my back, the tips of his fingers following the line of my naked spine.

"You're playing with fire, Samantha." The use of my name adds weight to the warning.

"Are you talking about Duke or yourself?" I force my eyes open to meet his. The irises are almost black. They'd seem soulless if it weren't for the flames of Hades burning in their depths.

Ba-dum.

Ba-dum.

Ba-dum.

His fingertips hit each vertebra like speed bumps, and my heart trips with each one.

The fabric of my dress is soft, silky…quiet. Yet the scratch of Jasper's thumbnail running over the stitching of the border of it is deafening.

My breath stills, not from asthma, but from the commanding way he slips under the material.

I bite down on my lip hard enough to draw blood, a needy moan desperate to break free while I'm more desperate to restrain it.

Arousal flares both in Jasper's eyes and my body as his gaze locks onto the movement.

I've fought this man at every turn. Pushed back at each attempt to bully me. Damn him for his ability to wreak havoc on my senses. Damn *me* for not being able to control my baser urges.

"*There's* my feisty Princess."

Why does the stake of possession send a rush through me?

"I don't belong to anyone—least of all you, Noble." My words are strong despite the lack of conviction I feel.

"Oh...that's where you're wrong." He chuckles, every single self-preservation instinct inside me screaming for me to run like they are watching a horror movie and I'm the dumbass walking up the stairs instead of fleeing out the front door.

Nostrils flaring, I hold my ground, the pressure inside my chest continuing to grow with each millimeter his fingers travel south.

He groans, lashes lowering when he discovers my bare skin. As in completely bare, no undergarment to be found. His next groan rumbles through me at the discovery, his grip on my ass bruising, fingertips creeping inward to follow the line of my crack.

"*Fuck*, Princess." Lower and lower he travels. "You were naked under here all night?"

He buries his face against the curve of my throat, my body arching into him, rubbing the hard-on digging into my stomach. This is so fucked, but I can't help myself.

"Panty lines didn't really go with this look."

"Panty lines," he growls, teeth raking down my neck.

What the hell is happening?

What am I doing?

Why am I angling my head to grant him better access?

Shut up and just go with it. I think I need to start taking applications for a new best friend because it is most *definitely* Tessa's influence that's to blame for these traitorous thoughts.

But do I stop him as he continues to travel south? No. Nor do I protest when he brushes my entrance with his fingertips.

"Fuck, you're soaked." Each guttural word rumbles through me with a direct line to my clit, only adding to the situation he's discovered.

"No-Noble." A warning? A plea? I'm not sure.

Everything about me is one giant exposed nerve. My racing heart. My constricting lungs. The way my skin crawls at the thought of him touching me all while feeling like I'm going to burst out of it if he doesn't.

"Jasper," he commands.

"Wh-What?" I wheeze.

"My name is Jasper. Say my name, Princess." He bites my pulse point, sucking hard and flicking his piercing against where I'm sure there's a new mark.

Say his name, say his name. Oh, now I'm channeling Destiny's Child.

"Say it." He taps his finger against my entrance.

I press my lips into a flat line, refusing to give him what he wants.

"Say it, and you'll get a reward."

God, his words are like liquid sex.

Come on, Savvy. We love presents. Say his name.

How am I supposed to formulate words when the only thing I can focus on is the continued tapping on my most sensitive area?

He's toying with me. With his words. His touch. His presence alone is one big tease.

Saaaaaaavy.

I roll my eyes. *Fine.*

"Jasper."

I barely get the last syllable out before his finger plunges inside me, the coming-from-behind angle deliciously sinful.

What am I doing?

I don't know, but hell if I want it to stop.

I give in.

Shove away the doubts, the worries that this is categorically wrong, and let my wanton desires take control.

Pump.

Pump.

I rise onto my toes with each one.

"Ah, Princess," he drawls.

Pump.

Pump.

My pussy flutters, my walls doing their best not to let him go.

"You can utter your denials until you're blue in the face." A second finger joins in the fun, a slight burn accompanying the stretch. "Your body wants me."

My teeth snap together, and my head thrashes against the wall, my hair becoming a tangled mess. Grr, I wish I could argue that he's wrong. "Shut up." It's weak, but it's all I've got.

He chuckles, a new gush of wetness coating the digits inside my body.

His hips rock forward, mine rocking back instinctively to ride his fingers.

"That's it, baby." I jerk at the endearment and the casual way it slips off his sinful lips.

His hand fans out, his thumb stretching back, pressing against the rosebud of my ass while one of his other free fingers brushes the steel bar of my VCH piercing.

"*Fuuuuuck*. Me. Princess, you're *pierced*?" My lips twitch at how painfully shocked he sounds.

Pressure mounts inside me as he breaches my final barrier. I flush hot then cold, overwhelmingly full as he holds me like a bowling ball.

It's naughty and dirty, and if it's wrong, I don't want to be right.

More.

I want more.

No. I *need* more.

"Jasper."

I don't think I've ever been this close to coming this fast in my life. If saying his name gets me an orgasm, it's a price I'm willing to pay.

"Jasper."

He scissors his fingers, flicks the piercing at the top of my clit, and that's all it takes.

Light explodes behind my eyelids. Blood rushes through my veins. Oxygen has officially abandoned my lungs, and I'm coming. Pleasure crashing, rolling, building in a never-ending wave.

"Princess."

Without a strap to secure them, the backs of my stilettos fall away from my feet as Jasper fingers me in earnest. It's violent, delicious, each *slap-slap-slap* of his hand driving against me punctuated with a squish of my audible arousal.

He releases my wrists, fingers dragging down the side of my face until he pinches my chin between them, tilting it up, adding an extra bite to it when I don't automatically open my eyes.

"You are so *goddamn* beautiful when you come. Did you know that?" He's smug.

I should smack him. My hands are free. I could do it. But an orgasm isn't the only thing he set off; the asthma attack I've been a few breaths away from is now fully fledged.

"Jas—" Gasp. "Jasp—" Choke. "Jasper."

I need to get out of here immediately. Wes is probably here already, waiting for me. He couldn't care less if I'm late, but if I show up displaying symptoms of an attack, he and Carter are going to rage.

My lungs are screaming, and black spots start to dance in my vision. Hypoxia is beginning to set in.

Finally…

Finally!

Jasper slips his fingers from my body, and I scramble to retrieve my clutch from where it dropped earlier.

Blind instinct and self-preservation have me stumbling down the hall and slapping a hand on the call button for the elevator. With numb fingers, I fumble with the clasp of my bag, the *ding* announcing the elevator's arrival sounding a second before I manage to separate the metal prongs from one another.

The smooth plastic of my rescue inhaler hits my palm, and I shake it to activate the medicine inside while the doors of the car slide closed.

CHAPTER 25

HAND COVERED in Samantha's cum, dick beyond painfully hard and at risk of busting through my pants like the Kool-Aid man, balls bluer than a Smurf and screaming for release, I watch in *What the fuck is happening?* confusion as she runs away from me and disappears into an elevator.

Bringing my fingers to my mouth, I lick them clean, savoring the musky, sweet taste that is pure Samantha. It hits my system like an injection of heroin, and I'm instantly addicted.

Unsure how long it's been since I followed her back here, I know I'll need to make a quick pit stop appearance back at the gala before I put in the work to charm the hotel staff into granting me access to the penthouse residence for the St. James family.

I slip through the service door, my return successfully going unnoticed.

A quick scan of the room shows Dad in a corner having a heated discussion with Coach and Governor Delacourte and

Mom near the edge of the dance floor with Mrs. Delacourte and Mrs. St. James. I'll have to have Mom make my excuses to Dad because I don't have the time to risk getting pulled into what I'm sure will turn into the inevitable debate about the upcoming hockey season. Scouts are the last thing on my mind at the moment, and I don't feel like dealing with Dad's disapproval of that fact.

No surprise, Duke is at the bar with the guys. I catch his eye as I make my way over to them, and he straightens, sliding his glass onto the bar top and stepping away from the group. "Sup?"

"I'm heading out." I tip my head to the side.

Duke studies me, blue eyes missing nothing. He shifts, angling so our backs are to the others and allowing our conversation to be private. "Want me to come with?"

I hesitate and think of how best to answer, the hand that was inside Samantha flexing with my indecision. A tagalong is the last thing I need when I find Samantha again, though there are a couple of advantages to taking Duke with me. For one, he'll dip out if I ask him to, and another is he might have more success with the front desk than me. He could easily say his father left something in the penthouse during his meeting with Mitchell St. James last week and asked him to retrieve it.

"Yeah." I nod. "That Gucci?"

"Yup." He spins on his heel to face the others again and throws up a peace sign. "Deuces, assholes." He starts to walk backward as they respond with similar goodbyes. "I take it we're going to rescue a princess?" he asks as we fall into step.

My lips begin to curl, and I give him a sideways glance. "You say that like *we* aren't the things she's in danger from."

A devilish gleam I'm sure matches my own takes over his expression, and he rubs his hands together in glee. "Fee-fi-fo-fum, here we come."

We swing by to say goodbye to the moms, and a few

minutes later, we enter the polished lobby of the St. James Hotel.

"Well, well, well," Duke muses, and it takes me a few steps before I realize he's stopped walking.

I double back, meeting up with him close to the fountain that sits in the heart of the lobby. When I make it over, I follow the direction of his chin jerk and spot none other than Wesley Prince posted up at one of the large marble pillars that create the entranceways of the cavernous space.

Jealousy spikes brutal and swift. I can still smell Samantha on my skin, taste her on my tongue. Is she really leaving with this guy after I made her come?

"Is it just me, or does he seem…off?" Duke asks.

Shaking off the fuzziness that goes hand in hand with my anger, I narrow my eyes and study the Royal who has been the cause of most of my discontent in the last month.

Hmm…

Duke might be right.

Even from a distance, I can see the furrow of his brow, his mouth turned down as he speaks to someone on his phone, his motorcycle helmet bouncing off his knee repeatedly. He definitely seems agitated. Could he already know what Samantha did with me? Would she have told him?

Prince's "*Fuck*" is easily read as it falls from his lips, his relaxed posture jackknifing away from the pillar. He ends his call and pockets his phone in the next second, every ounce of his focus shifting and sharpening. This is the version most everyone fears, the fierce defender and protector of the Royals who made a name for himself in underground fighting rings.

There's only one thing…one person who could shift his attention and demeanor on a dime…*her*.

Trudging across the marble floors is a version of Samantha St. James I haven't witnessed yet. Gone is the swagger that is synonymous with the sassy spitfire. Feet clad in a pair of those gray Uggs that look like they're made out of a sweater with big round black buttons on the side barely rise from the ground with her steps.

Her long legs are encased in stretchy black leggings, the mesh panel down the sides giving a hint of skin, but the baggie BTU Hockey hoodie she changed into hangs close to her knees and prevents me from appreciating her ass the way it deserves in the tight pants.

There's a number stamped on the back of the sweatshirt, but both the large hood and her long hair prevent me from making out *whose* number it is. *The only number she should be wearing is mine.*

I stumble back. This shit is starting to get out of hand.

Still…

I can't recall her ever mentioning being a hockey fan during the conversations I've overheard—okay, I shamelessly eavesdropped—her have with Tinsley. It's been mostly cheerleading and football talk. Could we actually have something else in common? Why does that thought scare me more than the possessive ones I've had?

Wesley folds Samantha into his arms, his forearms stacking around her lower back, her face burrowing into his chest. The embrace doesn't last long, but the way he brings both his hands up to cup her face sets my teeth on edge. There's an easy affection there that makes the beast inside me roar.

With his head angled down, I can no longer read Prince's lips, but there's no missing the way he brushes his thumbs over the curves of Samantha's cheekbones.

Long minutes pass as the two speak while Duke and I watch, transfixed by the sight. If I thought we could get away with it without getting caught, I would move in closer to hear what they are saying.

Finally, Wesley grabs the small duffel Samantha is carrying and puts an arm around her, tucking her close to his side as they make their way to the hotel entrance.

Now it's time for Duke and me to move, following behind like a pair of shadows.

Parked close to the valet stand, Prince's matte black motorcycle gleams under the lights, but neither move in its direction. What are they doing?

The roar of a throaty exhaust system echoes in the acoustics of the ornate overhang that offers protection from the elements as guests exit their vehicles, and a matte black Dodge Challenger Hellcat pulls to a stop directly in front of the hotel.

The door is thrown open, the tires still rolling slightly as Cisco Cruz, another Royal, rushes Wesley and Samantha, pulling the latter from the former's arms and completing a similar inspection. Something prickles at the back of my consciousness, whispering I'm missing…something.

There's an intensity in the way the Royals study Samantha. I noticed the night we crashed the Royal Ball, but this is different. I can't quite put my finger on it.

Cisco ushers Samantha to his Hellcat, holding the door open, hand cupping her elbow as she lowers herself into the bucket seat. He even goes as far as crouching beside her and stretching across her body to clip the seat belt in place before pulling back and curling a finger under her chin to turn her face toward him.

Needing to know what they're seeing that I'm not, I move to close the distance, only Duke's arm cross-lining my chest stops me before I can make it a step. "Not now."

Swallowing down the urge to argue, I set my foot back and shove my hands into the pockets of my tuxedo pants. I rock back onto my heels, and we watch as Prince tears out of the lot, followed by Cruz close behind.

"You're losing it, man." Duke eyes me warily as I continue to stare long after the taillights have disappeared.

Again, I want to argue but can't. I'm known for my control, revered for it. It's why I dominate both on the ice and in the halls of BA. Nothing challenges it. Not my father's demands, my mother's attempts at matchmaking, or familial obligations that feel like they take a piece of my black soul. *Nothing!*

Until…Samantha St. James.

CHAPTER 26

ANOTHER THIRTY-SIX HOURS consumed by thoughts of Samantha, and I'm no closer to getting any answers.

The games stop *now*.

We're hashing things out *today*.

I've wanted her since the moment I saw her. Knew—even if I refused to admit it at first—she is the only one worthy of sharing the crown with me from the first time she refused to bend to my commands.

I've lusted after her, jerked off to fantasies of her giving in to my control more times than I can count. Now that I've had a taste of her, witnessed her falling apart, felt her trembling in my arms, heard the way her breath hitches, seen the way her lashes fan across her cheeks, brows scrunch, and lips part when she comes—it's official. She is mine.

I don't give a fuck what the Royals have to say about it.

It's a bold statement, but it doesn't make it any less true.

There's a slight chill to the air one would expect for October in the northeast as I lean against BA's stone siding. By lunch, it'll be gone, and the summer that refuses to fully give way to the fall will have most everybody ditching their uniform blazers.

The lot in front of the school isn't overly large, reserved mostly for visitors, the handful of students who don't board here, and the upperclassmen who choose to drive over from the dorms (primarily athletes). I let my gaze roam over the collection of luxury vehicles as I wait for a familiar silver Bentley.

Precisely five minutes before the late bell is set to ring, it makes its appearance, following the circle drive and pulling to a stop at the base of the wide stone steps. Adjusting his suit jacket, the St. James' chauffeur rounds the hood, walking around to the back passenger side door to open it for his charge.

I straighten, shifting from one foot to the other, impatient for my first glimpse of Samantha.

Seconds pass, the bobbing of the driver's head while they speak ratcheting up my level of agitation. Without Duke here to keep me in check, I'm close to storming down the steps and yanking her from the car myself when a flash of black nail polish precedes Samantha taking the outstretched hand of her driver.

Again I shuffle my feet. The top of a messy bun comes first, then black high-top Chucks topped by black thigh-high socks plant onto the blacktop, and slowly, almost gingerly, she makes her exit, purple-framed Ray-Bans shielding similarly hued eyes from view once she's fully upright.

She pauses, her chest expanding with a deep inhalation. She seems...unsteady? Her driver still has hold of her hand, waiting for her nod before letting go. There's another exchange of words then what appears to be a purposeful roll of her shoulders as Samantha faces the school head-on.

She makes it up one step before she spots me waiting for her, chin dipping toward her chest, coffee carrier in hand tilting precariously, and I swear I can hear the sigh she expels from here.

Done waiting, I close the last of the distance between us, not stopping until I'm on the stair one up from her. I choose this purposely, letting my already taller stature tower over her in another example of my dominance. This time when she sighs, I do hear it, and I despise the defeated tinge to it.

What's got you down, baby girl?

"Can we *not* do this now, Jasper?"

Well…shit. If what I heard in her sigh wasn't enough to cause me concern, the fact that she called me Jasper certainly is. She *never* does that. I had to push her until she was teetering on the brink of orgasm to finally hear those two syllables fall from her lips.

Hooking a finger under her chin, I press until I can see myself in the black lenses of her glasses. "What's wrong, Princess?"

"Nothing." She tries to smack my hand away, but it lacks the typical power.

None of this makes sense. First the weird way the Royals were treating her at the hotel, now this. If anything, I would have thought she would double down on her conviction against me. Where's her fight? Her defiance? Her…spark?

No, something is most definitely wrong.

Pinching the frames of her sunglasses between my fingers, I push until they sit like a headband on her head. Dark bruise-like circles stand out like thumbprints underneath her tired eyes.

Leaning back, I notice she's pale, and not in a creamy Snow White sort of way, but in a sickly should-be-in-bed-under-a-heap-of-blankets kind of way. The urge to make her soup hits like a check to the boards, never mind that I don't know how to cook.

Ghosting a knuckle across one of said dark circles, I let my touch linger, unfurling my fingers to tangle in the hair pulled back on the side of her head and cupping her face in my palm. The instinctive way she nuzzles into my touch has my heart clenching inside my chest.

"Are you sick? Is that it?" Her skin doesn't feel hot or clammy to the touch, so I don't think she has a fever.

She jerks as if just realizing I'm touching her, only to lose her balance. Athletic reflexes have me hooking an arm around her middle, tugging her to me before she can take a header down the stairs like the coffees in the carrier do.

Again there's a delay to her reactions, and seconds that normally wouldn't pass do before she flattens her hands on my chest. Another atypical response has her leaving her hands on me, not to linger in her touch, but like she's using me to support her. Acid rolls in my gut at how wrong this entire exchange is.

"Listen…" She shakes her head, trying to find her bearings, but her eyes seem unfocused when she forces them to meet mine.

"Princess…" I swallow down the sudden and unexpected ball of emotion that rises in my throat. "You're scaring me."

"Just because I look like shit doesn't mean you have to lie to me, Jasper." There it is again—my name. I'd bask in it, but the wheeze that's tacked on the end has another pang of worry squeezing me like a human-sized stress ball.

"I'm not lying," I challenge.

"You have to care about a person for them to scare you." She pops her elbows out to the sides and shrugs out of my hold. "And to care, you have to have genuine feelings."

I wince, and despite the heaviness in her gaze, she catches it. *Feelings.* Damn, the word is like a curse. Feelings lead to emotions, and emotions make you weak, vulnerable to outside influence.

"See?" She flops a hand through the air as if I made her point for her. And, fuck…maybe I have. To be fair, this is all new to me. I don't know if I could classify what I've been feeling as *feelings for her*, but it's nothing like anything I've experienced before.

Duke is the only person—outside of my mom—I've allowed others to know matters to me. Though with him, if push came to shove, I know his father would be able to handle anything or anyone that dared threaten his son.

"I'm pretty sure I told you how I feel about you at the gala," I call out to her retreating back.

She stops, and this time she's the one on the higher step, causing us to be close to eye level with each other. "You can make a person come without having feelings for them." She shuffles closer, the tips of her sneakers now hanging over the edge of the step, her nose brushing along the stubble on my jawline, freaking tingles sliding down my spine at her breath blowing across my ear as she whispers, "I could make you come in under five minutes guaranteed." She pulls back, locking eyes with mine. "And I most *certainly. Don't* like you."

I momentarily forget about how off she's seemed this morning at the familiar spark of fire in her gaze—until it's extinguished and the corners of her eyes turn down the next instant.

"Again, Princess"—I grip her by the nape, keeping her close when she tries to run away again—"do you need me to remind you how you *liked* me just fine Saturday night?" I tug her closer, bringing my forehead to hers. "You *soaked* my hand. I could taste you for *hours* after I licked it clean."

Her entire body trembles, a flush of heat finally adding some color to her deathly pallor.

"Come on," I say as the warning bell rings, "let's go before we're late." I thread my fingers with hers and guide us to the entrance of the school.

Her hand wiggles in my hold, fingers stretching as if that's all it will take for me to let her go. *Fat chance.* I glance at our connection, the first pure and innocent one in all of our interactions. And...I...like it. *Huh?*

"What are you doing?" Her voice is husky as she voices a question I'm not close to having an answer for. The sound would be sexy if it weren't for the scratchiness that's causing the throaty quality, the strain evident for anyone choosing to listen hard enough.

"Somebody has to make sure you make it to class alright." I do another quick scan of her. For the first time ever, it's not the physical I concentrate on—the full tits, the slim waist, the flare of the hips, the long legs—and I'm not liking what I'm seeing in the least.

From day one, Samantha St. James has been a puzzle I've been trying to piece together. First, it was to make her heel. Now...maybe...it's to make her mine?

CHAPTER 27

FEELING LIKE A WALKING ZOMBIE, I let out a labored breath of relief when the last bell chimes, bringing an end to this farce of a school day. I've barely managed to stay conscious, let alone retain any details from today's lectures.

It usually takes a few days for my body to recover from an asthma attack. Having had this one so closely on the heels of the last one, though, has made the lingering hungover beat-up exhaustion worse. There will be no avoiding a checkup visit to the doctor this time either. *Fun times.*

Tinsley has stuck close to my side all day, and I love that my instincts about her were right. Chick is loyal as hell. Real Royalty-type stuff.

Wanna know what has me off my axis more than my recovery?

Jasper Noble.

Like, seriously? What the fuck?

I can't make heads or tails of him. He's been hovering, acting all protective-like in a way that has my head spinning.

He's also been…sweet. By the time second period started,

he was sliding a to-go cup of coffee across my desk. When I asked him what it was, he only shrugged, mumbling about how I never got my morning fix since I dropped the carrier outside. I mean, come on. That is *so* unlike him. Who is this man, and what has he done with the alpha-hole formerly known as Jasper Noble?

Sure…he wasn't completely absent, laying out his taunt about making me come at the gala and how much he thoroughly enjoyed it. Oh, boy…what an experience that was too. It was crazy, unexpected, and so unlike me that I had trouble recognizing myself in the mirror.

I shouldn't have done it. I should have never turned around when he called my name, should have kept walking to the elevator and gone on with my night like planned. Instead, I let him goad me and gave in to temptation. Now I'm still paying the price for the karmic bitch slap I was served in the form of an asthma attack.

That's twice now I've ignored the signs and allowed Jasper to trigger an attack that, if I'd listened to my body, if I'd heeded the warning signs, could have been avoided. If that doesn't tell you he's bad for my health—literally—I don't know what would.

I haven't told a soul about what went down in the service corridor at the St. James…well, except Tessa. Bitch took one look at me, ignored my pale skin, the sweat dotting my brow, and the bouncing rhythm of my chest trying to get my breathing under control, and somehow managed to spot the postorgasmic flush underneath it all. I've said it before, and I'll say it again—the girl reads too much.

I'm sure it doesn't surprise you because it sure as shit doesn't surprise me that there's a matte black vehicle parked in front of BA when I step outside. I knew there wasn't a snowball's chance in hell Carter would let me go back to Natalie's after school, but I wasn't expecting Lance's GMC Acadia to be the one waiting for me.

The hairs on the back of my neck rise, and sure enough, when I look to my right, Jasper's eyes are locked on me. My eyes bounce between the SUV and him, waiting for that familiar scowl to grace his expression, except...it never comes. *Hmm.*

"Wanna come over?" I ask Tinsley, keeping my arm linked with hers.

It takes her a moment to answer, her attention locked on Jasper and his group as well. At least I'm not the only one confused about the less-than-hostile air we've experienced from the guys all day. She's got that tiny *Anyone wanna tell me what's going on?* wrinkle between her brows. "Sure?"

I chuckle at how it comes out more question than statement, rubbing circles over my sternum and the twinge of pain the good humor affords me.

"Hey Lancelot," I call into the car after opening the back passenger door for Tinsley.

"Hey Savs," Lance returns, only to follow it up with a quick "*Jesus.*" He's out of the car and around to my side in a blink. "Are you trying to get me killed or something?" His hands cover mine, stopping me from trying to move his large gear bag out of the way.

"Aren't we a *wee bit* dramatic this afternoon?" I tease, stepping back and letting him take over.

Lance one-hands it, tossing it to the back row like it doesn't weigh as much as if there were a body in it, and straightens to give me an incredulous look. "You may be the queen of our crew, but that won't stop your brother from going all *Off with his head* if he heard I let you struggle with my shit while you're supposed to be taking. It. Easy." The emphasis on the last few words has me folding my arms across my chest in defiance.

"Some queen," I mutter, lips tugging down in a frown. "Being issued a babysitter"—I bounce my gaze up and down

Lance's BTU-Titan-hoodie-covered torso with an eye roll—
"*really* speaks to my power, don't you think?"

"Aww, Savs." He chuckles, voice pitched low to prevent
others from overhearing my "real" name like Carter decreed,
and he wraps his strong arms around my body, tugging me in
for a brotherly hug and kiss to the forehead. "You're his
whole world. Don't be mad at him for worrying about you."

The reminder is enough to douse the heat of my anger. Lance
is right. Carter worries about me; he always has. I think my new
living arrangement might be harder on him than it is on me.
From a young age, Carter has craved control. Not in a *Let me be
your master* sense—and if he channels his inner Christian Grey in
the bedroom, I don't need to know; there are some things a sister
does not need to have knowledge of regarding her brother, thank
you very much—but in the *I need to be the one to call the shots* way.

Sorta like a certain someone else I know…

As descendants of a founding family, there has always
been a level of respect, a sense of consideration given to us
that most other kids aren't afforded around town.

I was nine years old when Dad died and threw our entire
world for a loop. Natalie grieved—and I mean that in the
loosest sense possible—for a whopping month before she
started the hunt for husband number two.

As Dad's life insurance diminished, Natalie's neglect only
grew until things came to a head two years later. A then
sixteen-year-old Carter was left "holding the bag" when it
came to raising me, and the trajectory of his life changed
forever. Sure we had the Falcos, but if our godfather, Anthony
Falco—Chuck's older brother—insisted we sleep over too
much, Natalie would cause problems.

Guilt I'm well acquainted with causes me to shiver and
Lance to frown down at me. Assuming it's a side effect, he
pulls his hoodie from his body and tugs it over my head.
None of the Royals wear a lot of cologne in an effort not to

trigger me, so all I smell is the scent of ice and fresh cotton as I bury my face in the collar of the sweatshirt.

Lance waits until I'm settled, hands shoved into the front pouch before giving a small nod of approval. "Come on, Mini Royal"—he tucks an arm around me, spinning me around— "let's get you home."

As he guides me toward the passenger side door, I glance over the curve of his bicep and get an unexpected—and more so confusing—pang of guilt at the way Jasper's eyes take in Lance's hold on me.

Tinsley and I have each changed into sweats and T-shirts— short-sleeved for her and long-sleeved for me—by the time Tessa arrives in her typical whirlwind fashion.

Her backpack lands on the floor like a ton of bricks, stuffed with more textbooks than should be legal for one person to have. Her shoes go flying in opposite directions as she kicks them off. It's only the bag carrying her laptop that gets set down with any gentleness before her arms pinwheel and she flops back onto the couch by my feet.

"Hurricane Tessa has made landfall," I joke in my best impression of a weather person as she brushes her wild red mane out of her face and flips me the bird.

"Eh...she's only about a category two right now." Wes smirks as he makes an appearance and takes one of the over-sized leather recliners. "I wouldn't worry too much."

"Hilarious, Charming," Tessa says dryly.

"You're welcome." He mock bows, his upper body folding over his extended legs.

"If only your jokes were as funny as your face."

Wes eases back in his seat, crossing his feet at the ankles. "Your insults are reflecting your age, Buttercup."

Tessa executes a textbook-perfect hair flip. "Only trying to match *your* level of maturity, Charming." The overexaggerated smile she flashes him is anything but sweet. Tinsley, Cisco, who entered sometime during their banter, and I ping-pong our gazes between them like we're watching a tennis match.

Three beeps sound again, and the door from the garage opens, announcing my brother's return.

"Oh, man." Leo Castle, the final member of the Royalty Crew, waves his arms in front of his face like he's trying to rid the air of something foul. "The tension in here is *thick*." He perches himself on the arm of the couch next to me and chucks my chin in greeting. "What did we miss?"

"Just these two sparring like usual." Cisco bounces a finger between Tessa and Wes, guzzling down a Gatorade in three gulps. "We haven't hit the *I'm rubber, and you're glue* portion yet, so it's still early."

"How 'bout we skip that part?" Carter suggests, then asks Wes, "Bennett gone already?"

"Yup," I answer instead. "He rode off on his noble steed after delivering the *fair maiden*." Oh, did that sound sarcastic? Whoops.

"*Oh*"—Tessa feigns disappointment, shooting me a wink as she does—"Lancelot left before I could wish him good morrow?" She snaps her fingers. "Shucks."

"You two are such smartasses," Carter declares, but there's a tilt to his lips he can't entirely conceal. "How are you feeling?" He squats in front of me, eyes searching, assessing, probably seeing more than I would like.

"Okay." I lie through my teeth.

"Liar." He calls me out with a chuckle, tapping my knee before pushing to stand and taking the free recliner next to Wes.

I'd argue, but there's no point—he's right. I feel like death warmed over and could totally go for a nap. I *don't* mention the last part. He'd throw me over his shoulder and carry me upstairs himself, tucking me in bed with a freaking stuffed animal like I'm still five if I did.

"How was school? Any issues?"

I smash my lips together, knowing what he's *really* asking. I'd be annoyed, but honestly? All the question does is make me sad. Why is *he* the one who's checking in? Why is it my *brother* who cares about my well-being? Granted, I'm not saying a sibling can't care, but you know what Natalie said when she saw me before I left for school? It wasn't *Are you sick?* or even an *Are you okay?* Nope, she took one look at my pale skin and the dark circles under my eyes and suggested I put on more concealer before leaving. Isn't she a gem?

"It wasn't my first time going to school after an attack, Cart." I sigh, relaxing back into the couch cushions, the exhaustion making it too difficult to sit up and rest my head against Leo's jean-clad thigh.

"I'm well aware, Sav." The dark edge creeping into his tone tells me it's time to redirect this convo before he falls down the rabbit hole of Natalie's failures as a parent.

"I have a question of my own." I raise my hand and hold up a finger before circling it in the air. "What are you *all* doing here? Don't you two have class or work?" I fold my three middle fingers down toward my palm and make a Y with my pinky and thumb, using it to point at Leo and Cisco at the same time, the latter now sitting on the edge of the coffee table, legs manspread. "Or better yet…" I'm back to holding one finger up as if pointing can help emphasize whatever point I think I'm trying to make. "Why was it Lance picked me up when it should have been easier for one of you"—I V my fingers to indicate Carter and Wes—"since he had to rush off to practice?"

All four males share a look that has me sitting up, intuition making me hyperfocused. That was their *There's something we're not telling you* look—a glance to the left, avoid all eye contact, roll our lips between our teeth so we don't spill anything to Savvy type exchange.

I hate it. More because it fans the flames of insecurity about my place with them than the actual fact of them keeping something from me.

"Carter?" I say his name slowly, dragging out both sylla-bles as I wait for him to make eye contact.

His left eye twitches, and his jaw pops before he lifts his narrowed eyes to mine. There are the tiniest of wrinkles near the corners of his eyes, his brows drawn, his mouth flat. This is his *Carter King* face, the one he employs as the leader of the Royalty Crew. When will he learn it doesn't work on me? I stare at him flatly and wait for him to realize this simple fact.

"We had a meeting at the mayor's office. We wouldn't have made it across town in time for your dismissal." Carter's words are rough like gravel, like they're being ripped out of him.

"And what did Chuck E. Cheese need on a random Monday in October?" Tessa jumps in to ask.

"Only you, T." She preens, taking my comment as the compliment I meant it to be. Chuck may be considered an uncle sort to Carter and me, but only she can get away with using the name of a giant mouse as a nickname for a man who holds the title of mayor. I bring my attention back to my brother and wait for him to answer my earlier question.

"I'll answer that. But first—" He leans forward, also spreading his knees. He clasps his hands and lets them hang loosely between his legs.

He's attempting to come across as relaxed and non-confrontational. I don't buy it for a second. I see the way his shoulders are hunched toward his ears.

"—why don't you clue me in on everything that happened at the gala?"

Shit!

His lips curl, and both eyebrows bound up his forehead as

if to say *Gotcha!* "You are forgiven for not doing so Saturday night since you were asthmatic"—his expression flips to a disapproving dad frown—"but it *sure* sounds like there was a detail or two you should have shared yesterday."

There's no way he's talking about Jasper and me... right? *Ooo, so now there's a you and Jasper?* It takes every one of my tired muscles *not* to glance at Tessa at that particular question. She's itching to say she told me so the second I admit that *might* be true.

"What do you want to know?" I hedge instead. "It was a *lavish* event more suitable for a wedding than a school fundraiser. Natalie had me following behind her and Mitchell like a well-trained puppy while she lived her trophy wife dreams."

A murmur of *I bet* rolls through the room.

I continue to tick off the highlights of the night—or better yet, lack thereof—on my fingers. "I was mostly by myself since Tinsley wasn't there." I pause. "The food was delicious. The chefs at the St. James really are top-notch." I should know since every meal I eat when I stay with the Momster is catered in from one of the hotel's restaurants. "Aside from that, the only bit of entertainment I got was watching Chuck ruffle Natalie's feathers."

"Ah, yes." Carter strokes his chin. "He told us about that." The identical smirks blooming on the guys' faces make me think my brother wasn't the only one to hear the tale. "Though..." *Uh-oh.* The knowing gleam in his eyes has goose bumps springing to life as a sense of foreboding slinks in like smoke. "That's not the *only* thing he told us."

Shit! Shit! Shit! Shit! He *totally* knows about Jasper and me. Oh god, how embarrassing. Heat floods my cheeks while the rest of me goes cold. When I'm not in the middle of a mini-meltdown, I might—lots and lots of emphasis on *might*—find the humor in this. *Fuck!* Embarrassing isn't strong enough. I'm *mortified.*

"Who knew Natalie was such a fan of reality TV," Wes muses.

My head spins with the random change of topic, and the girls and I give him matching *WTF* faces. And yes, before you ask, there is a difference between the standard *What the fuck?* face and when it's said in IM-speak. Stripping expressions down to the acronym is an honor typically reserved for Wesley Prince.

"And to think"—he shrugs, ignoring our mass confusion—"I thought they canceled *The Millionaire Matchmaker*."

"They did," Cisco confirms, displaying his obsession with trash television. From *Dance Moms* to *The Kardashians*, there isn't a reality TV show I haven't seen him have on in the garage. "Years ago."

"Um…" Tessa raises a hand like this is class and she's waiting to be called on. She's adorable. "Can someone explain why this conversation has taken a detour to an outdated channel guide?"

I snort, which unfortunately triggers a coughing fit. *Ugh.* One hand balled into a fist covers my mouth while the other goes to my chest to rub at it. All eyes laser in on me, a range of concern to panic in them.

"I'm fine." I wave Carter away from my bag when he goes to grab my inhaler. I'm not having another attack. I'm just sore, my lungs always more sensitive in the days that follow having one, like they were scraped raw with steel wool.

"Bullshit," he counters, but he abandons his mission. "I don't care what you say—you're going to the doctor tomorrow to get checked out. Do I make myself clear?"

"Aye-aye, Captain." I'm the one who says the sarcastic retort, but it's Tessa who gives him the military salute. I love that chick something fierce. "We're getting off track." I return my attention to my brother after shooting my bestie a wink. "What is it Chuck told you?"

Outwardly, I'm the picture of unaffected calm. Internally?

I'm freaking the eff out wondering if someone who's like family saw me being diddled by a guy I'm not sure I even like and *then* told my *brother* about it. It gives me the willies.

"How Natalie was *all* about suggesting you spend your time with the governor's son." His brow curves upward as if asking, *Is this true?*

Wait…

This is about Duke?

It takes me a few to backpedal from once again jumping to the Jasper conclusion. Why do I keep doing that? *Because he's on your mind…* I despise how singsongy that particular thought is.

"If you mean did she arrange for the Delacourtes to sit with us at dinner, then yes." If anyone was *all about* setting Duke and me up, it would be *his* mom, not mine. Sure, Natalie seemed to almost crack a smile at Mrs. Delacourte's comments and suggestion we dance together, but that was it. Natalie's entire reasoning for me sitting close to Duke at dinner was to get me away from Chuck.

Although…

There is…*something* niggling at the back of my mind, but it's gone before the thought can fully form.

"Duke?" There's a hitch, a two-octave jump to Tinsley's voice that has me knuckling my ear. "I thought it was Jas—" Her words cut off when my head whips around to face her, and color fills her cheeks.

Shit!

I squeeze my eyes shut, color dancing behind my eyelids from the force. With a deep breath, I peel one lid open and chance a glance to my right.

Carter's eyebrows look like they are attached to his backward hat they're lifted so much, and the dimple forming on the side of his mouth screams *You have been keeping things from me, Samantha.* I *hate* when he calls me Samantha, even if it's only in a facial expression.

Tinsley starts to fidget, and I lay a hand on her thigh and give it a reassuring squeeze. She didn't do anything wrong; that's the *last* thing I want her to think. It's certainly not her fault I have an overprotective brother who is used to knowing *all* the things. I was able to redirect him away from his inquiry the day he picked me up from school, but I wasn't foolish enough to think he forgot about any of it.

I watch in horror as Carter transforms in front of my eyes. Gone is the broody asshole he is ninety-nine percent of the time, and in his place is the charming lady-killer no sister needs to see. *Eww.*

Tinsley's eyes flare wide, her jaw going slack while her body goes rigid. She sways the slightest bit as she falls deeper into the spell that is the Carter King charm. It's gross, and I'm seriously contemplating throwing my body between them to sever the connection.

I know. *holds up hands in defeat* I realize I sound like a hypocrite given how much I flirt with Wes on the reg, but…*yuck!*

"No!" I moosh Carter in the face, squishing the end of his nose flat. "Oh, *gross!*" I squeak when he licks my palm and wipe off his slobber on my sweats.

Cisco tucks his face into his shoulder and Leo pulls the collar of his shirt over his nose as both of them attempt to hide their laughter. Wes and Tessa? They let theirs fly.

"I want a name, Savvy," Carter demands.

My eyes jump to the three-story ceiling, my lips mashing to the side. Doesn't he realize I *hate* being ordered around?

"You know his name," I hedge. "You said it yourself."

Both Carter's lips and eyes go flat. He is *not* amused.

Fine…

I'll tell him. Honestly, I'm not quite sure why I've kept Jasper's name from my brother…

Lies.

Maybe if I do tell him, he'll let it go. "Jasper." The tilt of

Carter's head to the left says, *Keep going.* "Noble." Recognition flashes across his face, but how or from what, I have no clue. That's not the point. We're getting off track, and I have the sneaking suspicion *that* was Carter's goal.

Frustration and exhaustion war inside me like a game of dodgeball. For every time I'm told I'm a full-fledged member of the Royals, I can give at least one example of why that feels like a false claim.

I understand that I'm the youngest, and I was at school when they had their meeting. Lance clearly missed most, if not all, of it since he was tasked with playing chauffeur. Actually...as a Division 1 athlete, he has commitments that prevent him from being present for many things, yet he's more up to date on the day-to-day details than I am. There's also no doubt in my mind he knows the details behind Carter wanting me to be Samantha St. James at school.

"Look"—I slash a hand through the air—"Noble isn't the issue—"

"The fuck he's not," Wes mumbles under his breath, and I cut him a glare.

A headache forms behind my eyes, and I rub my temples in a circular motion to alleviate the tension. I can't be mad at their anger. Like I tried explaining to Jasper, bullying is not something the Royals condone. To have one of their own be subjected to such treatment is an insult of the highest order.

"You told me you trusted me to handle it." This time my glare is accusatory as it swings back to Carter. Was he lying to placate me?

"I do," he says, but a part of me doesn't believe him. I hate it, hate how that small kernel of doubt takes root inside me.

"Then let it go." I wait until I get four nods. "Now tell me what happened at Chuck's."

They do, and like a Facebook relationship status, it's complicated.

CHAPTER 28

I EXHALE and lean back against a row of lockers, the metal cold enough to seep through the high-quality cotton of my uniform's button-up. I ditched my jacket hours ago, the uneasy agitation simmering beneath my skin making even the soft cashmere restrictive.

"Jasper." Someone calls my name, but it sounds like it's coming from deep in a tunnel.

I kick a foot out, my heel scuffing the floor as I cross one ankle in front of the other, dropping my books with an audible *thunk*. My pen dislodges from where it was hooked on top of my notebook, and I absentmindedly watch it roll down the hallway as my thoughts stray to Samantha for what feels like the millionth time today.

She looked to be faring a little better than yesterday. Some of the healthy flush had returned to her skin, the dark circles under her eyes less prominent.

Duke did manage to get an eye roll out of her, but most of her plucky attitude is still absent and that defeated slump to her shoulders remains. I hate it and *hate* that I hate it.

"Jasper." This time when my name is called, I look up to see Banks approaching.

"Hey, man." I straighten, reaching out a hand to exchange a bro shake, then settle back in place.

Banks props a shoulder against the lockers, leaning to the side to face me. "Not coming to lunch?" He jerks a chin down the hallway as if I forgot where the cafeteria is.

"Waiting for Duke." I tilt my head in the direction of the classroom behind him. Our physics teacher asked Duke to hang back after class, and I figured this would give us a chance to speak privately. Guess that's not going to happen with Banks here.

"So…" Banks toes the ground, his focus on the way the rounded edge of his Ferragamo sneaker rocks back and forth on the marble. "Your girl hangs with Lance Bennett, huh?"

Ah…I'm not the only one with Samantha's latest chauffeur on the brain. My lips twitch upward at Banks's *your girl* reference while my fingers curl into my palms at the memory of another man's name on her back.

This…

This right here is why my head has been a mess. Neither of these reactions is like me in the least, nor is the relief I felt having figured out *whose* hoodie she must have had on Saturday night—not that it means I *like* it.

"Ugh." The door slams against the wall as Duke exits the classroom, saving me from having to come up with a response I don't have for Banks. "I need food to wash down that bullshit."

"I take it that didn't go well?" I point toward the once-again-closed door and scoop up my books from the ground.

"It's too damn early in the school year to be worrying about my grades," Duke grumbles.

"Truth," Banks agrees as we fall into step on our way to the cafeteria.

"Do we have to worry about your eligibility?" As much as

we all bitch about school, maintaining a C average is a requirement we must meet if we don't want to ride the bench when our season officially starts next month.

"Nah." Duke waves me off.

"You sure?"

"Yeah." He runs a hand through his hair, the tension leaving his shoulders as they fall away from his ears and his happy-go-lucky smile returning. "I think it was more Dad making the rounds with his phone calls last night."

Ah, yes. The parental check-in is the other reason I can't get a certain silver-haired siren out of my head.

Thanks to Duke being held back, we're the last to arrive in the cafeteria. Most everyone's already seated and digging into their lunches.

We make it through the line for chicken marsala in record time and are approaching our usual table when I decide to make a detour. Both Duke and Banks realize my intent and follow me outside. Banks grabs the end seat perpendicular to Tinsley with Duke taking over both across from the girls, ass in one, feet kicked out into the other. Samantha's pouty lips turn down at the corners as they do, and she swivels around in her chair a beat later looking for me—as if she *knows* I wouldn't be far behind.

A spark of something unfamiliar but not at all unwelcome lights inside me at the realization. She puts up a wall, fights me at every turn, yet she's attuned to me. Thank fuck I'm not the only one dealing with this...pull between us.

Sliding my tray next to hers, I lift and move the other end chair until it's touching hers, and I sit, my slack-clad thigh pressed against her bare one. Thank Christ for short uniform skirts.

"Are you guys lost?" Long silvery strands fall into Samantha's face as she rests her head on her propped-up fist, her torso twisting toward me.

Without thought, I reach out and tuck them behind her

ear, my fingertips skimming her soft skin as I do. Her eyes darken to a deep plum that brings to mind the color of her dress from the gala, which then triggers another memory of how her body felt writhing against mine as I fingered her to multiple orgasms.

My dick hardens behind my zipper. I need to make her come again. Need to taste her directly from the source this time. It's not the fact that we are in school—though it should be—that keeps me from acting on the impulse immediately, but that there's-just-something-off instinct.

There's another momentary nuzzle into my touch before she jerks away, her hand coming up to rub over the spot repeatedly.

"You know…" My elbow slides across the smooth glass on the tabletop as I mirror her body position, my height automatically giving me the upper hand even seated. "You sure seem to be concerned about my navigation skills. Are you afraid I won't be able to find you?"

"I dream of the day that happens," she says in a monotone.

"I *knew* you dreamed about me." I wink.

She rolls her eyes, her hand slapping the table as she shifts away and lifts a french fry from her plate. "Why doesn't it surprise me that *that* was your takeaway?"

I watch transfixed as she brings the fry to her mouth, the crunchy golden slice of potato slipping between her lips like temptation itself, until her straight white teeth rip into the fried spud, my dick jerking at the threat.

I'm beyond fucked when it comes to this girl, and not in the way I want to be.

"*Some*one's got their panties in a bunch," Duke singsongs, circling his fork to indicate Samantha.

"Can you *not* think about my panties?" she retorts while I lean in, my lips brushing the shell of her ear and stretching into a grin at the way her body trembles when I ask, "What about the lack thereof?"

A tapping sound draws my gaze across the table to where Duke is kicked back like he's on a lounge chair by a pool waiting for a cabana boy, or in his mind, a scantily clad cocktail waitress to bring him a frozen beverage. His knee bounces as his foot continues to tap out the staccato beat that captured my attention to begin with. When he meets my eye, he gives me an exaggerated wink, jaw hinging, mouth gaping open in a lopsided O, the side with the winking eye falling lower as the edge of his lip on the other curls inward.

I flip him off, which only has him breaking out into his trademark shit-eating grin.

"That"—Samantha stabs another fry in Duke's direction—"does *not* give me the warm fuzzies."

Duke shrugs, one-hundred-percent unaffected. "That's only because you refuse to give in and be our friend."

Samantha scoffs then starts to cough, thumping her chest twice with a fist. Tinsley jerks away from the latest flirt-tease-torture Banks is partaking in and watches Samantha with worry-filled eyes. She reaches for the bag hanging on the back of Samantha's chair but stops at the head shake Samantha gives. I'm not quite sure what all that was about; all I know is it prickles at my own earlier concern.

It takes three attempts at clearing her throat and a hefty swallow of water before Samantha can respond. "Why in the *world* would I *want* to be friends with people who have made it their mission to bully me into submission?"

The way the word submission rolls off her tongue has my dick twitching again, the pang in my balls a visceral reminder of the blueness I needed to alleviate myself Saturday night.

I was the one who pinned her to the wall.

The one who had *my* fingers inside *her* body.

I was the one in charge of her pleasure, keeping her on the edge of it until I got what *I* wanted.

Still…

When all was said and done, it was tinged with an essence of Samantha topping from the bottom.

She fought saying my name.

She ran from me the instant I released my hold on her.

I highly doubt there's a submissive bone in her entire delectable body. But a man can dream, right?

A coming Samantha was a sight to behold. A submissive Samantha, my name falling from her lips, coming undone around me, under me while admitting she's mine…

Fuck!

It's the last part that has me equal parts close to coming in my pants right here right now and nearly throwing up.

"It's been over a week since we've bullied you. It's old news by now." Duke says this in such a factual, come-on-you-should-agree-with-me way that would make his politician father proud. "Plus J gave you a ride that day you needed to help your friend…" His words trail off and he shoves a heaping spoonful of food in his mouth.

"Oh yes," Samantha agrees with the driest sarcastic deadpan I've ever heard in my life, and I have to bite my lip to keep from laughing. "One act of kindness erases *all* the other shit you assholes have put me through since day one."

"Two," Duke mumbles around a mouthful, holding up two fingers for clarification just in case. Thankfully he finishes chewing and swallowing before tacking on, "He also bought you a new coffee when you dropped yours yesterday."

From the side, I watch the way her lashes interlock at the corners when her eyes narrow. The pink of her tongue becomes visible as she runs it over the front of her teeth, the tip of it pausing at the corner of her mouth as she brings her attention back to me.

"What's it going to take for my lunch to be douchemon-key-free again?"

I fold my lips between my teeth to restrain another laugh.

"Nothing." Smoothing out my features, I drop an arm to the back of her chair, emphasizing how much I'm *not* going anywhere. "Besides…you should think of this week as practice, Princess."

Her eyes bounce between mine for a beat. "Practice for what?" Caution bleeds into her words, and this time I give in to the urge to laugh.

"Do you remember how dinner was at the gala?" She pauses as if thinking. "How you were borderline rude to Duke and me whenever we tried to engage you in conversation?"

"Was this before or after you were trying to feel me up under the table?" she retorts with an arched brow as the memory of touching her out of sight heats my blood.

Needing to redirect before things get out of hand and I do something that would most definitely get me expelled but unable to fully disengage, I stretch further, curling my fingers around her side much the way I did that night at dinner. Unfortunately, the silk of her uniform shirt greets me instead of the bare skin like then.

An innuendo is on the tip of my tongue. The urge to remind her how much she likes my touch and claim her in front of an audience is more powerful than the engine in my F8.

I swallow it down.

A certain sense of satisfaction blooms when it's clear I've caught her off guard by doing so. Point for me.

Samantha sighs and I smirk, the curve of my mouth only growing when her eyes fall to it and the dimple in my chin beneath it.

"Are you going to tell me what I'm supposedly practicing for?"

"How to make polite conversation with your peers." I chuck her under the chin just to be a dick.

"I'm perfectly capable of making polite conversation. Hell,

Tinsley and I were doing just fine until you three"—bounces a finger from Banks to Duke then me—"forgot that your table is in there"—her hand brushes the side of my face when she points toward the main portion of the cafeteria—"and decided to crash our lunch."

I wrap a hand around her wrist before she can pull hers back, my thumb stroking across her not-so-steady pulse. I push against the pressure point, her teeth biting down on her bottom lip as I use my eyes to telegraph, *See? I told you your body can't lie to me.*

"That might be true." She tries to tug her hand free, but I hold firm. "But it's not Tinsley's family joining yours for a dinner party this weekend."

I wait for the shock to set in, for the *Oh shit!* realization to drop her jaw and widen her eyes. Except...it never comes. There is a small crinkle that forms between her brows, but that's it.

"Families?" With her hand still trapped in mine, she can't bounce that finger again. Instead she looks first at Duke then back at me. "As in *both* of yours?" We nod. "Great." Her tone says it's anything but.

"Question." Duke drops his feet and leans his elbows on the table. "Is your hot friend gonna be there?"

Banks and I glance at Tinsley while Duke and Samantha maintain determined eye contact. I become so invested in watching the scene unfold that Samantha manages to free her hand, mirroring Duke's position, fingers steepling, chin resting on the cradle formed by her overlapping thumbs.

"There's a *teeny, tiny* part of me that *wants* to ask Tessa to come, *just* so I can watch you crash and burn"—she shakes her head—"but I won't do that to my best friend."

"What makes you think I'll crash and burn?" Nothing flips Duke's cocky athlete switch like telling him he'll fail at something, *especially* when it comes to a conquest.

Samantha snorts, eyes flitting my way briefly. "I thought I

was supposed to be practicing making *civil* conversation with you."

Duke nods. "Isn't that what we're doing?"

"Sure." Samantha rolls one shoulder forward. "But if we continue to travel down this road, it's going to turn into me telling you *all* the ways you and Tess will *never* happen, and" —she makes a rolling motion with her hands—"it will only snowball from there."

"How do you know she won't like me? My best friend"— he jerks his chin at me—"may be an asshole." I flip him off when he pauses to chuckle. "Doesn't mean I can't be charming."

The adjective seems to set Samantha off; her lips purse into a scrunched-up pout as her whole body bobs with quiet laughter.

I get a whiff of her lime scent when she twists around and pulls her phone from her bag. She silences Duke with a finger when he tries to ask another question and taps the screen with another until she's connecting to a FaceTime call.

"Bitchy!" The excited voice matches the ear-to-ear smile filling the screen as the pretty redhead comes into view. "Hey, Tins," she adds with a finger wave a second before her eyes go wide as hockey pucks when she spots me on the other side of her friend.

"Hey, T," Samantha returns with one of the softest smiles I've seen from her.

"Umm…" Tessa's finger bends and extends repeatedly toward the corner of the camera where I'm visible as she drops her voice to a stage whisper. "You do know Mr. Dick For Brains is sitting right next to you, right?"

That sound of tinkling bells rings out as Samantha releases one of those rare giggles and falls over to the side, her head dropping to Tinsley's shoulder as she joins in. Having witnessed it once before, I'm not slack-jawed at the sound like Duke and Banks, but I'm no less affected.

Also, Dick For Brains? Really?

"I just love you," Samantha says to her friend, wiping a tear from under her eye. She places a hand to the center of her chest, inhaling a deep breath. Was that a wheeze? No matter. This is the best, the *healthiest* she's looked in two days. "And yes, I'm *painfully* aware of my lunch crashers. That's actually why I'm calling."

I shit you not, Tessa's dark blue eye sparkle as she perks up like a prairie dog and starts to shadowbox with the hand not holding the phone. "Need me to kick some ass?"

There's another snort from Samantha, and it's genuinely difficult to reconcile this playful version of her with the tough-as-nails one I experience day in and day out.

"You may spend your nights tossing girls in the air like it's no big deal, T, but you aren't the one I'd call if I needed someone to fight my battles."

There's a weighted silence as the two share some kind of wordless female communication, punctuated by a shy grin from the redhead. "Yeah, yeah, yeah." She purses her lips and runs a hand through her hair with a huff. "You have Charming for that. I get it."

"See?" Duke cuts in. "She already knows I'm charming."

"She's *not* talking about you," Samantha says dryly.

My teeth grind when I realize they must be talking about Prince given his reputation in the underground.

"Is that Dick For Brains' sidekick?" Tessa's head tilts to the side, her expression turning serious.

"Yup," Samantha answers as Duke screeches, "*Sidekick?*" She flips the phone around, both the camera and the screen now facing Duke. "Tess, this is Duke. Duke, this is my it's-never-gonna-happen bestie Tessa." Samantha makes the introductions off camera.

"I'll have you know I'm *no* sidekick," Duke is quick to explain.

"It's cute that you think *that's* the reason I wouldn't Grinch you," Tessa responds with a head-scratching retort.

"Bruh." Duke snaps his fingers inches from my face repeatedly. "Look that shit up on Urban Dictionary. I need to know what the fuck it means to Grinch someone and exactly how *dirty* it is." His expression is stone-cold serious.

"It's not a sex act." Samantha's tone is dry and I can tell she's trying to act annoyed, but there's the smallest tilt to her lips that gives away her amusement.

Duke pouts, laying the boyish charm on thick with a slump of his shoulders and dropping his head into his hand. His muttered "Fuck" and lean forward to rub the shin I kick help clear away my own annoyance at his flirting. I also tack on a warning glare when he lifts his gaze to mine.

"You would think with your fancy-schmancy education, you boys would be better versed in Christmas carols," Tessa's voice teases while insulting us.

Samantha spins the phone back around to see her friend. She attempts to fit the whole table in view of the camera by extending her arm but can't quite manage. My hand covers the back of hers, a spark shooting up my arm, and her eyes jump to mine, the dilating of her pupils giving away that she felt it as well.

I allow myself one more second of our connection, my thumb drawing a full circle over the soft skin before liberating the phone from her grasp and angling it at the best viewpoint. I didn't expect the grateful twitch in her cheek, but I'll take it.

"Tins…" Tessa's mouth forms an O and her eyebrows jump when she spots Banks. If the knowing gleam is anything to go by, I take it my friend has been a topic of conversation. Interesting.

Tessa visibly brings herself back to the current topic of conversation with a quick shake of her head, eyes searching out Duke in the group. "As the narrator of the classic Grinch Christmas carol explains—"

Samantha leans both elbows on the table, linking her fingers together and resting her chin on the flat platform they create like she's about to watch a show. I swear if the culinary staff came around with popcorn she would be settling in with it.

"—I wouldn't touch you with a thirty-nine-and-a-half-foot pole."

"That seems a bit excessive," Banks comments, which Tinsley answers with, "Tessa is nothing if not extra." The person in question beams at us from the small screen.

A bell chimes in the distance and the students in the background start to gather up their belongings. "Whoops, guess I gotta go." The video wobbles as Tessa starts to do the same. "Guess Sa—" She cuts herself off with a small pause then finishes with, "Sammy gets to take *great pleasure*"—the two ladies share a conspiratorial smirk—"in filling you in on *all* the additional reasons you would *never* have a chance with me."

Samantha beams and gives a collective *Told you so* flutter of her eyelashes. I know she's *loving* being able to prove she was right while thoroughly putting us in our place, but I can't help but feel an immense sense of satisfaction at this display of playfulness.

"Wanna hit up EP after school?" Tessa asks, only to cut herself off with a snap of her fingers. "Oh, wait…his Royal Highness is escorting you to the doctor today, isn't he?"

I whip around, raking my gaze over Samantha—twice. I fucking *knew* she was sick. I do a third pass, trying to suss out what the issue could be, a panicky concern I'm completely unfamiliar with building in my system like grains of sand pouring into a vase. Not even the fact that the head Royal is the one picking her up is enough to deter my thoughts. What is wrong? And why won't she tell me?

Why should she?

Her plump lips press into a flat line and she nods. "I can

have him drop me off there after and we can hang until it's time to go to The Barracks, as long as you're cool to drive me home."

"Duh." Tessa adds an eye roll for good measure. "See you later. Love you, Bitchy."

"Love you too, T."

After Samantha disconnects, Duke peppers her with questions until our bell rings while I sit silent trying to figure out what could be wrong that would mean she would need to see a doctor when she's healthy enough to be in school. More importantly, though, why *do* I care?

SAVVY KING

CHAPTER 29

THE ELEVATOR DOORS haven't had a chance to shut when my phone rings. I may be shaking my head at what is clearly ridiculousness, but that doesn't mean I'm not smiling as I swipe to answer the call. "Should I call you my stalker or something, T? It hasn't even been a full minute since I left you."

"Fifty-three seconds. I won the pool," Kay calls out in the background.

"Is it so wrong that I want to listen in on the drama?" Tessa asks, ignoring her sister's taunt completely.

I'd argue her point, but maybe being on the phone when I finally return to the penthouse upstairs will help ease some of my frayed nerves.

Five days ago, I could have said with complete certainty I would be dreading tonight.

But...

Now...

Well...

I can't say I'm looking forward to it, but those two sly

motherfuckers managed to do the impossible and make me *not* hate them.

Four days of lunches together steadily progressed from *Why are you here?* to those first stages of civil conversation before shocking the shit out of all of us in surpassing that milestone.

I now...*holy shit!* Dare I say, actually...*enjoy* how Jasper and I can speak to each other on a level deeper than verbal sparring? Who knew, right? And, no—that wasn't a pig that flew by.

Just because I'm not absolutely abhorring the idea of this upcoming evening doesn't mean I'm not wishing I was doing something...pretty much *anything* else. That's probably why I am officially late. *Whoops.*

Natalie is going to bitch—what else is new? She was pissed when I made my escape to hang with Tessa's family this morning, but I needed a fucking break. The last three days I felt like I was being held hostage in the penthouse. It was all *This is how to act* and *Here's how to make a good impression* and *You will dress like...* and on and on. It felt like I was in a movie montage mashup of *Pretty Woman* and *The Princess Diaries* on proper etiquette, except Natalie had a way of making it feel like it was trending more toward the hooker side of the spectrum.

Thankfully I was able to slip out while she was too distracted with bossing around the hotel's staff tasked with transforming the penthouse for this evening to put up too much of a fight.

No matter how hard I've tried, I haven't been able to work out what her true motives are behind tonight's guest list. This is as much as we know:

1. Mitchell St. James and Frank Delacourte have been friends since their BA days.

2. Mitchell has been the governor's biggest campaign donor for years.

3. Since returning to New Jersey and making the St. James flagship hotel his home base of operations, Mitchell has decided to take on a more active role in state politics.

It's the last one that has led us to suspect that is why the Nobles and Chuck were invited to dinner tonight. Walter Noble has been the governor's campaign strategist for a few years, and Chuck is the local political connection.

I couldn't believe Chuck accepted the dinner invite. Sure, he's practically my uncle since his older brother is my godfather and was best friends with Dad when he was alive, but the King-Falco friendship never extended to Chuck and Natalie.

It turns out this dinner is what Carter and the Royals were meeting with Chuck about. Still salty about feeling like I was being left out of the conversation—it's not the same getting your info secondhand—I may have enjoyed sending countless *Godfather* and other favor-type GIFs to them all until they threatened to block me.

"Put me on video chat," Tessa demands as the elevator *dings*, announcing its arrival at the penthouse.

"Not happening." Lord knows Duke would steal my phone if he knew she was on the other end of the line, let alone in the building.

Not only is the St. James a premier hotel in the state, it's also an official hotel for the NFL. Any team that plays one of the two teams from New York (don't get me started on their stadium being in Jersey) stays here when they travel. Coincidence or not, I'm beyond grateful that the Baltimore Crabs (Eric Dennings' team) are in town this weekend. It's nice knowing there are friendlies a few floors down should I need them.

My heels clack a steady beat as I step out onto the marble floor in the foyer, and I can't stop another grin from forming when I glance down at the classic patent leather Mary Jane Manolo Blahniks. The revamping of my wardrobe to match the designer brands Natalie spent all our money on growing up may be because she thinks it will help me play whatever role she's casting me in, but I can't say I'm mad at it.

Voices filter in from the other room, and I take a moment to compose myself and double-check I have everything I might need.

Sliding a hand down the black off-the-shoulder skater dress I changed into, I'm thankful the fit and flare skirt allows for pockets to put my inhaler in. Knowing tonight is sure to be like walking an emotional tightrope of the unexpected, I'm taking zero chances of setting off another attack. My lungs are still raw and my ribs give the occasional twinge when I move a certain way from last week's episode. It doesn't help that I hear the concerned voice of my doctor in the back of my mind warning me to watch my stressors any time I can't take a full breath.

Pausing at the threshold where the hall meets the open main floor of the penthouse, I marvel at how it's been transformed from a few hours ago.

Instead of the small wet bar in the living room, a full bar—staffed with a bartender—has been brought in. The gorgeous African-American woman is already hard at work mixing drinks, a dewy glow on her ebony skin, the thin braids of her hair coiled into a large bun at the base of her skull as she shakes a martini shaker in one hand while dropping a skewer of three olives into the chilled crystal glasses waiting to be filled for Mrs. Noble and Mrs. Delacourte.

The biggest change to the space is the long cherry oak table, big enough to fit the dozen Jeanette black-velvet-uphol-stered dining chairs that were brought in to replace the more modest six-person arrangement.

Honestly, I don't understand why we needed to rearrange the furniture when we could have easily had this meal in one of the private dining rooms in one of the two top-notch restaurants downstairs. Natalie waved me off like *I* was the ridiculous one when I voiced the question and instead instructed the staff to polish the chrome buttons inside the tufted material and the nickel nailhead trim. Now you understand why I escaped earlier, right?

"I'll call you later," I say to Tessa.

"Promise?"

"Promise." I disconnect and slip my phone into the other pocket of my dress.

Natalie and Mitchell are near the lit fireplace in what looks to be a serious discussion with Governor Delacourte, Mr. Noble, and Chuck if the enthusiastic hand gestures are anything to go by, the former's bloodred painted lips curling at the edges when she spots my entrance. An icy chill shoots down my spine, and I cross an arm over my ribs and curl my hand around them with a squeeze.

Deciding to give them a wide berth, I continue deeper into the room and almost take out a server carrying a tray of hors d'oeuvres.

"Careful, Princess." Jasper's voice wraps itself around my senses the same way his arm does my back to pull me out of the way of disaster.

I have to shuffle step, my hand falling to his hard stomach to keep my balance.

"Thanks." Based on the way those pearly eyes widen, he's as taken off guard by my gratitude as I am, and by how I don't instantly pull away from him.

My fingers spread, the muscles of his abdominals jumping as they do, my gaze falling to where we're connected by my own doing.

Oh my god, he's wearing a vest.

The black material is cinched tight, emphasizing his trim waist. Time loses meaning as I rotate my hand, my nails scraping along the matte black buttons, the purple color of the nail polish Natalie will scold me for choosing picking up the thin pinstripe of a similar color hidden in the weave. That's my color. He's wearing my favorite color.

I snap my gaze up to his before falling back a step and dropping it to inspect the rest of him.

Damn. The Jasper Noble who showed up to this farce of a dinner party is *not* the version I expected. A quick glance at Duke confirms what I would have expected: perfectly cut designer suit, Windsor knotted tie, pocket square, shiny dress shoes.

Jasper? He has the whole elegance of the three-piece factor going for him, but he's sans tie, and the slim-fit tailoring of his pants is capped off with a fresh pair of black and white Chucks.

Why the hell does it feel like he's taking small parts of me and integrating them into himself?

More importantly, why do I like it?

Distantly, I hear Duke chuckling, but it barely registers as Jasper takes his turn raking his gaze down my body.

He starts at the top of my freshly re-dyed silver and blown-out hair, bouncing over my understated yet flawless makeup—both courtesy of Bette—pausing briefly on my nude-glossed lips then sliding down to where the black diamond rests in the hollow of my throat.

I swallow as his attention lingers there longer than anywhere else, the catch in it having nothing to do with my recovery and everything to do with what I'm coming to call the Jasper effect.

My blood warms and I feel my skin flush as he burns a heated path across the bumps of my collarbones, which are visible above the straight neckline of my dress, over the swells of my breasts, and locking onto the two strips of mesh material encircling my waist before the flowy skirt flares at my hips.

The hem of the skirt hits only a hairbreadth shorter than

my uniform skirt at mid-thigh, but Jasper stares at my legs like it's the first time he's ever seen them.

His inspection of me is so acute I start to fidget, my fingers worrying the hem of my dress, my heels rising as I turn my toes inward. Again, so unlike me.

It's my turn to glance at his mouth when he runs his tongue over the front of his teeth, the barely visible clear acrylic ball of his tongue ring managing to catch the light just right. It's easy to forget he has a piercing without it being your typical silver steel ball bearing, and it's jarring every time he's used it on me. An electric current zaps through me at the flash of memory of him doing so twenty-two floors below a week ago.

"*Damn*, Princess," Jasper murmurs breathily, his Adam's apple bobbing with a hard swallow.

Necks aren't particularly sexy—I'm more of a forearms, abs, and those sexy little hip indents type of girl—but like everything else about Jasper Noble, this body part seems to do it for me. Tessa takes great pleasure in telling me he has me dickmatized (her word, not mine), but then I get the joy of reminding her his dick hasn't come anywhere near me.

By the darkening of his irises and the pinch of his fingers on my side, I take it I'm not the only one who's liking what they're seeing. At least I'm not alone in this...*thing*.

"Samantha." My name snaps out of Natalie's mouth like the crack of a whip, popping the Jasper-haze bubble.

I lean to the side, peering around Jasper's large frame to meet the—surprise, surprise—disapproving glare of my Momster. I don't bother questioning what I did to earn it. Lord knows simply existing is enough most days.

CHAPTER 30

MY FAMILY MAY HAVE BEEN INVITED TONIGHT, but from the moment we stepped off the elevator and into Mitchell St. James' residence at his hotel, I've gotten the impression his new bride did so reluctantly. It's not anything obvious. On the surface, Natalie St. James is the perfect hostess; it's more an underlying vibe I'm picking up.

Duke and his parents arrived before us, and he was all too happy to abandon the conversation he'd been roped into participating in with them and the St. Jameses after all our greetings were exchanged.

Dad jumped at the opportunity to talk with the governor and Samantha's stepfather while my jaw clenched when I recognized the mayor of Blackwell was also here.

While Mom was whisked away by Mrs. Delacourte to the bar, I scanned the room for Samantha, not wanting her out of my line of sight with *Mr. Mayor* around. It wasn't until Duke slung an arm around my shoulders and guided us to our own space where we would be able to speak freely that I snapped out of it.

The click of heels is secondary to the way my blood hums any time Samantha is near. My body is attuned to her unlike any other, and with the time spent together this week—without trying to kill each other—that sensation has only gotten stronger.

She was a smokeshow at the gala in that gown, and I still haven't been able to get it out of my mind—or how she was completely bare underneath it—but there's something about the simplicity of her look tonight that is breathtaking.

Fuck me I'm starting to sound like a pussy thinking things like that.

It doesn't stop me from appreciating her effortless beauty, noticing details of her appearance I generally wouldn't. Her hair hangs loosely around her shoulders, and the way most of it is flipped to one side makes me suspect she recently ran a hand through it without thought.

Where her makeup at the gala was badass vixen with the heavy eye shadow and black lipstick I never got the chance to smear, tonight she has a more girl-next-door vibe I didn't think could *ever* be associated with Samantha St. James.

Like her gown, this dress also molds to her tits, but it's the long bare expanse of exposed leg that is my favorite. I'm thoroughly enjoying the way her heels make her calf muscles flex as she walks. I would bet good money those toned thighs of hers would squeeze my waist, the spikes of her heels digging into my back while I drove myself inside her.

My dick jumps, more than on board with that particular thought.

I used to be annoyed by my attraction to her, but now it's all this other…stuff that drives me mad.

Things like how I'm looking for signs if she's still sick, or how frustrated I am that I haven't been able to find out any details about what was wrong with her in the first place or how her doctor's appointment went earlier in the week.

How I can tell she's distracted before she almost takes out a server and would have if I didn't rescue her.

The worst of it all is the way my blood simmers, my body coming alive in every place it touches her. From where my hand cups her side to where my arm is banded across her lower back, the multiple layers of fabric that separate our skin are not enough to detract from the intensity, nor are they where her fingers brush across the jumping muscles of my abdominals.

There's a naked wonder passing between us. I experienced something similar the day I went with her to BP and the time I interrupted Midas when he was fucking with her. But this? It's more. It almost feels like we are seeing each other...*really* seeing each other for the first time.

What in the...

"Samantha." A disappointed scold from her mother causes her to jump, severing the connection winding around us.

Keeping with the unexpected theme of the night, Samantha doesn't pull away from me, only shifting to the side to acknowledge her mother. When she doesn't say anything, I twist my torso, and...*dayum.*

I'll be the first to admit I don't always feel like I have the most conventional relationship with my own parents, but *hell* if I don't feel the chill of the shade Natalie St. James is sending her daughter's way.

There's a rigidity, a strained tension to Samantha that's never been present in the countless times we've sparred. I don't like or understand the surge of protectiveness that slams into me at the realization, but that doesn't stop me from wanting to do something...anything to put an end to it.

With a shift of my weight, I close the little bit of distance between Samantha and me, lowering my mouth to her ear and whispering, "I don't think she likes me very much."

I catch the familiar scent of lime, my nose twitching as a

few stray hairs tickle it when Samantha lifts her face, her cheek pressing to mine. "I wouldn't take it personally." I force myself to focus on her words and not how much I like that it feels like we're exchanging secrets. "I don't think she likes *me* most days."

She moves to go around me and I give her side a squeeze, looking over her head at Duke.

"Oh, hey Duke." Samantha greets him as if only just realizing she never said hi. Not gonna lie, a sense of male pride beats in my chest at being her sole focus.

"Hey, Sammy." Duke winks.

Samantha pulls a face. "Ugh, don't call me that." The shit-eating grin that spreads on Duke's face tells me he's only going to do it more. *Asshole.*

The clearing of a throat breaks into our little moment, and I look up to see it's *Mr. Mayor* interrupting. I run my tongue across my teeth, forcing myself to take a breath before I do something that will have my parents laying into me for being inappropriate.

That particular struggle gets infinitely harder when Samantha turns his way and the two hug.

Right.

In.

Front.

Of.

Me.

"Got a minute?" Mayor Falco asks.

To my ever-growing annoyance, Samantha doesn't even acknowledge my presence, only glancing over toward her mother before nodding.

The volume of *What the fuck?* inside my head increases to a deafening roar as I watch them walk away and disappear into what I assume is a bedroom.

CHAPTER 31

I MAY COMPLAIN—A lot—about what I call overreacting and overprotecting from those who have known me most of my life, but I appreciate the reprieve Chuck's little check-in will allow.

Using the heel of my palm, I press down on my breast-bone. Ten minutes—I've been back under my mother's roof for ten minutes and the tightness in my chest is already worrisome. How am I supposed to make it through the rest of the night, through *hours* of who knows what Natalie has up her Armani sleeve?

The frequency of my current attacks has made me more conscious of even the most minor symptoms when they present themselves.

My fingertips start to tingle as my hand wades through the fabric of my dress, only confirming a hit from my inhaler is the best course of action. At times like these, when I know I'll struggle to keep my emotions in check, prevention is the name of the game if I don't want to have a full-blown attack.

I have the plastic device in hand, already giving it a shake to activate and bringing it to my mouth as I step inside my bedroom, Chuck following close behind.

I pull in as deep a breath as I can manage then exhale in three harsh bursts, tilt my chin up, teeth biting down on the small hard plastic bridge, and depress the plunger on a ten-second inhalation, holding my breath for another ten before I release. The nearly immediate response to my medicine tells me I stopped the symptoms quickly enough to stave off an attack.

"You good?" Chuck stares at the inhaler cradled in my hand, but I appreciate his calm, even tone, and I nod.

"Do I need to call Carter?"

Still focusing on my breathing, I shake my head. My brother is already feeling a certain kind of way about tonight; we don't need him to know how bothered *I* am. Not after I promised I could handle whatever way Natalie plans to use me to further Mitchell's political aspirations.

Having known me long enough to be able to recognize signs of an impending attack, concern etches its way across Chuck's features.

I clear my throat, return my inhaler to my pocket, and say, "I'm okay. Promise. That was more preventative than anything else." He eyes me skeptically. "Really, Uncle Chuck." A smile teases both our mouths. "It's like taking Advil when you feel a headache coming on."

Chuck's cheeks puff up as he blows out an *If you say so* breath, shaking his head and shoving both hands in the pockets of his trousers for good measure.

"Don't take this the wrong way or anything..." I glance toward my bedroom door, lowering my voice when I notice he didn't fully close it behind him. "But it didn't seem like Natalie was too happy to have you included in the conversation."

My comment gets me one of those brotherly, annoyed

laughs, and he pulls me in for a hug. "You mean she didn't seem enthralled by my charming personality?"

I snort, barely managing to swallow back a *Yeah right*, though I think the way my eyebrows fly up my forehead says it for me.

"Yeah, didn't think so either," he agrees, releasing me. "It's weird…" He paces away, coming to a stop at my dresser and leaning against it, feet crossed at the ankles. "She's trying to show her influence in town, but *only* by connecting herself to me and not…" His words trail off and a hand swipes in front of me.

Huh? Why would she do that?

This feels a little bit like trying to get to someplace new but the GPS doesn't work.

I'm not naive enough to think the way I grew up was normal. Blackwell still acknowledges the five founding families generations later. Natalie married into one of those families. She may not be involved in anything that has to do with Royal Enterprises, but the family business is *the* prominent business in town and in the state. The King name means something, so why is she so insistent on distancing herself from it?

"She married Jeremy King—I'm so confused why she tries to pretend she didn't." I run a hand through my hair and let it fall haphazardly around me.

"Beats the hell out of me." Chuck places a hand on his chest. "Your guess is as good as mine." He flops his hand forward. "But…then again…" He shrugs. "When has Natalie ever been known to live in reality?"

Let's see, Dad died in…

"Exactly." Chuck makes finger guns at me, having read my thoughts. In Natalie's…quest for more social status, she actually ended up lessening what she earned by marrying into a founding family.

"This is the part I'm struggling to understand…" A noise

from the hallway has me going quiet and Chuck straightening up.

With a pointed look to the hand I slapped over my now racing heart, Chuck closes the distance between us. "Who knows? Maybe tonight will be the last night I'll have to call you Samantha."

"Whoopie," I answer dryly. Whether or not I get to attend BA as Savvy King, I'll forever be Samantha to the Momster. Calling me Savvy would be admitting to her failures as a parent.

With the same kind of familial affection that earned him the Uncle Chuck title, he places a kiss on my forehead, telling me he'll see me out there, and leaves.

I should follow, but I need to take a breath—a non-literal one—and I beeline it for my en suite, moving to the sink to run cold water over the insides of my wrists. Elbows braced on the speckled granite of the countertop, I lean forward until my body is bent at an almost ninety-degree angle.

Breathe, Savvy, I remind myself again. It's something so simple, a biological function most everybody—including me—does unconsciously. The powerlessness that comes with needing to remind myself to do something so basic is as crippling as an asthma attack itself.

I let the tap run for a solid minute before twisting it off and drying my hands with the towel hanging on the wall. God, what I wouldn't give to be able to go back down to the seventh floor and hang with Tessa's family again instead of my own. If I did that, I wouldn't be constantly teetering on the verge of an attack, that's for sure.

I turn, staring at the closed door to the bathroom while I take another pause to reset my emotions. My eyes fall closed and my chest expands as I pull in the fullest breath I can to carry me through the next few hours. A full eight-count passes as oxygen travels in through my nose then out my mouth.

I blink the room back into focus. Despite the lingering weakness in my legs—another side effect of my symptoms—I feel resettled.

Time for dinner.

It's a meal; I can handle it.

Just a few more hours—tops.

CHAPTER 32

DUKE DRAGS me to the bar while I try, and mostly fail, to not think about Samantha with *Chuck…alone.*

A few minutes pass as my mom and Mrs. Delacourte pull us into a conversation about…I couldn't even tell you with my thoughts fully focused down the hall.

The bartender pours our drinks before I finally have enough. Thank god Duke can read me as well off the ice as on because he distracts the adults for me to make my escape.

Somehow I'm slick enough to go unnoticed, and I stalk down the hall to the room I saw Samantha and *the mayor* disappear into.

I'm not sure if I'm more grateful for the door not being shut because it means they are less likely to be fucking each other, or because it makes it possible for me to hear snippets of their conversation.

It's the former, but we'll pretend it's the latter.

"This is the part I'm struggling to understand—" Samantha's still slightly raspy voice filters out to me, cutting off suddenly when a shift of my weight has a floorboard creaking and I step back to not be seen.

After a pause, I move back in place just in time to see Chuck kiss Samantha's forehead.

Black.

I see black.

I clench my hands into fists, ready to start throwing punches for a girl I have no official claim over.

Except…

When *Chuck* steps out, the motherfucker smirks upon seeing me standing out in the hall, shaking his head and leaving without a word.

That was…odd.

I'm ready to lay into Samantha in the most epic blowup, but when I enter the room, it's empty.

Where the hell did she go?

The sound of running water hits my ears, and I wait for her to be done in the bathroom.

And wait…

I have no idea what I'm going to say or why I'm even in here, but none of that matters.

The door opens, and the second I see her, animal instinct takes over.

Mine.

I'm on her in an instant. My hand wraps around her throat and I spin her, slamming her back against the wall.

Both her hands fly up to wrap around my wrist. I ignore the bite of her nails as they dig into my skin, relishing the way her eyes flare wide in panic.

My grip loosens, squeezing but no longer cutting off airflow, maintaining my control. I step into the final bit of space between us, my forearm flat against her chest as my other arm moves to sandwich it on the other side.

Her lips part as she sucks in ragged breath after ragged

breath, my gaze locked on her tempting glossed lips while I inhale her sweet lime scent.

I hold her there, the curl of my fingers pressing into the underside of her jaw until I have every ounce of focus from those purple irises on me, where it belongs.

"*You.*" I press closer. "Need to *stop* playing games," I command, my voice like gravel.

Samantha rolls her eyes, her mascara-coated eyelashes brushing against the crease of her eyelids from the force. "Who says I'm playing games?"

She's acting innocent with her question, but all I hear is that goddamn defiance that drives me insane. *She* drives me insane.

"I fucking mean it, Samantha."

"Well in that case…"

Fucking hell. I'm the one in the position of power here. Would it kill her to agree with me? My hand is literally wrapped around her throat. All it would take is a squeeze of it and I could choke the life out of her. Does she care? Except for the sting of what I'm sure are going to be crescent-shaped wounds on my wrist, I would say no.

Why is it so hot?

My dick is harder than it's ever been, and it's about fucking time I do something about it—time *she* does something about it.

I kick her feet apart with one of mine, instantly stepping into the small space I create and bringing our bodies flush from chest to pelvis, her heaving tits flattening against me with every labored breath.

Bending my knee, I grind my thigh into her, the heat from her pussy burning me. My lips curl into a grin. She's wet—for me, from me.

I tilt her chin another hairbreadth, my eyes locked on hers, not blinking while I devour her with my gaze as I lean down until my lips brush hers. We've been in a similar position multiple times before, this almost kissing but not quite.

"I'm dying to taste you, Princess."

She shifts, the movement minuscule but enough that it's only the corners of our mouths touching now. "And I'll die before I ever let that happen, Noble."

Son of a bitch. Always with the Noble shit.

My jaw moves along hers. "Wanna bet?" I flick the skin behind her ear with my tongue, letting my piercing drag a second longer. I wait for her to argue again, but it never comes. I do get a moan of acceptance.

I press my lips to her neck, biting around the vein pulsing erratically, kissing down the length of it.

I rake my teeth across her collarbone, grinding my thigh onto her pussy again, followed by a thrust of my hips, my dick leaking precum inside my boxer briefs at the contact with her soft belly.

"No—" I freeze at the choked word until she finishes, "—ble."

My free hand curves around her nape, my long fingers stretching behind her head, tangling in her hair. Straightening to my full height, I fist her long locks and tug sharply, the crown of her head thunking against the wall.

"Jasper," I command.

Nothing. She stays silent. Brows rising as if to say *Nice try.*

She. Is. Infuriating.

With a growl, I slam my mouth down on hers in a kiss so brutal our teeth clash. Releasing her throat, I hook my arm behind her back, my hand curling around to the front of her, grabbing her just beneath a tit and hauling her body up closer to mine, forcing her onto her toes.

She hisses from the pain of her hair being pulled, and I steal the opportunity to plunge my tongue inside her mouth.

I kiss, bite, lick, and suck, fucking her mouth with every

part of mine so thoroughly not even amnesia could make her forget it.

Her hands are trapped between us, but that doesn't stop her from fisting them in my shirt when she starts to kiss me back.

There she is.

I let her tongue find mine, rolling it against hers and licking inside her mouth, consuming the essence of her taste.

Before she can take control, I break the kiss, lowering her down until her feet are back to being flat on the ground.

Her eyes slowly blink open, lust burning in her gaze behind blown-wide pupils. Her skin is flushed, her breathing rapid, and if I thought her lips tempted me before, they have nothing on what they look like now, swollen after being ravaged by mine.

"Jasper," I instruct.

"Noble," she counters.

I run my tongue along the front of my teeth and cup both sides of her neck as I debate how best to break her to get what I want again.

"Fine." I stroke both thumbs down the center of her throat, feeling her swallow beneath them as I do. "We'll play it your way."

A little V forms between her brows as she tries to work out what I mean. My palms glide over the curves of her shoulder, her eyes bouncing between mine as I take my time.

It isn't until my thumbs hook inside the edge of her dress that I make my move, yanking down until her tits spill free. There's also the added benefit of her arms being trapped at her sides thanks to the way the material folds down, cutting her off at the elbows in a restricting band.

"Noble," she warns.

I tsk. "Wrong again, Princess." I cup both her breasts, thumbing her nipples and twisting until she hisses.

I push and squeeze, maneuvering until I have both in one

hand, keeping control of both them and her by clamping the now erect buds between my fingers.

Maintaining my hold, I take one step back and palm myself through my slacks while I study her at my mercy and debate how I want to take her.

Bending, I drop to a knee, letting one of her tits fall free while the other fills my palm completely, and use it to pin her in place.

There are so many ways I could take her. The hours I could spend showing her the error of her ways and teaching her why it's to her benefit to utter those two syllables I want to hear... Unfortunately, now is not the time. Who knows how long I have before someone comes looking for us.

I lift the bottom of her skirt and damn near come on the spot at the teeny tiny purple panties that greet me. They sit low, the jut of both hip bones visible above the skinny string encircling them, the front panel a shade darker than the rest of the lace, giving away how much Samantha wants me.

"Tell me no," I challenge, pressing a finger to the front of her pussy and flicking over the hard metal of that sexy-as-fuck piercing she has hidden underneath. "Samantha," I growl. I'm not playing fair, and I know it. I'm demanding consent but touching without waiting for it. I'd feel guilty if it weren't for the way her legs are trembling on either side of me. "This is your only chance." I draw a T on her clit, the mini ball bearings on her piercing punctuating how I cross the letter. "Tell. Me."

"No..." Her lips quirk. "...ble."

Fucking hell.

That's the *last* time I accept my last name falling from her lips. Her hands thread into my hair, and that's good enough for me. I hook a finger in the lace, tugging it to the side with enough force to hear a stitch pop.

I seal my mouth over her, my tongue lapping at her from

entrance to the top of her clit, biting and sucking the piercing between my teeth.

"*Noble.*"

My efforts instantly double, hissing as she yanks on my hair and I spear her with two fingers, scissoring them and drinking down the gush of wetness like sweet honey. The tightness that greets me has my eyes falling closed, her walls hugging my digits like a fist.

In. Out.

My tongue works her over as I stretch her with each pump of my fingers.

She swells, her walls beginning to flutter, and I can tell she's close. "Say my name," I demand against her pussy.

"No—"

I look up the length of her body: back arched, pink nipples standing at attention, head thrown back as her torso rolls like a wave, hips thrusting her center against me harder, seconds away from coming.

"—ble."

Fucking hell.

A cry falls from Samantha as I rip myself away and jump to my feet. I curl my hands around her shoulders and spin her around to face the wall, crushing her against it.

"I was about to come," she complains.

I'm well aware. I press a hand between her shoulder blades, forcing her back to arch, and flip her skirt to rest above the swell of her ass before spanking one of the pale cheeks. Leaning in until my chin rests on her shoulder, I whisper in her ear, "You don't get to come until you say my name."

CHAPTER 33

THIS IS WRONG.

Now is neither the time nor the place.

He is not who it should be happening with.

I should put a stop to it. Ask me if I will though.

Since the end of August, my life has not been my own, others making most of my decisions for me—where I'll live, where I'll go to school, social engagements I'll attend.

I wouldn't even be here to be in this situation if it weren't for Natalie dictating my schedule—again.

I don't think so.

My life is spinning out of control to the point that it's almost unrecognizable. The line my emotions have been teetering on for two months is razor thin, my asthma flaring up the worst it has in years because of it.

It seems like everyone around me is trying to tell me what to do. Natalie, Carter, the other Royals, and now Jasper Noble thinks he gets to tell me when I get to come or not.

Yeah…I repeat: I don't think so.

The painted drywall is smooth under where my cheek

pillows against it and cool when my nipples brush it with each inhalation I work to achieve.

A second slap echoes in the acoustics of the bathroom, warmth radiating from where my ass was spanked, spiking my arousal to new levels.

Most of me may not like Jasper the majority of the time, but I haven't missed how Natalie seems to abhor him. With his tattoos, tongue ring (no matter how hard it is to see), and showing up in Chucks, a shoe I'm known to favor, he is not worthy in her eyes.

Fine by me.

Fucking Jasper will be like my own personal *Fuck you* to Natalie. If this asshole thinks I'm not going to get an orgasm out of it, he's out of his mind.

I angle my chin and do my best to meet his gaze over my shoulder. His eyes have darkened like storm clouds, his hair in disarray, and his mouth shines with my juices. It's erotic as hell, and I feel another pull deep in my core. I need him inside me.

"Noble," I warn. "Fuck me."

He chuckles, the sound dark and full of naughty promise. "Oh...I'm gonna fuck you, Princess."

His knees press into the backs of my legs, keeping me pinned in place as he shrugs out of his suit jacket and lets it fall to the ground without a care.

There's another push between my shoulder blades, his fingertips skimming down the line of my spine before he snaps his arms out and efficiently starts to roll his sleeves, his ink visible, standing out in contrast against the white fabric.

"If you want, I'll pound you through this wall." His hand disappears into his pocket, a foil packet pinched between his fingers when it makes a reappearance.

I swallow, lungs and heart working overtime, my adrenaline still on a high from using my inhaler earlier.

Unable to watch, I look away only to have my gaze redirected back to Jasper when he fists my hair and cranes my neck at a not-quite-natural angle, my gaze locking onto the gold foil held in his teeth.

The fabric of my dress digs into my arms uncomfortably when I bend my elbows as best I can, pressing my palms to the wall for a little bit of leverage.

My lower half is exposed, dress thrown up my back, thong still hitched to the side, air wafting against my wet center as he works first his belt then his zipper open.

Bent and held the way I am, I can't see his cock when he pulls it free, the pang of disappointment because of it something I'll worry about at a later date, but I sure as hell feel it as he drags it along the line where the curve of my ass meets my thigh, painting my skin in his sticky precum.

"But…" He rips the condom open, sheaths himself, and lines up with my entrance. "You don't get to come unless you say my name."

What little breath I was able to manage is stolen from my lungs as he plunges inside me in one brutal thrust until his balls slap against me.

I attempt to bite back a moan and fail, my hands scrambling for purchase on the wall, skin too clammy to manage it with much success.

The emotional torrent, the adrenaline high, the close call of a looming attack—all of it adds up to me being one big exposed nerve ending.

My head is yanked back further, scalp burning from the roots of my hair giving a valiant effort to remain attached. I'm panting and gasping, the line of my throat curved outward, my eyes falling shut as my body goes along for the ride.

Jasper sets a punishing pace, only slowing when he feels I'm close to coming. The millisecond I've edged away from the brink of release, he picks up speed, the *slap-slap-slap* of skin on skin the background beat to the animalistic moans, groans, and curses volleyed between us.

"Say my name, Samantha."

I can't manage much thanks to his grip, but I shake my head as much as physically possible. If I don't get to hear him say the name I want to hear, why should he? Don't give me any crap about him not knowing it either.

His hold on my hip is bruising, and I bet I'll be wearing the imprint of his fingers for days to come.

Thrust. Thrust.

The edges of my vision grow blurry.

He buries his face in the curve of my neck. "Princess," he growls against my skin.

"Noble," I taunt, because I can.

He releases my hip, clutching at my breast, twisting my nipple until I see stars and another wave of wetness adds to the ease at which his cock is pummeling me. I may not have decided how I feel about Jasper, but my body has zero doubts. Except…

I need to come—badly. Desperately. Like need it more than my next breath, and that's saying something.

I'm on fire, burning up from the inside out.

He abandons my breasts, my nipples now sore enough that when they brush the wall with every pump of his hips, a spark of delicious pain streaks through me.

"Say. It." His hand is on my pussy, his dexterous fingers sliding between my lips and clit, leisurely rolling to the ball of my piercing in his pinch-grip.

"N—" I can't even manage to get out the full first syllable of his last name. For a man who claims he won't let me come until I utter his name, he sure as shit knows how to make me feel like that's an impossibility.

"Do it." He nips at my back, shudders racking through me. "Give me what I want." He tugs my hair again. "And I'll give you want you *need*." The gravelly way he rolls the last word the same way he is my piercing almost does me in.

"I doubt you *could*," I taunt, refusing to break.

He growls, pumping into me harder. I push back, swirling my hips as much as I can to find that *spot*.

"Fucking *hell*." Jasper latches onto my neck and I detonate, coming hard and long. The force of my orgasm is so great I barely notice how Jasper's speed and power triple in intensity. If not for him releasing my hair and hooking that arm underneath my arm then spreading his hand over my sternum, he might have actually succeeded in his promise of pounding me through the wall.

He roars his release, his forehead falling to the center of my back as he comes down.

I'm not sure how long we stay like this—me with my upper half smooshed to the wall, back arched in a cow stretch, ass stuck out, and him with his arms coiled tight around me, head resting on me, his breathing as ragged as my own.

I bite down on my lip to restrain a cry when he finally slips from inside me.

On wobbly legs, I straighten, adjusting my thong and dress back into place while Jasper ties off the condom and dumps it into the small garbage can in the corner.

Neither of us says a word—verbally. But our eyes? They devour each other like we didn't just have the hottest hate sex of my life.

Fine…I'll rephrase that to be the hottest *sex* of my life since I don't regularly go around screwing guys I don't like. Jasper Noble is the one and only person to hold that honor, seeing as I'm drawn to him in a way I can't seem to put a stop to. I know—*holds hand up*—I don't want to analyze what that says about me.

A glance to my left reveals a disheveled reflection. A part of me wants to leave this room and return to this farce of a dinner with my sex hair and smeared makeup. Natalie would lose her shit. Might be worth it?

Unfortunately, I know I won't follow through on that plan.

The repercussions *wouldn't* be worth it. Instead, I move to the counter, picking up the hand towel I discarded earlier, and use it to clean up the mascara smudged under my eyes and the smeared lip gloss surrounding the outside of my mouth.

Warm weight meets my back and strong arms bracket my body from behind. Slowly, I lower the towel, my hands curling over the countertop, chin falling to my chest. Neither of us says a word, Jasper's forearms my sole focus, the swirls of black ink decorating his skin a dangerous kind of beautiful. *Kind of like him.*

"So fucking stubborn," Jasper murmurs into my hair.

My body is all out of whack, my breathing and heartbeat irregular from the dual adrenaline surges, one involuntary, another in an effort to control the other.

Swallowing repeatedly, I will the saliva to rid me of the cottonmouth I have going on. I reach for the glass on the counter, my hand shaky as I do.

"We should probably get back."

I nod, surprised Jasper isn't pushing me harder about not saying his name. I set the glass back down and focus on inhaling and exhaling measured breaths.

It'll be fine. I'll be fine. I can totally get through the rest of this night without losing it fully.

"Since you refuse to say my name"—*There it is*—"the first thing you're going to do is stop letting other guys put their hands and lips on you."

I snap to attention, my stilettos clacking as I do.

Yes, we had sex, and yes, it's making me feel all kinds of ways I'll need to examine at a later date.

But…

He *does not* get to tell me what to do.

Shooting an elbow back, I muscle my way free and storm out of the bathroom.

"Samantha," Jasper calls out, but I ignore him.

I'm sick of people trying to tell me what to do. What

makes him think he can? It's one thing when he tries to do it at school. I can shrug it off as his misguided sense of entitlement.

The muscles in my back seize and that familiar band tightens around my chest as those earlier symptoms start to return.

"Princess." It's more warning than anything else.

I whirl around, rubbing at my breastbone. "What makes you think *you* can *tell* me what to do?"

His expression turns stormy. Brows lowered, eyes narrowed, that dimple in his chin extra deep with the clench of his jaw.

"You're fucking *mine*." He stalks to me, hands cupping either side of my face and jerking me to him. "Not *Chuck's*. Not Wes's. *Mine*."

This time when I go to take a breath, I cough, a muscle spasm taking hold that I can't stop. My forehead falls to Jasper's chest and I know I'm in trouble. I'm going to need my inhaler, and if I don't get away, I'm going to need it in front of him.

"I—I'm not theirs." I pull in air, but it never reaches the bottom of my lungs as it should. Chuck? Is he kidding me with that? Like, Wes I can understand; I've used him enough to torment Jasper. But Chuck? What? Really?

"Fucking A."

That's not what I meant, but another coughing fit takes over first. "I'm not *yours* either."

Thumbs push under my chin, holding me in place. Normally I would jump at the challenge staring down at me, but I've passed my threshold and need to act before it's too late. Fumbling with my dress, I search around for my inhaler.

It isn't until he feels my arm shaking to activate my medicine that he steps back, eyes locking onto the plastic device cradled in my palm.

"Sam—" My name cuts off as he watches me go through

my routine. One hit doesn't do it, and I depress the plunger a second time, inhaling a second puff.

I close my eyes, uncomfortable with the concern and panic I see swimming in his multicolored gaze. I just handed him my biggest vulnerability on a silver platter. Where's the spark of victory?

CHAPTER 34

SHE DIDN'T SAY IT. She managed to get off without saying my fucking name. Then watching her pull herself together like nothing happened frays the last bit of my control.

Because pretty much hate fucking her was…what? I shove the question from my conscience to the deepest part of my mind to examine…well, never.

The straightening of her dress knocks me off center. Her fingers combing through her hair and untangling it only ties my guts into knots. And when she fixes her makeup, cleaning up the last bit of outward evidence of what happened between us, something shifts inside me. It's elemental, a core-deep change that rebels against how I've lived my life.

I've tried to ignore it, to brush off every surge of possession as no big deal, a phase that would pass once the newness of her wore off.

Except…

It's not wearing off. The longer I know Samantha, the more time I spend in her presence—it only causes those urges to happen more frequently and increase in intensity.

In a last-ditch effort to reclaim my sanity, I thought maybe I could fuck her out of my system. Thought it was only a case of wanting something I couldn't have or because she was the new shiny thing.

Fuck was I wrong.

My dick isn't even dry and I want her again—I *need* her again.

There is a Louis Vuitton store's worth of baggage to unpack between us. We've essentially been enemies, choosing opposites sides of a proverbial line, not to mention her association with the Royals. Most would say that's the last group of people whose direct crosshairs I want to put myself in.

Fuck that.

I'm Jasper fucking Noble.

I race in their races, gate-crash their events, help organize the pranks against their school, and mess with their favorite rat on the daily. Officially stealing Samantha would just be one more check in my badass column.

She thinks I'm trying to tell her what to do. Sure, I can admit it, I am—but why can't she see that she's *mine*?

Samantha lets me pull her to me as I cup her face in what is probably the most affectionate gesture I've ever made with her. Defeat enters her eyes a second before her forehead falls to my chest.

She starts to cough, and I'm reminded of how concerned I've been all week and the unknown details of her doctor's appointment.

She's antsy in a way I haven't witnessed before, agitated so that she's struggling to breathe.

"I'm not *yours* either," she manages to get out between coughs.

Using my thumbs, I tilt her face up to mine, ready to lay out on the line all the scary things that have been brewing inside me, but her arms knock into me, a rogue elbow getting me in the gut as she runs her hands over her dress.

I have no clue what she could be looking for and almost fall on my ass from shock when I see her pull out an inhaler.

She has asthma?

The *whoosh* of the medicine dispensing and the wheeze of her inhalation are amplified by the panic taking root inside me.

Why didn't she tell me she has asthma? *Holy fuck!* Is what we did in the bathroom responsible for what's happening now?

"Sam—" She takes a second hit of her inhaler, looking anywhere but at me as she starts to pace.

I've spent more time watching Samantha St. James than I'd like to admit, but this is different. I study her, looking for all the signs I've missed without realizing it.

"You have *asthma*?"

She thumps at her chest, rolling her shoulders back and shooting me a death glare to end all death glares. It is elementally wrong given her current situation, but all I want to do is wrap my hand around her throat again.

"Fucking hell, Samantha!" I shout. "This is the kind of information you tell a person."

That glare sharpens, and I almost move to check to see if I'm bleeding. "And *why*, pray tell... would *I* tell *you* of *all* people I have a condition you could use against me?"

Son of a bitch. My hands flex with the urge to strangle her.

"Do you really think I would do such a thing?"

She laughs an ugly, humorless, barking sound that sets off another coughing fit. She holds up a hand to stay me when I start to move toward her. "*Puh-lease.*" She rolls her eyes. "I think you've more than proved your asshole-ness to me."

"THIS IS DIFFERENT!"

She arches a brow and shoots a worried glance at the open door.

Way to make a scene, Noble.

"Oh yeah..." Sarcasm bleeds into her tone. "I bet you and your boys are *real* concerned about a person's health when you're telling them they're going to be on their knees for you."

You would think I didn't almost black out from an epic orgasm minutes ago with the way blood rushes to my cock. If the current topic of discussion weren't so important, I would point out that the only one on their knees was me, but doing that will only help her downplay the issue at hand.

"Princess..." I try for a different approach and her shoulders fall, eyes softening at my naked concern, and she starts to inch her way toward me only to halt when Duke enters with a "Dude."

His steps come to a stop. "Whoa. Did you two finally fuck?" He waves his arms through the air wildly. I clench my jaw at the way he perks up at the possibilities, neither confirming nor denying. "So much sexual tension in here."

"Great...your sidekick is here." Samantha shoves her hands into the hidden pockets of her dress, and I notice it's her way of hiding her inhaler.

I roll my lips between my teeth at how Duke bristles at once again being labeled my sidekick.

"I'll show you—" Duke shakes his head and redirects his attention to me. "Not important." Another head shake. "You might want to rejoin the festivities before this one's"—he hooks a thumb at Samantha—"mom blows a gasket."

"Yeah, because it's not like that's a daily occurrence or anything," Samantha mutters, exiting her room and leaving us behind.

I get a *What do you think that's about?* head tilt from Duke and answer with a *No idea* shrug before moving to follow.

I don't know if it's because she's moving slower after needing to use her inhaler or not, but Duke and I easily catch up with Samantha and have fallen in step with her by the time she makes it over to where the adults are talking.

"Samantha." There's a haughty reprimand in Natalie St. James's tone, her gaze running disapprovingly over her daughter as she takes in her appearance.

"You rang?" Samantha drawls like Lurch from *The Addams Family*, and I have to scratch a knuckle underneath my nose to hide my amusement. I don't get to appreciate it much because it's usually directed at me, but she might have the driest sarcastic wit out of anybody I know.

"Really, Samantha." Natalie lets out an exasperated sigh but maintains what Duke and I like to refer to as political poise. You know, where you smile with your lips so onlookers think everything is that public relations perfection, all while your eyes shoot daggers and reprimands and cutting remarks hiss through your teeth.

Thanks to Dad's job, I've attended enough events to recognize the expression, but I'm taken aback when Samantha dons it. She is the least fake person I have ever met. Seeing her of all people playing this role is jarring, and I hate it.

Natalie's posture straightens, preening at the sight of Duke with her daughter. The tilt of her lips drops the tiniest millimeter when she notices I'm on the opposite side.

Yes, I know you don't like me. Ask me if I give a fuck.

"Hillary, Frank, you remember my daughter Samantha." Mitchell makes introductions, holding a hand out, palm facing up toward Samantha, and it's not the first time I've heard him refer to her without using the step title.

The three nod while Mrs. Delacourte looks at Samantha with hearts in her eyes. In my peripheral vision, Duke and I share a *Gird your loins* mantra, both more than familiar with his mom's expression. Mine isn't any better, and normally I find amusement in Duke having to suffer through his mom's matchmaking attempts, but not this time. Samantha is not available.

Samantha rolls her shoulders back and brings a hand to rub at her chest. It's something I've noticed her doing a lot more frequently, as well as the cough and constant clearing of her throat. Now I'm aware of why she does it.

A glass of water appears as if out of nowhere, and my agitation levels rise when I see it's the mayor with the offering. They jump again when Samantha croaks out, "Thanks, Chuck E."

To my further irritation, he doesn't respond right away, instead studying her much the same as I have all week. I hate him a little bit more for clearly having old knowledge about her asthma when I only just learned about it.

"I *love* when you guys use that particular nickname for me, Sav—" Samantha whips her head around so fast the water in the glass splashes over the rim and onto her hand. "Sam," he finishes.

It's not the first time, and he's not the only person I've caught cutting themselves off when they say Samantha's name. That's odd, right?

"Being equated with a homicidal children's toy will really help me in the polls come election time," he adds dryly. The look the two of them share has me rotating my wrist in an effort to shake off the urge to punch the guy.

"To be fair, that's Chucky with a Y. When I say it, it's with an implied E for a middle name.."

Chuck *E's* jaw falls open, and I long to ram my fist into the open space in his mouth. "Like. The. *Mouse?*"

The arch of her brows and the press and curl of her lips to restrain her amusement are facial tics I'm familiar with. I'll never admit it to her, but I'm starting to live for them. I don't want them used with someone else. They're mine.

"As much as I would *love* to take the credit for it, that particular gem comes from Tess."

"That doesn't surprise me in the least." They share a laugh, Samantha tossing out a "Never gonna happen" to Duke when he perks up at them discussing her friend.

There's a furrowed *What's that about?* brow from Chuck,

and Samantha shakes her head before his expression sobers and he asks, "You alright?"

Again I study Samantha. I swear I'm going to tie her down and force her to tell me exactly how bad her asthma is. Her blasé attitude is starting to mess with my sanity.

"Of course she's fine, *Charles*." Natalie manages to sound both offended he would ask her daughter such a question and put out by it. There's a haughty air to her sigh that has the mayor's jaw and mine clenching.

It may not be noticeable to others, but having kept close to Samantha, I notice when she shifts, her weight moving the slightest bit until her back brushes my arm like she's seeking...comfort? I don't know, nor do I care. Instinctively, I accept it and offer it, twisting and rising until the flat of my palm rests against her lower back.

There's a push, and this time I'm sure it's not a subconscious move; Samantha is actively seeking me out, wanting my touch.

I spread my fingers, covering as much of her back as I possibly can, and use the tip of my fingers down to the first knuckle to clutch her. We've been adversaries, enemies from the jump. Here? Now? This? I don't question the lure, the draw to unify in this confounding moment.

Natalie's eyes meet mine, the ice in them having nothing to do with their blue shade and everything to do with the naked disdain she transfers from Chuck to me. If I didn't suspect she thinks eye-rolling is beneath her, I'm sure I would have received one of those before she slid her gaze over to Duke, her entire demeanor morphing.

Malevolent gleam brews inside her irises, and the slow curl to her lips is more sinister than the bloodred color they are painted in.

"I really hope you don't coddle her like the rest of these men do once the two of you are married," Natalie says casually to Duke. My brain screeches to a stop like a record being cut off mid-song.

What did she just say?

She didn't say what I think she said...

Did she?

DID. SHE?

I freeze. Samantha's body seizes beneath my touch, and there's a rattle, a strain when she inhales sharply with a hitch to her breathing.

"Sweetheart." There's a slight reprimand to Mitchell's tone as he clears his throat. "That's not how we planned on bringing up the topic."

Natalie transforms right in front of me. Her eyes go oh-no-I-didn't-mean-to-spill-the-beans wide, one hand rising to cover her mouth with the tips of her fingers while the other grips Mitchell's arm. "Oh my goodness." She spins, searching out the Delacourtes with please-forgive-me eyes. "It just slipped out."

"It's kind of exciting, though. I get it." Mrs. Delacourte agrees with a hand resting over her heart, those hearts beaming proudly in her gaze.

"It is." I don't believe the sweet, loving smile Natalie sends her for a second. "Again though, I do apologize."

The sweet moment between the two matriarchs is broken up by Samantha. "Wha-what the fuck did you just say, Natalie?" The disbelief in her tone when she voices her question matches my own. We have to be hearing things. But...both of us? Is that possible?

"*Language,* Samantha." Her gaze bounces nervously to the Delacourtes.

"Cut the shit, Natalie." Samantha passes off her glass then shakes out her hands, flicking them as if they're wet. This is also the second time she's called her mother by her first name, and the disapproving pout it receives and the absence of correction gives me the impression this isn't the first time she's done so.

"I'm not going to stand for your insolence, young lady."

"Insolence?" The last syllable breaks off on the end as Samantha gasps for a breath. The smack of her hand hitting her chest rings out loudly in the otherwise silent room. "Repeat." A sucked breath. "What. You. Said."

Again, Natalie checks with the Delacourtes. Duke's father watches the scene with a calculating intensity, and where I would think his mother would be looking anywhere else given her general avoidance of uncomfortable situations—not necessarily the best trait for a politician's spouse—she's beaming at Duke with maternal pride.

"I was only trying to advise the young Mr. Delacourte that he'll want to keep a firm constitution when it comes to your marriage." Down at her side, Natalie flexes her left hand, admiring the way the light reflects off the giant rock on her fourth finger. "If he continues to spoil you the way your *brother* and his *friends* do—"

She cuts a glare to Chuck, and my mind spins over the fact that Samantha has a brother I didn't know about. Is he older? Younger? I want to assume he's older since Natalie insinuated he spoils her, but where is he? Maybe he's in college and his school is out of state? Questions continue to fly at me, but I shove them aside so I don't miss a thing about this current madness.

"—it'll make for a lopsided union. It's one thing dealing with it in a child, but in a spouse…" She tsks. "That's one of the quickest ways for a marriage to fail."

There's that M word again. She's most definitely saying marriage. Why the hell is she bringing up things like marriage and spouses to her teenage daughter?

"Wh-why are *you* of *all* people offering up marriage advice?" Samantha slashes a hand through the air.

Again Samantha starts to shake out her hand, intermittently bring the tips of her four fingers to her thumb like she's pretending to have claws before repeating the pattern. Is this her asthma flaring up?

"No." Shake. "Wait." Claw hands. "Back up." A thump to her chest. "Why is my name"—cough—"coming up when"—wheeze—"marriage is the topic?"

Natalie expels yet another of those heavy sighs. "We're really going to have to work on your listening skills, Samantha." Her head falls forward then she shares a conspiratorial look with Mom and Mrs. Delacourte. "Teenagers."

I slide my foot across the floor until the front of my leg is pressed to the back of Samantha's.

"Mom?" Even Duke sounds unsure as he speaks up for the first time.

"Duke…sweetheart." She reaches out a hand for his. She glances at her husband, waiting for his nod before continuing. "Your father has decided to make a run for the White House when the election rolls around in a few years."

Duke nods, and I find myself bobbing my head along with his. This isn't earth-shattering information. Governor Delacourte has been a favorite of his party for years, and one of the reasons he hired my dad to take over as his campaign strategist was to help facilitate this goal. It would be more shocking if he wasn't planning on making a bid for the presidency, and Duke says as much.

"What I don't get is what's with all the marriage talk?"

Natalie cuts in before Mrs. Delacourte can answer. "After much discussion, we've decided it will be mutually beneficial to all parties involved for you to marry my daughter."

Okay, okay I totally hear your shouty capitals before you even type them. I'm sure you're like WTF ALLEY!!! I need to know what happens.

Good news! Book 2 is available for preorder and will be out in June. And there's no cliffhanger!!!

Ruthless Noble A Royal Crew Duet Book 2 PREORDER HERE!

Prefer to borrow it for FREE in Kindle Unlimited?

CLICK HERE to sign up for a one-time alert when *Ruthless Noble* goes live. (You will not be subscribed to my regular newsletter.)

Need emotional support? Need a place where you can WTH did I just read and HOLY SHIT Alley really took her Evil Queen status to a whole new level?

Maybe you just have some crazy theories to run other like minded people? Want to help plan Natalie's death? Join the SQ Spoiler Group.

Are you one of the cool people who writes reviews? Savage Queen can be found on Goodreads, BookBub, and Amazon.

Randomness For My Readers

Whoops, I went and gave you guys another cliff. But before you go and yell at me at least book 2 is done and will be out in June and you can PREORDER HERE!

This book wasn't supposed to be my next release, but now that you've met Savvy King, I bet you can understand how she forced her way to the front. Damn that Tessa Taylor for encouraging her lol.

I was a little nervous, and by a little, I mean SOOO much, to write these books. I love me some bully romances, but Savvy was such a badass she certainly made trying to dive into writing one a hell of a challenge.

But of course, I had to have my favorite coffee shop from my BTU Alumni series make an appearance.

So now for a little bullet style fun facts:

- I have a major girl crush on Savvy King.
- Tessa Taylor might be the most ridiculous character I have ever written…and that's with both Lyle and Duke being side characters of mine lol.
- I watched so many YouTube videos about Ferrari F8s I need to make millions so I can have one lol.

- I know a bunch of people were probably freaked out about Merlin, but boas really are sweet snakes.
- Joey and Kennedy my cover models are a couple in real life.

If you don't want to miss out on anything new coming or when my crazy characters pop in with extra goodies make sure to sign up for my newsletter! If my rambling hasn't turned you off and you are like "This chick is my kind of crazy," feel free to reach out!

Lots of Love,

Alley

Acknowledgments

This is where I get to say thank you, hopefully I don't miss anyone. If I do I'm sorry and I still love you and blame mommy brain.

I'll start with the Hubs—who I can already hear giving me crap again that this book also isn't dedicated to him he's still the real MVP—he has to deal with my lack of sleep, putting off laundry *because… laundry* and helping to hold the fort down with our three crazy mini royals. You truly are my best friend. Also, I'm sure he would want me to make sure I say thanks for all the hero inspiration, but it is true (even if he has no ink *winking emoji*)

To Jenny my PA, the other half of my brain, the bestest best friend a girl could ask for. Why the hell do you live across the pond? I live for every shouty capital message you send me while you read my words 97398479 times.

To my group chats that give me life and help keep me sane: The OG Coven, The MINS, The Tacos, The Book Coven, and Procrastinors & Butt Stuff (hehe—still laugh at this name like a 13 year old boy).

To all my author besties that were okay with me forcing

my friendship on them and now are some of my favorite people to talk to on the inter webs.

There needs to be an extra shout out to Laura and Julia, for without them I wouldn't have finished this book. Laura you've been stuck as my cross-country bestie for years but thanks for bringing Julia into my crazy!

For my beta readers and their shouty caps as I played around with the cliff and story.

To Maggie for being my asthma sensitivity reader and letting me ask her question after question as my inside source for Savvy and never thinking it was weird when I'd text her with "Question" at 2 a.m.

To Sarah and Claudia the most amazing graphics people ever in existence. Yeah I said it lol.

"To Jules my cover designer, for going above and beyond, then once more with designing these covers. I can't even handle the epicness of them.

To Jess my editor, who is always pushing me to make the story better and giving such evil inspiration that leads to shouty capitals from readers.

To Caitlin my other editor who helps clean up the mess I send her while at the same time totally getting my crazy.

To Gemma for going from my proofreader to fangirl and being so invested in my characters' stories to threaten my life *lovingly of course*.

To Dawn and Ellie for giving my books their final spit shine.

To my street team for being the best pimps ever. Seriously, you guys rock my socks.

To my ARC team for giving my books some early love and getting the word out there.

To Amanda and Wildfire PR for taking on my crazy and helping me spread the word of my books and helping to take me to the next level.

To Wander and his team for being beyond amazing to

work with and this custom shoot for Savvy and Jasper's books. And Joey and Kennedy for being the perfect models! Seriously I think the world can hear my fangirl squee whenever I get to message with you both on IG and I love that you guys are a real life couple!

To every blogger and bookstagrammer that takes a chance and reads my words and writes about them.

To my fellow Covenettes for making my reader group one of my happy places. Whenever you guys post things that you know belong there I squeal a little.

And, of course, to you my fabulous reader, for picking up my book and giving me a chance. Without you I wouldn't be able to live my dream of bringing to life the stories the voices in my head tell me.

Lots of Love,

Alley

For A Good Time Call

Do you want to stay up-to-date on releases, be the first to see cover reveals, excerpts from upcoming books, deleted scenes, sales, freebies, and all sorts of insider information you can't get anywhere else?

If you're like "Duh! Come on Alley." Make sure you sign up for my newsletter.

Ask yourself this:

* Are you a Romance Junkie?

* Do you like book boyfriends and book besties? (yes this is a thing)

* Is your GIF game strong?

* Want to get inside the crazy world of Alley Ciz?

If any of your answers are yes, maybe you should join my Facebook reader group, Romance Junkie's Coven

Join The Coven

Stalk Alley

Master Blogger List
Join The Coven
Get the Newsletter

Like Alley on Facebook
Follow Alley on Instagram
Follow Alley on TikTok
Hang with Alley on Goodreads
Follow Alley on Amazon
Follow Alley on BookBub
Subscribe on YouTube for Book Trailers
Follow Alley's inspiration boards on Pinterest
All the Swag
Book Playlists
All Things Alley

Sneak Peek of Writing Dirty (BTU5)

MADDEY- CHAPTER 1

"Don't you *dare* think of stepping one foot inside this house in gray sweatpants, Ryan Donnelly." I point an aggressive finger toward the glass sliders leading to the back deck, all while not looking up from the computer screen in front of me.

"Don't be like that, Madz." Ryan pouts when I finally look. It's not a look a twenty-seven-year-old man should be able to pull off, but with his Chris Evans good looks, he totally does.

Not for the first time—perhaps for the millionth, for that matter—I curse my stupid heart for not being able to get its shit together and accept his proposal. *Nooo,* it had to stubbornly, *stupidly* insist on not being able to figure out how to love.

Well, that's not true. I love my family, my friends—Ryan included—and my dog, but I haven't figured out what it actually means to be *in* love.

Sure, the voices in my head can tell me how they feel. My characters pretty much craft all sorts of shouty-capitals-worthy happily-ever-afters in my books themselves.

I'm constantly having to tell them to stay in their lane when it comes to whose story it is, but when I try to phone a friend with them, they're all, *New phone, who dis?*

"Don't even try it, mister." I wave my finger side to side, still not fully looking up. "You do and I'll sic my attack dog on you."

Warmth leaves my lap as Trident, my yellow lab, lifts his head, knowing I'm talking about him. He may be able to teach a master class on being a well-behaved canine and can scare off any would-be attackers (aka the mailman and such) with his bark, but he's a big ball of mush for Ryan and my other friends.

He lazily lumbers to his feet and heads straight for Ryan, only further proving the point.

The NHL golden boy bends down to love up on my fur child while actually following my orders and staying in the open doorway, the breeze from the ocean bringing in the comforting scent of salt and sea.

"Who's a good boy?" Ryan wraps both hands around Trident's ears, scratching behind them. "You are, aren't you, Tri? Yup, I know you are. You're keeping your mommy company while she ignores her real friends for the ones in her head, huh?"

My "attack dog" has a hind leg scratching in the air and is melting into an almost-hundred-pound puddle right there on the floor. Granted, I'm not super far behind as I watch the display. Why did I have to look up?

No, Madz. The question you should be asking yourself is why aren't you with this sweet, sweet man?

Jiminy can be a real son of a bitch.

Really…is it my fault I can't get my heart to fall in line?

"Can you please stop telling my dog lies? I'm not *ignoring* you guys. It's only six in the morning—almost everyone is still sleeping."

Over the head of my blissed-out dog, blue eyes a few

shades darker than my own find me. "Yes, but if *you're* up at six *AM*, it means you've been up all night and will end up ignoring us to sleep."

Is it wrong that I kinda wanna hit him for being right?

"Semantics."

The sound of joints popping as Ryan rises to stand fills the silence before he finally braves going against my orders and walks into the house. He lifts my feet from the chair they're resting on, settling into the seat with them in his lap.

"What are *you* doing up this early anyway?" I ask, reaching down to pet Trident as he retakes his spot at my side.

"I came to pick up my running partner before I set off."

My gaze automatically falls to watch the way the muscles in his arm pop and flex as he stretches to run a hand down Trident's back. My dog lets out a sigh, and I can't blame him. I have firsthand knowledge of how good it feels to have that particular body part do the same to me.

Stop that right now, Madz. You do not get to think those things anymore. You and Ryan are only *friends now.*

God, I need sleep. It's only when I'm overtired like this that I beat myself up over what at times I think are my bad life decisions. I really am fucked in the head.

"You do realize it's the offseason, right?"

There are days I question if the word offseason is even in his vocabulary with the way he trains year-round. His work ethic rivals that of my brothers, and their *lives* depend on their physical fitness.

Hmm…

I saw Justin just last week and he'll be down the shore again this weekend, but when was the last time I spoke to Tyler or Connor?

Tyler is stateside right now, but it's been a few days since he responded to the family group chat. I'll bug him later.

Connor's team is currently deployed, so his additions to

the chat are few and far between. I shoot off a quick email—since that is sometimes more reliable—asking when we can video-chat again. Hopefully the conversation will end on a better note than the last one.

A girl gets herself an overzealous fan and everyone is all up in arms about it.

I swear I'm too old to still be dealing with big brother overprotectiveness.

They have a point, Madz.

Oh, leave her alone, Jiminy.

Yeah—the Die Hard Trilogy needs to take a chill pill.

The metal of Trident's collar tags jingles when he tilts his head at my growl.

Bed.

I need bed.

"We're not gonna bring the Cup back to Jersey without putting in the work," Ryan says, answering my earlier question.

I'm surprised my dog is the only one he's enlisted to run with him. What about his teammates?

"Jake and Chance are lucky I didn't pull their asses out of bed." It's scary how well he can still read my thoughts.

"I agree about Chance since you live in the same house, but I call bullshit on Jake." He arches a brow at the mention of his brother-in-law. "There's no way you would risk facing the wrath of your sister if you woke up any of her babies."

I don't bring up the fact that it's weird for a group of professional athletes—multi-millionaire athletes—to share a shore house together, even if it is a mansion. Those comments fall on deaf ears anyway. No use wasting trash talk on it.

"You got that right. I would prefer not to be the victim of one of JD's revenge plots, thank you very much."

"Plus, you run the risk of seeing her naked since she and Jake like to—"

"Not cool, Madz. Not cool at all." He is quick to cut me off before I can go on about his sister's sex life. Torturing brothers is one of my favorite pastimes, one that is also enjoyed by some of my fellow Covenettes.

Who are the Covenettes, you ask?

Only the most awesome women in existence. It started with the original six—the founding members, if you will—but we've added to our ranks the last few years.

"If you want, I can text her to see if it's safe?" I reach for my phone only to have it snatched away.

"No way. I don't need to be the topic of a Coven Conversation this early."

I snort, like I do any time one of the guys uses the name they assigned to our group chat. I highly doubt Ryan's brother Jase—Jordan's twin—and his best friend Vince knew what they were getting into when they gave us our nickname in college. Too bad for them we're the type of women to take the ball and run with it.

Plus, those Coven Conversations are life. It is seriously the best thing to happen on my phone, and that's saying *a lot*. Think about it; I write romance—can you imagine all the *research* I've conducted on it?

"Don't be a baby," I tease, poking him in the side.

"Let me see what you're working on anyway." He slides my MacBook Pro toward him as he squirms away from my tickling touch.

"Nope." I slam the lid shut before he can get a peek. Only my girls get to read the rough, hasn't-been-edited word vomit I come up with.

"No fun." There's that damn pout again.

I pop a shoulder and bite back yet another yawn.

"Come on, you." He takes one of my hands in his and pulls me to stand. "Off to bed." He cups his hands over my shoulders, turning me in the direction of the stairs that will take me to my bedroom.

"But—"

"Nope." He cuts off my protest, the captain in him taking charge. "I'll drop Trident at JD's after our run so you can sleep as long as you need."

Gah! Again he has to go and be perfect. I really am an asshole.

Pausing at the bottom of the stairs, I turn to watch my ex-boyfriend-turned-bestie corral my dog, wondering how I can be so good at writing other people's happily-ever-afters when I can't figure out my own.

Also by Alley Ciz

The Royalty Crew (A #UofJ Spin-Off)

Savage Queen

Ruthless Noble- Preorder, Releasing June 2021

#UofJ Series

Cut Above The Rest (Prequel) Freebie

Looking To Score

Game Changer

Playing For Keeps

Off The Bench- #UofJ4 Preorder, Releasing December 2021

BTU Alumni Series

Power Play (Jake and Jordan)

Musical Mayhem (Sammy and Jamie) BTU Novella

Tap Out (Gage and Rocky)

Sweet Victory (Vince and Holly)

Puck Performance (Jase and Melody)

Writing Dirty (Maddey and Dex)

Scoring Beauty- BTU6 Preorder, Releasing September 2021

About the Author

Alley Ciz is an internationally bestselling indie author of sassy heroines and the alpha men that fall on their knees for them. She is a romance junkie whose love for books turned into her telling the stories of the crazies who live in her head…even if they don't know how to stay in their lane.

This Potterhead can typically be found in the wild wearing a funny T-shirt, connected to an IV drip of coffee, stuffing her face with pizza and tacos, chasing behind her 3 minis, all while her 95lb yellow lab—the best behaved child—watches on in amusement.

facebook.com/AlleyCizAuthor
instagram.com/alley.ciz
pinterest.com/alleyciz
goodreads.com/alleyciz
bookbub.com/profile/alley-ciz
amazon.com/author/alleyciz

Made in the USA
Middletown, DE
11 May 2021